BEWARE THE WILD

BEWARE

THE

WILD

NATALIE C. PARKER

An Imprint of HarperCollinsPublishers

HarperTeen is an imprint of HarperCollins Publishers.

Library of Congress Cataloging-in-Publication Data
Parker, Natalie C.
    Beware the wild / Natalie C. Parker. — First edition.
        pages   cm
    Summary: A teenaged girl and her boyfriend must find her older
brother after he wanders into their town's swamp and a mysterious
girl appears in his place.
    ISBN 978-0-06-224152-8 (hardcover)
    [1. Supernatural—Fiction.   2. Swamps—Fiction.   3. Brothers
and sisters—Fiction.   4. Missing persons—Fiction.   5. Louisiana—
Fiction.]   I. Title.
PZ7.P2275Be   2014   2013047957
[Fic]—dc23   CIP
                                                             AC

Typography by Kate Engbring
14 15 16 17 18   LP/RRDH   10 9 8 7 6 5 4 3 2 1
❖
First Edition

For Tess,
who always believes

PART ONE

Beware the swampy places, child,
Beware the dark and wild,
Many a soul has wandered there,
And many a soul has died.

IT'S NO SECRET, OURS IS the meanest swamp in Louisiana.

Regular swamps are dangerous enough. Loud, stinking things, they hide their claws in the mud between cypress knees, beneath the surface of stale, brackish waters. There are a hundred ways to die all cloaked in the twist of pale trees—gators fast enough to catch a grown man, mosquitoes teeming with disease, stinging plants, hungry black bears, and nasty cottonmouths all filled with spite and patience. Heat so dense it collects in your ears, air so thick it coats the inside of your nose, and plenty of putrid, sucking mud that'll pull you down and fill your lungs with slow death.

But what's in ours is worse.

Ours is a creature all its own. We don't stare into its depths and we don't ever go inside. We live alongside it, tolerate it the way every southern town tolerates creeping vines of kudzu, and I've done my best to avoid it until today.

It's a million degrees, and I'm baking my butt on the cherry-red hood of Phin's old Chevelle. He's been fixing it up, and he'd get after me if he saw I was sitting on it, but I like the way the heat sears my thighs.

Only one week to go in my sophomore year. I should've been blowing off studying for finals because I was too busy painting my nails or spending a lazy afternoon at the race-track. But everything changed a few hours ago, and I'm blowing off studying for a totally legitimate reason, hoping Phin will come home just to cuss at me for sitting on his car.

My phone buzzes against the gravel on the ground where Candy Pickens sits. She scoops it up and screens the text. I can't be trusted to answer anything right now. Not without burning a whole host of bridges.

"It's Beale," she reports. "She's finally done with church and wants to know if she should come over."

I'm tempted to say yes, but I shake my head. Other than Candy, Abigail Beale's my closest friend. She's nothing if not calm and collected, and if I need anything at the moment it's to stay calm, but having her here won't make me feel any better. She'd only sit as powerlessly as I've been doing all day.

The front door opens. Voices spill into the yard.

Candy takes my cue and we keep quiet to avoid being noticed.

"You're sure you don't want to press charges? He's eighteen now. Not a boy anymore, and there isn't a soul in Sticks who'd think poorly of you for it, Gatty."

I recognize Sheriff Felder's lazy voice. He's been inside with Mama and my stepdad, Deputy Darold Gatwood, for the better part of the afternoon.

"No charges," my stepdad says. "It was an accident. Plain and simple."

"Maybe so, but he could've really hurt Sterling and I don't much like the idea of letting someone get away with hitting one of my deputies. Sets a bad precedent. A particularly bad one, if you know what I mean. I hope you'll reconsider."

I'd like to walk right around the corner and tell him to do his job and go find Phin instead of looking for excuses to arrest him, but Darold gets there first.

"Nothing to reconsider. That boy's had enough trouble in his life. It's not for me to add to it." He pauses. I strain to hear his next words. "He might be in danger, you know."

It's the sheriff's turn to pause. Then he says, "I can't send any of our men into that swamp. You know it, Gatty. I'm sorry. Let's wait and hope for the best."

Darold's muffled response is followed by the front door closing hard. Sheriff Felder comes into view, halting his slow stride to tip his Stetson. Sunlight flashes over the star pinned to the brim and he drawls, "Girls," before pouring into his cruiser like molasses.

"Hope for the best" is his way of saying he won't be looking for Phin, but he might feel bad about it. It's the same approach he uses for hurricanes or flu viruses, anything he feels powerless against. Or, in the case of my brother, anyone who's more trouble than they're worth.

But Sheriff Felder doesn't know Phineas like I do. Maybe he'd feel differently if he'd known Phin as a ten-year-old twig of a boy, willing to put himself in danger to keep me safe. Maybe he'd care if he'd seen Phin standing bare-chested and shaking brave in front of a man big enough to snap him like kindling. Maybe if he had, he wouldn't be ready to give up so easily. Or maybe he'd go on turning his eyes away from the swamp no matter what.

"I'm sorry, Saucier," Candy says from the ground, her hands pressed to either side of a volleyball. She's more gentle than usual with the syllables of my last name, SO-shur—the name Mama was born with, and Phin and I took after Dad left.

"Sorry for what?" I'm aware that being snappish isn't kind, but I lost kindness hours ago. "Even if they cared, they'd never have looked in the swamp."

This entire town would rather believe we're better off without him, that it was only a matter of time before violent Phineas Saucier crossed a line. When the story gets out, they'll care that Phin and I were fighting, and Phin got so mad he nailed the carport by my head. They'll care that when Darold grabbed Phin's shoulder, Phin spun and punched him in the face.

They'll care that Phin did what every man, woman, and child in Sticks knows not to do and crossed the split-rail fence into the swamp. Then, they'll shake their heads and cluck their tongues like it's such a shame, and if they're generous, they'll hope for the best.

I peer over my shoulder at the far edge of my yard where pine trees dust everything in shadow. Their branches bend down in a way they shouldn't, like greedy claws. We all know better than to cross that fence.

But the only time Phin gets dumb is when he's angry.

And he hasn't come back.

"They know what happened, Candy," I say. "The swamp ate my brother."

"Don't be dramatic or anything," she says flatly.

From beneath the pines, the air somehow winks both dark and bright. On our bit of fence, beads and Christmas lights glitter against the old gray planks. A tradition started by Mama's daddy, Grandpa Saucier, to remind the swamp that there was nothing for it beyond its edges. Mama adds more Mardi Gras beads every year, clearing the oldest and dullest ones to make room for new strings of black-and-red top hats, purple-and-green fleur-de-lis, peppers, gator heads, and whatever else was tossed during the parades. And now, behind that familiar sight, something shines in the dark.

Sweat slides down my spine and I rub my eyes to clear them. When I open them, the air shimmers again.

It's too early yet for fireflies, but the lights I see are unmistakable. They dance above the fence, a hundred glowing eyes.

"Do you see that?" I ask. "What *is* that?"

Candy's face is impassive. "You'll have to be more specific."

I hop off the Chevelle, my skin ripping from the hot chrome, and stalk to where the unremarkable split-rail fence is ghostly pale against the dark swamp. It's as easy to climb over as it is to scoot beneath, but no one does, and for some reason, the swamp stays firmly on the other side. A few brave plants may reach across the line, but by and large, the swamp keeps as much distance from us as we do of it.

I stop just shy of the fence. It's at least ten degrees cooler here, but that's not what makes my skin prickle. There, wrapping around every other tree trunk and dripping from the underside of broad, leafy plants, are lights as bold as fireflies. They swirl in and around the foliage, hover in the air, and thread through the tangle of Spanish moss. A chill races down my arms.

"I know you have him," I whisper.

The lights wink.

"What are you on about?" Candy calls from behind, running to catch up.

"What do you see in there?" When I rest my hands on the fence, little lighted fronds reach for me. They brush over my hands like butterfly wings. I snap them away.

"Nothing but swamp," she says, climbing boldly onto the bottom rung. "No sign of him."

"Nothing strange? No little lights?"

This time she doesn't even look. All our lives, she's told frightening swamp stories at sleepovers and on camping trips. She'd grin a cat-grin when someone screeched or woke from a nightmare, but now her frown is for me alone. "This is what happens when you starve your brain, Saucier. You get stupid."

"Well, I see something. What do you call the lights that are always leading people into the swamp? The ones from the Clary stories." If anyone knows the finer details of the Clary Tales, it's Candy.

She steps off the fence. Sweat has pulled her straight, blonde hair flat against her forehead and the bridge of her nose is beginning to flush pink. We've been outside too long, but there wasn't an ounce of me that wanted to sit and listen to anything the sheriff had to say.

"You mean the creeping lights people claim to see when they're drunk? That strand men and children deep in the swamp? The Wasting Shine. Or just Shine," she says confidently. "And they're easy to explain away with our good friend Science."

9

"That's it. That's what I see right now. Long, creeping lights like vines. Not at all like Science." I'm not usually quick to dismiss science, but this is different. The Shine beckons and blinks, beckons and blinks, turning the whole of the swamp into a living thing. I know I shouldn't say more, but worry makes me reckless. I ask, "What if there really is something different—dangerous—about our swamp?"

"That's called superstition. Or crazy. And that's no one's friend."

The screen door squeals. Mama pushes her head through enough to be visible. Her dark curls are as limp as her voice when she calls, "Time to wash up, Sterling. Dinner in ten." And then she's gone. I don't think she even saw us standing here.

"That's my cue." Candy squeezes my hand, pulling me halfway to the house. "Want me to see if I can weasel out of the Pickens' weekly drama and stay for dinner?"

Selfishly, I do, but it'll be miserable inside our house with or without her. I shake my head. "Thanks, though."

She nudges the heavy silver bracelet on my wrist and smiles. It's as much encouragement as she can muster. She retrieves her bike and pedals down the drive, leaving me alone in the middle of the yard.

I twist the bracelet, letting the silver push into my bones. Phin gave it to me early this morning before everything went wrong. This morning. He hasn't even been gone a full day. It feels impossible. He'd been proud as a robin when I opened the box.

"I found it up in the attic with Grandpa's old things," he said, grinning.

There's a reason Mama tucked it away when Grandpa died. It's horrid. A thick band of tarnished silver with a small gap where a wrist could squeeze through, embellished with a gaudy bloom of curling flowers. I frowned at Phin's grin. "You don't say."

"Sass," he said with amusement.

No one can dismiss my frowns like Phineas, and I felt the beginnings of a wretched smile respond to his teasing.

I picture his dark hair, charting an improbably choppy course around his head. It took more than one hair product to change his curls into the mess he preferred. The long line of his nose, the sharp angles of his jaw, the three freckles that trip down the left side of his neck—I know my brother better than anybody.

"Let him go," I whisper, looking into the swamp.

I feel the flood of sunset against my back, but my eyes stick on the dark place where Phin vanished. I should have gone after him; I shouldn't have let him carry that rage away. But there was a look in his eyes I recognized and it nailed my feet to the ground.

Darold told Mama that Phin only needed to blow off some steam. He'd be home before we knew it. Neither of them had been willing to voice the grim thought plaguing us all: the swamp always demands a price of trespassers.

And he hadn't come home. Not in an hour and not in eight.

Now, finally my eyes burn and panic balloons in my throat. Of all the stories we keep in Sticks about the dangers of the swamp, there's not one in which someone who went inside it returns unchanged. If they escape at all, it's with half a brain or madness in tow. Of course, those are just stories: tales kids tell to scare one another, but they wouldn't be so frightening if our parents weren't so guarded.

I'm certain that right now, something awful is happening to my brother and there's not a single thing I can do to help him.

Long after Candy has gone, I keep staring into the tangle. The Shine grows brighter as the light of day fades. Then, somewhere deep inside, I see movement.

I squint, clench my fists, and wait.

I want it to be Phin so very badly.

Surfacing through the dusk in flashes of white and green, a figure coalesces. I try not to breathe, not to move or do anything that might draw attention and make the swamp stop this person from emerging.

Its steps are slow. Mockingbirds shout their litany of songs at the setting sun. I smell something soft and sweet on the air.

It gets closer.

I see long hair and a dark green sundress, and I feel an icy pain in my chest. A girl. A girl, not my brother, is walking out of the swamp.

"Hello?" I call, disappointment heavy in my throat.

She pauses briefly, but doesn't answer before continuing her slow progress toward me.

"Hey!" A dozen swamp stories flash through my mind. *Is this even a girl?* Unnerved, I step closer to the house, putting distance between us. "Can you speak? I said hello."

But again, she doesn't answer. Her hand extends slowly and she hesitates before finding the fence. Dark hair hangs in her face, wild with curls and lovely in a way mine will never be. She climbs with something less than grace, fumbles with her dress, and nearly falls to the ground in my yard. She catches herself in a crouch, halfway to her knees. This clumsiness does nothing to relieve me.

All at once, the shining vines reach toward the girl, grasping for her as if they never meant to let her go. But she's beyond their reach. She rocks. Finding her balance, she tests the ground with her hands and feet before pushing up again.

Then, her eyes lock on to mine, and she heads straight for me.

I can't think of a single good reason for a strange girl to stumble out of a swamp. But to stumble out of *this* swamp?

My mouth opens to shout or scream or make demands when Mama's voice comes from behind. "Girls, what are you waiting for? Come wash up for dinner!"

When I turn, she's standing with the screen door pushed open wide, a steaming spoon in her hand, and no hint of weariness about her. She watches me expectantly before shifting her gaze to the strange girl.

"What are you waiting for?" she asks again. Her irritation is split evenly between me and the girl I've never seen before in my life.

"What?" I ask.

"Sterling." Mama points her spoon in warning. "Don't start tonight. You and your sister, pull that cotton from your ears, for Pete's sake, and come in for dinner."

"My *what*?" I ask, but she's already gone. The screen door slaps three times behind her.

There's a hollow feeling in my gut as I turn to the strange girl. Her hands are folded demurely, her face is pale and radiant in the light escaping the kitchen windows. She wears a simple and quiet smile. Behind her, the swamp is flat black against the dusted blue sky. In comparison, she's all watercolor and light. She doesn't look real and I think it's because she's not, but she steps forward and still smiling says my name, "Sterling," and then, "let's not keep Mama waiting."

And without another word, she walks past me, up the three brick steps to the screen door, and straight into my house.

MAMA'S CHEEKS ARE ROSY WARM and they carry a smile I haven't seen all day. She spins between the counter and oven with dishes gripped between hot pads. Darold makes a dive into the fridge for a beer, humming an unidentifiable tune. The bruise Phin left him, the one Sheriff Felder called a "fine piece of work" a few hours ago, is glossy and purple. Grinning at me, he takes a quick swig, then breezes down the hallway to pound his way upstairs. From the dining room, I hear the clatter of silverware as someone—the girl—sets the table.

None of this is as it should be. The rooms should be cold and dark and anxious. Mama should be stuck to her front room rocker, red-rimmed eyes watching for Phin to come walking down the road. Darold should be restless and irritable, glowering through his bloodied eye. All I should hear is the *tick-tick-tick* of the clock in the den, marking each second Phin is gone.

My house is too full and too strange.

"Mama, what's going on?" I push my hip against the kitchen table to stop the dizzy feeling climbing my limbs.

"Dinner is going on with or without you, so go wash up." Mama knocks the oven shut with her knee. It complains the whole way and she wrinkles her nose. "Darold! I need you to oil this door sometime this year!"

She pushes two serving spoons into a steaming casserole and carries it into the dining room. For a moment, I'm stuck. Staring down at the faux marble tiles, I take three deep breaths while Mama and the strange girl fuss over dinner in the other room. Whatever Mama said outside, I must have misheard her. There's no way she said "sister."

"Sterling!" Mama stops in the doorway. Behind her, the strange girl stops, too, that same, small smile on her pink lips. "Why are you still standing there?"

I push off from the table and point at the girl. "Mama, who *is* that?"

Mama and the strange girl frown together, but it's Mama who speaks. "Are you feeling okay? What have you eaten today?"

Anger muscles through my confusion. *How can she be*

thinking about food? She starts forward again and I circle away, pressing my back against the fridge. Strange Girl blocks the door, looking at me like she knows me well enough to care.

"I feel fine! I want to know who she is, why she's here, and why you're all acting like you know her. I watched her climb over the swamp fence, for crying out loud!"

"Now you're worrying me," Mama says. "Are you telling me you don't recognize your own sister?"

"Sister?" The breath I take is shallow and worthless. How can she not see this girl wasn't here five minutes ago? "What about Phin?"

Mama opens her mouth and I wait for the sorrow to surface and pull the color from her cheeks, for the dread of impending loss to cloud her blue eyes. She presses her lips together. For a second, her eyes move out of focus and I think she's remembering, but then she says, "Honey, who's Phin?"

There's a storm in my ears when I look away.

Behind me, the fridge slips on the floor as I press my back into it as hard as I can. "My brother," I say and then again, "Phineas Harlan Saucier is my brother and he ran into the swamp early this morning," but Mama is unblinking.

Frantic, I search the front of the freezer for the photo I stuck there two years ago. I'd taken it on his sixteenth birthday just after the tow truck unhitched the '68 Chevelle in our driveway. The car was equal parts rust and disaster, but in the photo, Phin is a smear of happiness on glossy paper. It's my favorite picture of him.

What I find instead is an image of the strange girl standing in front of the same car. Her eyes are closed, but she's smiling with the keys cupped in one hand. I feel my fury rise like the sun.

When I look for her, she still stands in the doorway. "What have you done?"

The clock dings seven times in the den. Darold comes tromping down the stairs and the strange girl in the room licks her lips. She unfolds her hands in front of her, offering me nothing.

"Sass, what are you talking about?" Her voice is a silky thing as she steps forward.

"Don't," I say, throwing a hand between us. "Don't call me that. Only Phin calls me that, and oh my God. Are y'all serious? All of you? No one remembers Phineas?"

No one gives me anything but a frown.

Every horrible story I've ever heard about the swamp flashes through my mind: the one of the two sisters who followed their dog deep inside only to be pulled beneath the mud by ghostly hands; the one of the woman who tricks you over the fence then eats your feet so you can't get home; the one of the trees that shriek so loudly your ears bleed, leaving you deaf to the cries of your loved ones; the one of the beast that steals your soul forcing your empty body to wander the swamp for eternity.

Now there's this story: the one of the dark-haired girl who crossed the fence and stole a boy's life. I haven't heard it before, but I'd recognize a swamp story anywhere.

"She came from the swamp! I don't know *what* she is, but she's *not* my sister!"

"I'm calling Dr. Payola." Mom digs in her purse for her phone.

"What's all this shouting?" Darold's face appears around the corner, creased with concern. Mama only shakes her head and keeps digging.

I want to run, but my legs don't feel attached to my body. I'm trapped in place, in this kitchen that's my own and yet not mine at all, while the girl, the *thief*, closes the distance between us. Her fingers are soft and warm against my skin. She wraps them firmly around my arm with a small shake as if to say, *Don't fight me.*

I yank my arm away. "Don't touch me. Nobody touch me."

Without another look at any of them, I leave the kitchen and climb the stairs as fast as my wobbly legs will allow. Then it's eight steps down the hallway to Phin's room. Inside are the same yellow walls I've seen my entire life, the same short dresser in the corner, the same poster of a '68 Chevelle tacked up over the bed, a giant copy of the periodic table of elements that matches the one in my room. A thousand memories skitter through my mind: Phineas praying to the god of Chevelles to be kind and grant him enough cash for a new set of shocks; Phineas covering the dresser with every flavor of bumper sticker; Phineas tossing a dart at the periodic table and quizzing me on the element it hit; Phineas singing, Phineas yelling, Phineas laughing.

It's all so nearly the same. But it's not his—no darts stick in the heaviest elements. Instead, the first elements have been decorated with sequins and fake jewels and bottle caps to stand in for electrons and neutrons. I remember laughing with her when she reached silicon and realized her plan to model each element would soon eclipse the entire chart.

No, I don't. I can't remember someone who doesn't exist. I can't remember that her favorite color is purple but thinks Chevelles look best in red. I don't even know her name.

Except I do.

Lenora May. May to her friends. Lenora to teachers and Aunt Mina. But Lenora May to me. Always Lenora May.

Panic grips me. Is this how it happens?

No. She can't have me, too. I won't let her—

Jewelry clutters the dresser top. I recognize a necklace I gave her two Christmases ago. The whole place reeks of a cloying sweet scent, a tacky, cheap perfume I've hated since she bought it last year. Everywhere I look, I see things I shouldn't recognize. My own mind is betraying me. Memories of Lenora May sit side by side with memories of Phin.

I know how she loves to bake, how she's saved every penny of babysitting money to improve the Chevelle, and that she's too generous for her own good.

There's a whole history of her inside my mind, but it's flimsy and thin. It's not real. She's not real. I know it even if her pale purple bedspread says otherwise.

I stare, gripping the door frame until my nails bend, and then I flee.

In my own room, I close my eyes and say Phin's full name aloud six times.

People don't just disappear. Not like this. Not from our memories. If they did, we'd have all forgotten Dad. Mama wouldn't hate the smell of whiskey. I wouldn't sleep with the window open. And Phineas wouldn't know how to be angry.

It's several minutes before I open my eyes and hit the lights. The floor is comfortably littered with clothes, shoes, hair ties, lip gloss, and magazines. I spot one with a car on the front that's been painted with fierce stripes to make it look fast. I snatched it from the neat stacks in Phin's room two weeks ago—Lenora May picked it up on a trip to New Orleans—because Candy was making a collage and needed one of the pictures.

I shove the magazine beneath the bed.

The knock on my door is sharp as a tack.

"Go away," I say, but the door opens on Mama's alarmed face. Behind her, Darold echoes her concern.

"Honey, Doc Payola's here. Okay if he comes in to chat?"

I feel my jaw go slack and stupid. They got Doc Payola to make a house call on a Sunday night. This is as serious to them as it is to me, except they aren't worried about Phin. They're worried I might be crazy.

Am I?

Phineas. Ten years old. Bravely fighting tears as Doc Payola set his broken arm.

I'm not crazy.

Never deal in secrets of the swamp, the old Clary advice echoes in my thoughts. I've never understood it as clearly as I do right now.

Nodding, I hastily tug the quilt over my bed and perch on the edge with what I hope is a sane expression. Mama steps aside and Doc Payola enters with a smile as broad as his shoulders.

"Evening, Miss Sterling. How are we feeling tonight?"

Angry. Confused. Scared. Betrayed. "Fine."

"No dizziness? Disorientation?" Setting a leather case on the foot of my bed, he removes a small flashlight and lifts my chin with a soft touch. He smells like barbecue and Tic Tacs.

I'm careful to avoid Mama's face as I answer, "Um. A little." Better to give them something to chew than let them believe I've cracked.

Doc flashes the light in my eyes, watching as my pupils retreat from the assault. "Got a bit of sun on your nose. Spend much time outside today?"

"Basically the whole day," I say, taking the opening. "Not the smartest thing, I guess."

He asks a few more questions—Did I knock my head today? Do I know what day it is? The year? What's my birthday? Can I spell my name backward?—then inspects my head for bumps before turning to Mama and Darold. I keep my voice level through it all and focus on him, his long nose, his dark skin, the familiar tenor of his voice, the many memories I have of sitting in his office side by side with Phin.

"Right as rain," he says. "I suspect this is a case of mild heat exhaustion, but if you're worried, I can set up a CT scan sometime this week. You'd have to drive to Alexandria or New Orleans, of course."

"That might be b—"

"No!" I spring to my feet. "Mama, I'm fine. I promise. It was the heat."

Mama looks unconvinced. I see a future of hospital visits and overbearing parental attention and no Phineas unspooling before me.

"I was just confused," I continue, sick with fear. "I know who Lenora May is. Of course, I know my own sister." Did she notice the tremble in that last word? The tremor in my lip?

I force a smile. Mama exhales and says, "Okay."

"Keep her out of the sun for a few days, Emma, make sure

she hydrates, and gets a good night's rest. And if anything like this happens again, we'll set up that scan. Agreed, Sterling?"

"Yes, sir," I say, offering his bag.

Satisfied, Darold takes Doc Payola downstairs for a drink. Mama follows more slowly, pausing to fuss with my pillows and plant a kiss on my cheek.

Finally alone, I flip off the lights and lock my door. The exchange with Doc Payola had an inexplicable calming effect. I no longer feel like a scream, but I don't know where that leaves me. In the middle of something too maddening for rational action. How do I even begin to think about what's happened without losing more of myself to this twisted new reality? I can't. Instead, I sit by the open window, with my eyes trained on the swamp, and anchor Phin's name in my mind with every memory I can summon.

My dreams are all kinds of haunted and I wake with an image stuck to the inside of my eyelids: Lenora May standing in our yard in some old-fashioned dress, hands resting on the slope of her petticoat, winsome eyes on my house. With the gloaming thick around her, she opens her mouth to speak, spilling murky swamp water and mud all down her pretty white dress.

I stumble to the bathroom. No matter how hot I make the shower, it does nothing to erase the dream from my mind. Everywhere I look, Lenora May's presence grows like spotty, black mold. The shower holds a new brand of conditioner, and there's a set of hair and face products I don't recognize on the counter. They aren't new. Each bottle or tube is in a different state of use, as though she's been here for months applying hair gel and using toothpaste. It's even Phin's brand, with the end rolled up to keep all the paste moving forward, just like he would have done. Behind it is a neat little caddy of makeup that doesn't belong to me.

"Phineas Harlan Saucier," I say to the shadow of myself in the foggy mirror. I cover the silver bracelet with my hand. It's wet from the shower, but there isn't anything in this world that'll get me to take it off. One thing, at least, the swamp didn't take.

"It's a charm," he'd said. *"It'll keep you safe."*

I hadn't thought much of his words. At the time, the bracelet was only a symbol of his intention to leave Sticks and me behind when he left for college in August. I'd wanted nothing to do with it, but now I study the florid design more closely. It's a tangled mess of coiling vines and blooming buds, each one finely sculpted.

Grandpa called it his "swamp charm." Holding on to it kept him safe, he'd said. Mama rolled her eyes and told us not to indulge him in nonsense thoughts, but after Dad left, Mama didn't deny Grandpa anything. Phin and I would sit at the foot of his rocker in the screened porch listening as he told us over and over that the swamp was a cruel, hungry place, full of magic so terrible he'd built the fence to contain it.

As a kid, I thought Grandpa was spinning stories, but

now I wonder what secrets he knew.

I'm relieved to find Lenora May's door—*Phin's* door—is shut when I leave the bathroom. Mama and Darold's door, too, is shut tight.

Beside my own door is a plate of food someone brought me last night. I consider leaving it, but the last thing I need is Mama obsessing over what I have and haven't eaten. In the kitchen, I scrape the dried food into the trash can, where it sits on top of everything else. Yesterday, Mama wouldn't have noticed. Today, though? I grab a paper towel and reach into the bowels of the trash can to bury my uneaten meal. Even holding my breath, I can feel the thick scents of day-old broccoli and peaches, oversweet sugars exhaling the scent of death. Moisture seeps through the towel, coating my fingers in old grease and rancid juices from whatever was in that casserole. My stomach lurches when the paper towel breaks and something mushy slips beneath my fingernail.

This is not a normal thing to do.

I'm keenly aware of the fact that I'm doing things like sneaking through my house and sticking my arm into days-old trash, all to avoid being seen. But I can't deal with Mama's concerns about my weight. Not right now. With my dignity somewhere behind me, I twist my hand and push the evidence of my meal as far into the can as possible.

It takes three rounds of hot, soapy water before I'm convinced my skin is clean again. By the time I'm done, the house has begun to shift and creak above me. Soon, they'll be hunting for coffee and eggs. I've got no desire to revisit the events of last night. I need answers, not another fraught conversation. I pull a travel mug from the cabinet, an apple and granola bar from the pantry, and slip through the door unseen.

The early sun is hidden beneath the tree line, casting light that's hazy and blue and still. Grass showers my legs with dew. Beyond the fence, those same lights wink quietly from within the fog, creating rings of light like ripples. But it's the fence that catches my eye.

Somehow the top plank of one section has been knocked from between its posts. It hangs at an odd angle, supported by the thin, green wire of Mama's lights. I've never seen any bit of the fence broken before. In every part of town, it's always been tall and steady as the day my grandpa built it, a solid, unbroken warning.

With the top plank down, the swamp feels closer than it was before. The Wasting Shine moves, weaving together until a clear golden vine runs into the wild. It looks like a promise. I shake my head, but can't get rid of the feeling that the swamp wants me to follow. The thought is accompanied by a cold sweat haunting the nape of my neck. Quickly, I walk around the side of the house and down the road leading to town: the only place I'm likely to find help.

⁜ ⁜ ⁜

Clary General Store is the center point of town. It's a squatting shack with its back to the swamp, a front porch built of unfinished logs, and might be the oldest building in Sticks.

Five rocking chairs sit on either side of Clary General's front door. Each is occupied by the local good ol' boys. Every morning, the old farmers and working men gather by 4:30 a.m. to have the same conversation they've had every other morning before. They rock slow and steady until the sun's proven itself and the first cars have passed, then they go their separate directions to work until dusk.

I've known most of them since I was eight, and Darold started bringing me with him for Saturday sticky buns. There's Sheriff Felder, who takes the prize seat by the door; the local cattle Baron, Mr. Tilly; construction tyrant Mr. Wawheece, whose sons are the scourge of Sticks High, to name a few. Mr. Clary himself takes the seat on the other side of the door and doesn't ever say much at all.

Darold's never been invited to join them. He says it's because he's not yet ancient enough to need a rocker, but I'm convinced half of them'll vote Democrat before they let a black man join their ranks.

As I approach the front steps, they toast me with steaming cups of coffee.

"Here comes trouble," says Mr. Marrioneaux, his mouth entirely obscured by a full beard. Featherhead Fred is what everyone around here calls him. Too much time hunting up natural gas has left him witless and brainsick, but harmless enough. He's the only one in town I've ever heard tell his own swamp tale, which is as much reason for his nickname as anything else. If he wore overalls and held a banjo, he'd be his own tourist attraction.

"Only if you get between me and my coffee," I call, winning a hoarse laugh and a knee slap.

Beside him sits Sheriff Felder, coffee mug on one knee, hat on the other. He gives me a nod and quick smile. "Mornin', Miss Sterling. Didn't manage to bring that deadbeat of a deputy with you?"

There's no hint of the sympathy from yesterday, no sign that I should have anything weighing on my mind. But I need to be sure. "I left the house early, sir. I'm sure he's not far behind. He's—I think he's waiting on Lenora May."

Hope stirs like nausea in my guts. I wait for him to answer, pinching my fingers into fists for patience. *I can't be the only one. I can't.*

"Sounds about right," he says in his slow, sleepy way. "She's in those advanced classes with all the exams this week, right? Smart genes in your family, Miss Sterling. Don't you let that go to waste."

My stomach threatens to revolt if I stay in this conversation much longer. "Yes, sir," I say with as much cheer as I can force. I take the front steps two at a time.

Inside, Clary General smells like coffee, pinewood, and

animal hide. With all the lazy fuss on the front porch this time of day, the interior is empty. The door groans behind me, and the floor beneath me. Clary General is an unquiet place, too full of memories to keep still.

The front of the store is designed to trap the ten tourists who come through Sticks each year. Every shelf is dedicated to swamp paraphernalia and local crafts. One is covered entirely in gator goods: dried heads, boiled skulls, teeth, claws, gator jerky, recipe books, and gator-skin purses. One carries all the sweets you can imagine coming from sugar and nuts: five flavors of pralines, candied pecans, butter toffee, chewy caramels, and chocolate gators. Another holds the full collection of Clary General's Tales of Sticks' Swamp, an ongoing series of books written, illustrated, and published by the Clary family for more than a century. Every few years they release a new one and even locals can't resist. Candy hordes them, adding each new tale to her arsenal with a delight born of scaring her friends stupid, but they've always left me with a shiver.

I pull the most recent from the shelf. The first page is the same in every volume, a note from the first Old Lady Clary, who started recording these tales in 1868:

I do not tell these stories to delight or entice. Rather, I tell these stories to entreat you—stay away from our swamp, but do not ignore it. Read

these stories, my loves, and remember. Secrets are never so dangerous as when they've been forgotten.
—Winona Love Clary

Obviously, Winona Love Clary isn't writing these anymore. This collection is the work of her some-number-of-greats granddaughter and current Old Lady Clary. I page through. All the stories are familiar. Unhelpful. Plenty of tales detail people going missing or getting stuck. But there's nothing practical about how to find them again. If anyone in town knows more than these stories are telling, it's got to be the author.

I only know Old Lady Clary is behind the tall counter by the sounds she makes as she tears plastic wrap to drape over her sticky buns, the quiet smack of her lips as she licks errant frosting from her fingers, the small chuckle of satisfaction that follows. As I press the lever on the coffee dispenser, her round face peers around the canister. An ever-ready smile hangs from the apples of her cheeks, her lips thin and glossy with sugar.

"Morning, Mrs. Clary." I set my mug and a five-dollar bill on the distressed wooden countertop beside a cluster of colorful seven-day candles. Each tall jar is painted with various Catholic saints and voodoo deities. More than once, I've seen locals take them through the back door and plant them along the ground at the base of the swamp fence.

She eyes the book in my hand and then me, curious. "Where'd you get that?"

I gesture to the shelves. "Over there. From your collection of swamp stories."

She makes a sharp, wet noise of displeasure. "Not the book, child. That." She points to my wrist where the bracelet sits.

"My bro—" I catch myself, suddenly unsure. "I mean, I found it in the attic. One of Grandpa's old trinkets. Probably belonged to my grandma."

Old Lady Clary's eyes narrow to slits, her mouth puckers. Everything about her goes still and she releases a slow "Mmm." Then, moving more quickly than I'd have thought possible, she sweeps my money into her till and counts the change. "You want the book, too? Sorry to say it, but I'm afraid this ain't enough."

"No, ma'am, I just had a question." I pause, flipping through the pages of the slender volume.

"About a prayer, shug?" she asks knowingly, reaching for one of the candles. It's decorated with an elaborate image of Marie Laveau dancing, a snake dangling around her neck.

"I think I'm past candles, Mrs. Clary." I hit her with my next words before I can think better of it. "The swamp took my brother and no one remembers him."

The candle thunks against the counter, and the whole shop settles into a thick quiet. I feel hope down to my toes. She's going to remember. She's the one who will help me, who will tell me what's happened, and how to fix it.

"My, my, my," she mutters. "Yes, you're beyond candles, child, far beyond the reach of candles. I'm so sorry, so very sorry."

It takes a moment for that to register. She's not denying what I've said, but what she's offering is so much worse. "No. How do I get him back?"

She shakes her head.

"You have to help me get him back!"

But Old Lady Clary gives another fierce shake of her head. "No, no. You stay away from that swamp. It's a fearful place and no good can come of it. Best to forget and move along." She cuts me off before I can voice a single word. "Nuh-huh. I don't want to hear any more, Sterling Saucier. You mark my words and keep a good distance from that swamp."

"Please," I beg. "You must know *something.*"

She lowers her voice, her eyes on my bracelet. "There's more than one kind of fog in that swamp. Keep clear of it. That's all I'm gonna say."

The door opens with an offensive creak, and Mr. Marrioneaux lumbers in.

"Dear Ida, I've come for a refill," he sings.

I don't move, but Old Lady Clary won't meet my eyes, focusing instead on Mr. Marrioneaux. It's like I'm not even there.

It's all I can do to step away and hold all this anger inside myself when I'd like to throw it at Old Lady Clary.

Through the open door, I spy Darold's cruiser pulling into the store's gravel lot, and then something I can't believe: Phin's Chevelle racing up the road toward school with Lenora May's grinning face at the wheel.

"Thanks for everything," I call sarcastically. And then I hurry after the girl who stole my brother's life. And his car.

Sticks High crouches at the top of the only land in town high enough to call a hill. A flat, redbrick building with bits of white trim to add a touch of southern flair, it's old and quaint and a tight fit for the two hundred and thirty-two students it serves. The Chevelle gleams in the student lot, the one place Phin swore never to park, not with the money he poured into that paint job. Took six months of after-school work at the auto shop to save enough to paint it the color of open defiance. Of all the things Lenora May's taken, this one seems the most unjust. After two seconds of staring at the shining chrome, feeling futile, I spin and let that anger carry me the rest of the way to school.

Locker doors slam open and shut with the sort of enthusiasm reserved for the first and last weeks of school. The air is electric and cold and too sweet. Someone crows at the other end of the hall.

I'm surprised to find Candy at my locker. Just as she's the first on the volleyball court during the season, she likes to be in her desk no later than fifteen minutes early to get herself organized for the day.

She greets me with a careful smile and an uncharacteristically gentle "Hey, Saucier."

"Hey," I manage, trying to fathom why she's so contrite this early in the day.

"So, I'm the worst friend. I got into it with my mom last night and in my brilliance, left my phone in the den. I missed every one of your texts. Forgive me?"

In the middle of the night, after hours of watching the Shine make eerie shapes and shivering in my bed, I'd sent her three 911 texts in a row. Now, I think I'm grateful she missed them.

"Forgiven," I say. "Last-minute panic about the final. I couldn't remember the name of Twain's first publication. L-Lenora May knew the answer."

She nods. Confirming what I already knew: she doesn't remember Phineas.

My stomach releases another angry yowl, reminding me that I haven't eaten since sometime yesterday. Candy is immediately fierce.

"When's the last time you ate? Did you get breakfast? I'll bet you didn't."

I produce the apple and retrieve my coffee mug. "Breakfast of champions."

Her frown is bone deep. "Champions of what? You've got to eat, Saucier, it's a basic function of the human body. We eat, we sleep, and we spike."

"Look. I'm eating. Mmmm, apple." I take a big bite of the fruit. It's sandy and mostly disgusting, but I force a smile. "So just leave it alone."

"You may not want to talk about this, and that's fine, but you can't hide the fact that you've been starving your brain for the past few months, and I need you on the court this fall—on *varsity*, so you can listen while I talk."

This is an argument we've rehearsed many times since the day Phin announced his intention to leave and I lost my appetite. I know how this conversation goes.

Candy doesn't disappoint. She launches into an account of my eating habits over the past three months, my slow but steady drop in weight, my inability to eat a normal meal, and ends with a statement about how "thin doesn't equal beautiful." She's gotten better at it, I have to admit.

"Beauty is a social construction. I'm your best friend and that means it's my job to tell you the truth, and the truth is that you were a helluva lot prettier three months ago than you are now, so snap out of this." She's gotten so passionate in her speech that she's turning heads. But she's immune to the attention.

"Keep your voice down, Candy, I hear you," I say.

"I'm not so sure that you do."

The first time she asked me about this, I'd tried and failed to explain that it wasn't about wanting to be thin; I couldn't think of food when the threat of losing Phin to college was so near. She'd cut me a little slack, but now that Phin's not even a distant memory in her head, that piece of our friendship is gone, gone, gone. How much of my best friend disappeared with my brother?

I'd rather not find out. I give her the only innocuous non-response I can think of. "It's not that simple."

"Whatever you say," she says with a defeated sigh, "but I'll be here whenever you're ready to talk. Promise me you'll still be here, too."

She says the words so casually that at first I don't understand her meaning. Where would I go? But then I get it. The constant pressure in my stomach becomes hard and pointed.

"I promise," I say, and it's true. It never occurred to me that avoiding a few meals might actually kill me.

Maybe it had occurred to Phin, though. The thing that made him angriest was fear, and he was furious in the moments before he ran into the swamp.

"Sterling," he'd said, his voice a caged bear. "Why are you *doing* this? Why are you starving yourself?"

The bracelet was a dead weight in my hands, my shoulders pressed to the carport wall. I answered, "What do you care? You're leaving."

He'd moved so quickly then. His fist flew at my face. I closed my eyes a split second before I felt the carport buck. Darold appeared out of nowhere, grabbing Phin from behind. That's when Phin spun and threw a second punch into Darold's eye.

I'd thought it was anger that made him take a swing at me. I'd thought he was angry with me for losing weight or for caring so much that he was leaving. I'd thought that he was angry because leaving wasn't easy. But maybe he was as afraid as I'd been.

I take another bite of my apple, hoping it will taste good enough to get me through the whole thing. It's grainy and gross and entirely unappetizing. Candy averts her gaze as I take one more bite and drop it in the trash.

The bell rings five minutes after I've handed in my exam. Candy snaps her pencil against the desk and turns hers in with a little more flourish than is strictly necessary. On her return, she bends to drop a tease in Abigail's ear. Abigail swats at her and continues frantically scribbling. Watching her makes me want to hold my own breath. Finally, she slides back in her seat, her shoulders relax, and she stretches her long, dark legs.

From her desk, Mrs. Gwaltney reminds us to turn in our books if we haven't and threatens the wrath of every writer from Thomas Malory to Mark Twain if we don't. It's the sort of joke she can only make at the end of the year, even then only a few of us paid enough attention to find the humor of it.

Finally free, Candy, Abigail, and I join the rush of bodies sweeping along the hall to the cafeteria.

"How'd you do, Beale?" Candy calls across my nose.

"None of your business," Abigail says, uninterested in competition off the volleyball court.

Walking next to her, I always feel a good two feet shorter than I am in reality. She's looming and serene with hundreds of dark braids coiled on top of her head adding a touch of regality. When Candy talks about beauty, Abigail's the person I think of. Put her next to her sharper twin, Valerie, and they're deadly gorgeous.

Candy scoffs. "Everything is my business," but she doesn't press. Precedent is against her strong-arming Abigail into anything.

The cafeteria is a long room lined with windows that face the football field, which stands between the school and the swamp. The walls are yellow, the floor a tightly checkered pattern of maroon and black and years and years of grease.

Lenora May is already here, seated at a table full of senior girls. I search their faces for any sign of discomfort at her presence, but I should know by now that I'll find none. Lenora May and the other girls move and talk in the rhythm of old friends. Her curls bounce while she laughs. Ketchup hangs from the little cluster of fries in her fingertips, and I hope with all my might that it'll splatter the front of her dress. She notices, dabs it lightly on her plate, and eats.

"Buying today?" Candy tugs me in the direction of the grease and canned veggies line.

The sight of Lenora May has killed any appetite I might have dredged up during finals. I pat my backpack. "I've got mine. I'll get a table."

"Whatever." She stops short of calling my bluff and leaves to catch Abigail.

The crowd is a smothering riot of laughter and anticipation of summer. I find myself enraged by how easily they accept Lenora May as one of them. Would Candy and Abigail so quickly relinquish memories of me?

This sparks an idea in me.

With a student body barely large enough to support the typical gamut of sports teams, it doesn't take long to figure out who your friends and enemies are. And in a place like this, you're either one or the other. In Phin's case, there are more of the latter thanks to his fists-first philosophy of conflict management, but he wasn't without allies.

Scanning the room, I find Cody Hays sitting at a table by the vending machines for those who prefer sugar to grease for lunch. He's been Phin's best friend since I can remember. If there's a chance anyone else in this entire town might remember Phin, surely it's him. I have to try.

Cody sits in the perfect center of his table, which will make this awkward no matter how I do it. I stop at the far end and push my hands into my pockets. Keeping my eyes steady on his face I say, "Hey, Cody."

"Hey, Sterling," he says with a grin, leaning back a little. All heads at the table turn toward me. I can't help but remember the two million times he's teased me about my pale legs while Phin smacked the back of his head—we all knew his teasing was an excuse to look. Beside him, his girlfriend, Samantha, narrows her eyes.

"What's up?" he prompts.

A weight heavy enough to stop me from speaking settles on my chest. Pushing my words past it makes their ends waver. "I wanted to know if you've heard from Phin."

There's a pause and, in a burst of hope, I think he's the one who will finally remember my brother. But then—

"What are you talking about? Who, now?"

"Your best friend? My brother? Phineas? You've been helping him rebuild his Chevelle all year?" His shrug pulls my throat tight. "He disappeared into the swamp yesterday when you were supposed to go to the track, remember?" My mouth is hot and my hands cold, but I keep going. Last chance. If Cody doesn't remember . . . "He loaned you thirty bucks two weeks ago because you said you needed gas money, but really it was because you thought Samantha was preg—"

"Hey!" The near-mention of Samantha's scare has him on his feet. Samantha's cheeks go red and she smacks his arm. "I give, okay. I *really* don't know who you're talking about. I wish I did," he says with a nervous glance toward Samantha, who's looking fit to be tied. "I'm sorry," he adds, but it's more for Samantha.

My tears are too fast for me. The first one is falling down my cheek before I can stop it.

"You have to believe me," I say, pleading. "The swamp took Phin and I just need someone to give a damn!"

Cody looks stunned, like I've called his mama a whore. He opens his mouth, but it's Candy who speaks.

"What the hell is going on?" she asks, inserting herself between me and the table. "Why don't we grab a Coke and sit for a minute?"

Heat rises to my cheeks. I should do as she says, but frustration is a waterfall and I'm already plummeting.

"No! Candy, you have to remember Phin. You had a crush on him in sixth grade. He's always in trouble, but he's stupid smart. He's planning to leave in the fall because he got that scholarship to Tulane and I've been mad at him for months. The swamp took him, Candy. The swamp took him away, it took his whole life away. Don't look at me like that. I'm not crazy. You know I'm not."

"Yeah, I know that, but honestly, Saucier, you're sounding a little crazy right now. Let's—"

"Candy, please!" Tears get in the way. "You have to believe me. Just say you believe me."

Candy looks away. I can't bear her silence. As students gawk, I head straight for the doors.

The little courtyard is full of noon sun that pulls the AC right off of my skin. I keep moving, slashing at the tears that fill my eyes. We're not supposed to leave the campus, but no one's around to enforce it the last week of school and I move easily through the courtyard, out the rear doors, past the teacher parking lot, and around the bleachers. I keep going until I'm on the far side of the football field, running right into the pines and all the way to where the swamp fence curls around on this side of things.

My breath catches painfully in my throat. I squeeze my eyes shut and concentrate on trapping my tears there, but they push through my lids and slide, hot as sunlight, down my cheeks.

Phineas is gone. He's not in any of the places he should be and the whole world acts as if it's fine and dandy for Lenora May to be here instead. *Am I crazy?* I think, and panic smacks my heart into skipping a step.

No, I decide, twisting the bracelet on my wrist. *Phin is as real as I am.*

I slam my open palm against the fence. "Give him back! I swear on my life I won't let you have him!" I cry, and slap the plank again.

I've bruised my wrist bone by hitting the bracelet against the fence. I study the piece of silver, the blooming red beneath it. I wonder if Phin really believed it would keep me safe.

Long minutes pass until somewhere far behind me, the first warning bell trills. The sound calls to mind the chatter of friends, the smell of lunch lurking in the air, and a hollow feeling in my guts.

I let the walk up the hill take as long as I dare. Inside, the hallways are crowded and anxious. Too many eyes follow as I pass. Not only does news travel fast in this school, but I probably couldn't have picked a better time to have a spaz attack or a better person to have it on. Even people who've never bothered to notice me take the chance to get in a good leer.

I'm trying so hard not to notice everyone noticing me that I don't hear the person calling my name as I walk into trig. I only stop because he pulls on my shoulder. Lightly and just once. His hands are already in the pockets of his faded jeans when I turn.

"Sterling Saucier," he says again. It sounds like an invocation and I think if he knew my middle name, he'd have included that, too.

"Heath Durham," I answer. One corner of his mouth twitches, a feint at a smile that doesn't reach his eyes.

We've shared a number of classes in the past two years. In fact, near the end of ninth grade, there was a moment when I thought we were heading toward a first date. Heath wasn't a talker, but when he did talk, the words we shared were sweet and supplemented with notes of the flirting variety.

And then he shut up.

For about three weeks, I cursed his name, but by the time sophomore year started, he'd taken a turn for the stoic and unattainable. Drugs are the popular theory, which only serves to make him that much more appealing to most. Not me. I've avoided him like death all year. Yet, I can't deny there's something about the cut of his honey-gold hair and the uneven slope of his shoulders that makes my mouth hunt for a smile.

"I heard about your—um—conversation with Cody," he says, and I stop him right there.

"It wasn't anything, okay? A mistake and frankly, none of your business." I'm more than a little irritated that the time he decides to break his stupor and talk to me again, it's to take a cheap shot at the girl who's losing it.

I turn so fast my hip slams into a desk hard enough to tip it. It crashes to the ground in cacophonous glory. Any eyes that weren't already on Heath and me surely are now.

"Sorry," Heath says loudly so everyone can hear. "I can be such a klutz."

I can recognize a kindness even when I'd rather not.

"It's okay," I say, turning to face him as he rights the desk. "And thanks."

His nod is barely visible, a quick wink of movement.

The room begins to fill around us. The imminent exam has siphoned their attention from the crazy girl. Now they frantically review equations and rules, rapidly quizzing each other. I should be doing the same, but Heath catches my hand and pulls me as far from the crowd as we can go. Dusty afternoon light warms my shoulders. But it's something else that makes my cheeks heat when he bends to speak in my ear.

"I believe you," he says, his breath stirring my hair.

"What?" I don't want to jump to conclusions, but hope is a weedy thing.

Just as close, he adds, "About the swamp."

I lean away enough to see his face. His eyes are tired but earnest.

"You believe me," I repeat because I want it to be true.

"Can I drive you home?" he asks.

"Yeah," I answer without bothering to think about it.

His brassy eyes brighten. "Okay. Meet me by the magnolia tree after school."

"Yeah," I say again.

Candy is full of significant glances when I sit down. Thankfully, there's no time to talk before the exams are passed around. And extra thankfully, this is trig and I can work most of it in my sleep, which is good because there are only three words in my head right now and they're the best I think I've ever heard: *I believe you.*

In Sticks, there aren't many people who actually need to drive to school. Regardless, the student parking lot is a boiling pot of alternately pristine and peeling chrome. Heath stands at the edge of the lot in the shade of the tall magnolia, hands in pockets, studying the ground with a steady gaze. He's oblivious to the ruckus around him as students tumble toward freedom. One boy gives Heath's arm a friendly punch as he passes. Even that gets little reaction. Just one slow nod of acknowledgment.

I contemplate the drug rumors.

I consider the talk that must be going around about me after today.

"Hey," I say, stepping from the sidewalk to the grass.

His eyes are glassy when he looks up, a statue coming to life. "This way."

Heath's truck is one more hand-me-down Ford lost in a sea of trucks. Green and cleaner on the outside than most, he hasn't made any attempt to fancy it up the way others have. No tacky license plate frame, no fake balls swinging from the hitch, no fancy rims on the tires. The only thing resembling decoration is a faded decal of the sun plastered perfectly in the middle of the rear windows.

Inside, the cabin smells vaguely of leather and lemons. The floors are lost beneath homework assignments, crushed soda cans, and the summer AP Literature reading list. Baseball caps, maps, and food wrappers cover the dash. I have to slide *Fahrenheit 451* and a seriously abused iPod out of the passenger side to make room for myself. I try not to notice the B's and C's on the papers at my feet. If they were mine, I'd have burned them, but they'd never have been mine.

Heath heaves his bag into the little space behind the seats. It lands on a duffel bag and a baseball bat, and I remember that he's big into baseball. A pitcher, and not a bad one. Before our year of silence, I used to go to the games with Candy and Abigail and watch how calm and sure he was at the center of all that tension.

It's hard to remember how brilliant he was back then. He was the sun and everything revolved around him until one day he went dark. And then he started showing up in the back of Darold's cruiser.

"Uh," he starts. "Sorry about the mess. It's sort of a chronic condition for me."

"I don't mind," I say, carefully setting my feet on top of his discarded assignments. "I prefer the disasters you can see."

He smiles and just like that we've reconnected.

"Coke?" he asks. "My treat."

I'm not much of a Coke drinker, but I find myself nodding. "Sounds great."

We have three options: Flying J, the only gas station for thirty miles; Sonic, the town's sole representation of mainstream dining; or Clary General, home of infuriating encounters with Old Lady Clary. He heads to Clary General. I'm unsurprised. He's a Clary General type of guy.

As we approach, I see that Phin's Chevelle is already parked in the gravel lot. My heart boils at the sight.

"You wouldn't happen to know how to hot-wire a car, would you?"

I feel Heath's eyes settle on me. The truck slows to a crawl, but doesn't turn in to the lot.

"No. But I've got ten minutes and a smartphone."

It doesn't take ten minutes. In less than five, we've discovered that classic cars like Phin's will turn over for a screwdriver, and have parked Heath's truck as far from the Chevelle as possible. We don't have to look any farther than the truck bed to find the same little red toolbox all the boys and men of Sticks seem to carry.

Heath taps the screwdriver against his leg, considering me or the car, I can't tell. He says, "You gonna tell me why we're doing this?"

"It's my brother's," I say, hoping he'll let this be enough. "The one the swamp took. I want to keep it safe." I want to keep it away from *her*, but I can't explain that, yet.

He nods once and steps into action. He retrieves his wallet from the truck, cracks the windows, locks the doors, and joins me, all with the same level of care. Mercifully, the Chevelle is unlocked. Heath slides behind the wheel.

Clary General is still quiet, but the sun is high and there are plenty of people passing on the street. I remind myself that it's not theft because the car didn't belong to Lenora May in the first place. It doesn't do a whole lot for my nerves.

Heath has his screwdriver poised for crime.

"Wait. Let me do that." I reach for the tool. "Scoot over."

He doesn't argue. I take his place behind the wheel, settling into the wide, leather seat, and verifying my feet reach the pedals. If this were a normal day, they wouldn't. Phin's legs are a foot longer than mine, but apparently, Lenora May and I are of comparable height. I grind my teeth at the thought.

With a little extra pressure, and one disturbing sound, the screwdriver fits neatly into the ignition.

Wincing, I twist the handle. The engine rumbles to life as the door of Clary General swings open. I catch a glimpse of

Lenora May's dark curls as I reverse out of the parking spot. Without another glace at the door, I kick the Chevelle into third as fast as I can. Gravel sprays behind us as we peel away.

Heath slouches in his seat, one hand on the window frame, the other on his thigh, a picture of calm in my speeding car.

"What do you intend to do with this vehicle?" he asks.

"Put it someplace it won't be found."

We take the side road by the swamp. Half a mile past my house, the road forks; in one direction, an ancient wooden bridge brings you over a wide swath of the Mississippi River, and in the other a gravel road bends around the far side of the swamp. I take the gravel road, slowing to accommodate the choppy, disused terrain.

No one comes here. Most folks don't even know it exists.

I turn down another narrow road that's nearly invisible below a sprawl of oak trees. The air is cooler here, the branches crossing every which way overhead to veil the sun, each of them bleeding Spanish moss. Fallen twigs snick and pop beneath the tires.

"How did you ever find this place?" Heath peers through the open window at the canopy above. I'm pleased at the appreciation in his voice.

"I didn't." Heath looks at me, an eyebrow arched in question, but I shake my head. He doesn't know what kind of story he's asking for. "This isn't even it. Just wait."

The trees open; behind them the sun splashes over a tall,

long-forgotten plantation house. White paint peels away in long scrolls, exposing pale, aged pine beneath. Wide-open porches and balconies crawl around every corner. It's remarkably intact: the roofline's square and not a window is broken.

I tuck the Chevelle around the side beneath a low-bending oak branch and then together, Heath and I get out and climb the five steps to the front door. An old metal plaque nailed to the right of the door says LILLARD HOUSE, 1778.

Heath tries the handle. The lock rattles securely. He cranes his head, following the arch of the door frame. "Ever been inside?"

"No. Everything's locked up tight and has been for years."

Heath's lost in the grandeur of this place. He walks the length of the porch, peering in windows, his hands cupped against the light.

I remember the first time I saw the house. It was late one summer night. Phineas and I had escaped one of Dad's drunken rages. Neither of us was brave enough to try the swamp. Instead, we ran and ran, and when the Lillard House loomed ghostly white in front of us, it was a relief. I collapsed on the porch and Phin sat with an arm around me while I cried myself dry.

But standing on the porch now, I feel an invasive memory creeping in. One of running through those same woods with Lenora May. She gripped my hand, helped me up when I stumbled, and when I couldn't stop crying, she held my face in her own trembling hands and said, "This is our place. It's safe." She pulled me away from the house, beneath the dark canopy of oak trees and said, "We're so safe here, we can scream our hearts out."

And then she screamed at the sky. It was a vicious and brave noise. At first, it frightened me. I thought Dad would hear, but when she did it again and nothing happened, I joined her.

She held both of my hands and we tipped our heads back and screamed.

Except we didn't.

It's not real.

The real memory is Phineas wrapping his thin arms around me and telling me I was safe, safe, safe as long as he was with me. The real memory is Phineas saying it was Mama's fault for not being strong and, even as he said it, we both knew it wasn't true. The real memory is leaning into that porch like it had arms to fold around us and falling asleep there.

Behind the house a little field spills away toward the edge of the swamp. This time of year, clusters of wild sweet William grow in blue patches, like the sky dropped down and left bits of itself behind. Heath eyes it all with a quiet focus that I suspect means he's thinking. If he wasn't, he'd pick a point for his eyes to stick to and fade away the way I've seen him do a thousand times from the last row of the classroom.

"Jezuz," he says, having explored the back porch from one end to the other. "How does a place like this fall off the map?"

That idea doesn't seem as strange as it might have a few days ago. If a mother can forget her own son, a town forgetting a relic of the past century seems easy as dying.

"The swamp's down there." I point to where a few pine trees mark the edge. They're older and more dense than the trees behind my house, the fence is hidden beneath their heavy, needled boughs.

A small shudder passes through Heath's shoulders. He doesn't speak right away. Just watches me with a little distance in his eyes. Then he says, "I don't know who you lost, but I remember what it was like. When no one believed me."

Quickly, I run through what I know about Heath and his family. The Durhams live in the wealthiest part of town, in the faux plantation-style homes, which sit on a few cozy acres of land, none of which touch the swamp. His dad's a farmer and his mom's an engineer or something else fancy like that, and he doesn't have any siblings. At least, none I've ever heard of.

"Nathan Payola," he says. He waits for me to react, but there's nothing for me to react to. Angrily, he adds, "He was my best friend."

Because I know what it feels like, I wish I could tell Heath I remembered Nathan, but the name sparks absolutely nothing inside me. So I say the same thing Heath told me that I found comfort in. "I believe you."

I commit the name to memory, Nathan Payola, anchoring it as firmly as I did Phin's. It's only familiar because there *are* Payolas in town. But Doc Payola and his wife never had childr—

As soon as the thought crosses my mind, a fog I hadn't known was there begins to clear. A memory shakes itself loose: a boy lurking behind his mother's desk with a stack of old books in Doc Payola's waiting room. His name was Nathan. The more certain I become, the more he settles in my mind. As with Lenora May, there are memories of the Payolas being childless sitting side by side with memories of their son.

"Heath," I say, unsure of my own mind. "I remember him."

His voice is wounded. "Sterling—"

"I didn't. I swear, I didn't until you said his name and somehow . . ." I gesture helplessly at the swamp. "Everything cleared and now I do."

"You're kidding."

"Not even a little!" Excitement rushes through me. If I can remember Nathan, there's hope. "Doc's son. A year ahead of us. Basketball, tongue ring, great laugh. Heath!"

My enthusiasm barely stirs him. His smile is cautious when he says, "That's him."

"How did it happen to you? To Nathan?" I ask.

Heath stares into the oaks and sinks into the memory. "We grew up together. When he got his license last spring, we drove to New Orleans. Because we could. Got all the way to the Quarter, but parking was so damn expensive we couldn't do anything other than turn around. It was late when we got back. We thought we'd take a few laps around the racetrack. See if anyone else was there."

The track is at the end of Candy's street and if you go to Sticks High, you've been there more than a few times. It's a sad piece of pavement that all the good ol' boys do their best to keep flat and functional, and it's about as far as you can get from the swamp without leaving Sticks. Phin's grand plan for the Chevelle was to have it fixed in time for a graduation loop of glory three and a half days from now. More than anything, I want him to be home in time to make that loop.

I'm glad I saved his car from that thief.

"We never made it to the track. Not even close," Heath continues, picking at a leather band around his wrist. "Someone came tearing down the side road and forced us into the swamp. They must've been drunk. We crashed nose-first on one of the fence posts—I still can't believe it didn't break." He pauses; the memory looks like it's closing in on him. "I blacked out. Woke up with blood in my eyes, a tree practically in my lap. All alone. I had to climb through one of the rear doors—mine was crunched shut." He makes a shape with his hands to mimic the destroyed door. "Whoever it was that ran us off didn't even stop and at first I didn't see Nathan anywhere.

"This is where it starts to sound crazy." He pushes his hands through his hair and that's when I see they're shaking.

"Heath," I say, being bold by taking one of those hands in mine. "I know you're not crazy."

His expression is guarded, but his hand settles, and he goes on with a little more confidence.

"The driver's side of the car had punched through the fence and was sinking in the muck. The swamp was full. It had been raining for days and there was so much water. There was nothing else to do so I waded in, looking for Nathan. I kept tripping because I couldn't see where I was stepping. I was soaked. Choking on swamp water—I remember how horrible it tasted and thinking that I shouldn't care about a thing like that, but I couldn't help it because it tasted *so* bad—but I kept trying to run. Jezuz, I was terrified that Nathan'd be floating there. Dead.

"I didn't see him at first because I didn't expect him to be on his feet and so far into the swamp. Just standing there."

I'm chilled to the bone. Suddenly, I see Lenora May's figure, a ghostly silhouette deep in the swamp. The horror is fresh as new.

"I yelled, but it was like he couldn't hear me. Twenty yards away and he couldn't hear me. I don't really know what happened next. I turned away for a second and when I looked again, he was gone," Heath finishes with a tight shrug.

"And no one remembers him except for you," I add, both horrified and relieved. There's some comfort in simply not being alone. "Did anyone replace him?"

The look he gives me is answer enough.

"When the swamp took my brother, it sent someone—some*thing* else to take his place. I don't know what Lenora May is, but she's not my sister."

"Are you shitting me?" Heath reels, stepping back a few paces. "She's not your sister? You don't have a sister? She came from the swamp?"

"Yes and no. I've never had a sister. Only a brother. Phineas. Phineas Harlan Saucier."

"Phineas," Heath repeats. And then he pauses, jerks a little, and frowns. "Phin Saucier."

"He only ran into the swamp yesterday and—"

"Wait, wait, wait," he says, pinching his eyes shut. With his hands braced against his hips, he keeps his eyes closed for a long minute.

"Heath?"

"Yeah. I just. I don't know." He looks at me, frowning hard. "Phin was a senior?"

"With a full ride to Tulane in the fall. I guess that's Lenora May's now, too," I say, letting my bitterness show.

"Dark hair, dark blue eyes. Like you," Heath continues, studying me so intently I feel myself squirm. "Quick temper. Better in a fight than the Wawheece boys?"

He can't be saying what I think he's saying. "You . . . remember?"

"I don't know." Heath rubs a hand over his face. "I don't know."

He stands then and paces over the weedy ground in the full sun, stopping with his back to me. He stays like that until sweat speckles his shirt between his shoulder blades.

"Heath?"

Slowly, he turns to rest glossy eyes on me. "I remember him," he says.

The moment tightens around me.

"Like you said. I didn't before," he says, caution rough in his voice. "I only remembered that you had a sister—Lenora May—until you said his name, and now"—he shrugs, casting around for the right words—"now, I can practically see him. We weren't ever friends, but I knew enough to be afraid of him. Especially after—um, well, after the summer I ditched you, I kept my distance."

At any other time, I'd be stuck on him admitting he ditched me. But now, all I can think of is Phin.

"Yeah," I say, nearly breathless with wanting this to be truth. "That's Phin. But why doesn't anyone else remember?"

"None of this has ever made any kind of sense to me. I

stopped trying to understand it a long time ago." He falls into silence, then adds, "Jezuz," drawing out the word. Finally, he says, "So, what do we do now?"

"I wish I knew." I try not to feel defeated. "We've got to start moving, though. It's a long walk to town even if we don't follow the road."

We don't dawdle, but it's early evening when we finally reach his truck at Clary General. He drives me home, idling at the end of my driveway. The whole truck rumbles like a pile of thunder.

"Thank you," I say. "For today."

He's the closest to a true smile I've seen in a long time. "I'm the one who should be thanking you. Grand theft auto, creepy old houses, and a two-mile hike in the hot sun? You sure know how to show a guy a good time. Next time, I'm thinking bank heist."

I know I'm blushing by the heat in my cheeks, but I counter, "Or maybe something really insane. Like going after Phin and Nathan."

We're both quiet and I can't decide if I'm glad or mad at myself for saying it.

Finally, avoiding my eyes, he says, "I haven't been hopeful in a long time."

At first, I think he means he's hopeful now, but then I realize it might be a warning. Maybe after a year, hope wears thin.

"Got your cell?" I ask.

"Um." He absently pats at his pockets. "Yeah."

"What's your number?" I ask. He recites the numbers, but when I start to give mine, he stops me with, "I still have it."

He kept my number. For an entire year, my name has been living in his phone.

I have the urge to confess that I technically didn't delete his, that it was Candy who did the deed, but instead I offer an "oh" and my second blush of the evening.

"Sterling," he says, uncertain. "Hey. I'm—sorry. Since Nathan disappeared, I've been kind of messed up."

"I remember," I say, thinking of how many times Darold was called in the middle of the night to track Heath down, how often he and Sheriff Felder discussed Heath in hushed voices at my kitchen table, how often he'd been pulled from class by a scowling principal.

"Right," he says. "I guess your stepdad won't be thrilled if he sees me here."

Gravel crunches behind us and we both jump, but it's only Candy's white Ion. Not a police cruiser, but maybe not much better.

"Gotta run," I say, pushing the door open and sliding to the ground. "Remember me tomorrow?"

"I promise," he says without a pause.

Suddenly, we both freeze, neither of us realizing how serious the request was until after. Now, I hold the door for a moment longer than necessary. The truth is neither of us can make that promise, because we can't fight something we don't understand. But I remember what Heath said about hope. I'm not going to let the swamp have that, too.

I run my fingers over my bracelet and make my voice firm. "I promise, too."

"I HOPE YOUR RADIO SILENCE is a sign your fingers have been twisted up in those golden locks," Candy says, resting her chin on my shoulder. It takes me a minute to realize she means Heath's golden locks.

From a few feet away, Abigail answers for me. "You can't go judging what other people've been up to based on your own personal scale. The thing only goes from easy to slut."

"Better than a scale of freezing to nun," Candy counters with a grin. Their snipes may carry sharp edges, but we all know it's only combat training. There'll be no mercy for the person who calls any of us a slut and means it. "Or have you been keeping secrets? Did you ask Shannon out and not say?"

A blush spreads on Abigail's dark cheeks. Discretion is one of her principle virtues, which isn't always easy for a girl who prefers girls in a small town. Even with her best friends, she finds it difficult to talk about her love life.

"What are you doing here?" I ask.

"Ouch, Saucier. A boy walks into the picture and we're suddenly gutter trash?" Candy grasps at her heart. "C'mon, don't be that girl. I've got no time for that girl."

I look to Abigail for help. "It's Monday," she offers.

Monday.

Monday has been our study night all year. It's the night Mama goes to church to prep meals for the eldest members of Sticks, and Darold goes with all of the other deputies to play pool at Mean-Eyed Possum's House of Beer and Cues. This is the night Phin would make his signature grilled cheese and Tabasco sandwiches. Candy and Abigail would come over and we'd study, polish our nails, and listen to whatever music Abigail had discovered during that week until one of our parents called an end to things.

It's not exactly that I forgot. It's more that it was something I thought would've disappeared with Phin.

"Right. Sorry. Study night. Sure."

"First things first. Spill," Candy commands.

"What, Heath? There's nothing to spill," I protest.

"B and S," she returns fire. "You've been gone for hours with the Greek god of all things stoic and beautiful. This is the guy who abandoned you last year without a word. There better have been an apology or he's got a world of hurt coming. So. Spill."

"Leave the girl alone," Abigail says, coming to my defense. "Sterling, don't answer her."

"I'm not holding out on you, I swear. We talked and yes, he apologized. That's it."

Abigail's had enough. She derails Candy the only way she knows how. "Know what I heard today? Quentin Stokes is totally into you."

Candy looks at Abigail with signature suspicion. "Prove it."

"All I know is he's planning on making a move at the track Thursday night, so you might want to put a little effort in."

"That's not proof," she says pointedly. "Did he tell you to your face? Write it down? Is my name tattooed on his beautiful bicep? No? Then I don't believe you. Saucier, this thing with Heath—"

"Look, Candy, I don't want to talk about boys," I say, suddenly impatient with everything. "Unless we're talking about my brother, Phineas."

She and Abigail share an uncomfortable look.

"That's the boy you say disappeared?"

"It's the truth. And if you were really my friends, you'd at least give me the time of day."

"Why don't we study?" Abigail suggests. She tugs on our hands, making a gentle plea for peace in her calming way. "I know you both need help with history."

But Candy's not having any of it. "You want the time of day? Here's a minute or two!" As I protest, she grabs Abigail's hand and drags her across the yard and over the broken section of the fence. "Let's settle this."

The Wasting Shine glimmers at their approach. Pine branches bob in the breeze like a great gaping maw. A nightmare descends. They can't really be in the swamp.

"Candy, c'mon," I urge, "this isn't funny. Please, come back."

"Why?" She moves deeper into the woods. "This whole town thinks there's something horrible hiding in here, but it's *just* a swamp, Saucier. Louisiana is lousy with them. They smell like shit and they're full of gators and ducks, but you know what they're not full of? Demons and ghosts."

She smacks her palm against the trunk of a skinny black gum tree and swings around it until she's facing me again. Shine skitters away, avoiding her touch as if she were a negatively charged magnet.

"Hey!" she shouts. "Demons of this sweltering mud pit, if you exist, come forth, I summon thee!"

When nothing happens, Candy splays her hands as if that's proof of anything.

"I hate to agree with her when she's being so obnoxious, but I think she's right." Abigail's moved off a little ways, down the fence where blackberry bushes have always grown just beyond reach. She plucks a few and eats. "Ugh. Except maybe fear these blackberries."

"Okay, great. You've made your point, both of you, now please come back into the yard."

Long ropes of Shine lash at Abigail's ankles and lick up her calves, but she doesn't notice them. She tosses the berries away and begins to move a little deeper into the swamp as though the Shine guides her.

"Do you guys see that?" she calls. Cypress trunks block my view of her tall form.

This must be what happened to Phin. And to Nathan. Now, it's happening to Abigail right here in front of me and I'm too scared to cross the fence.

"Candy, please go get her," I plead, trying to keep as much of the fear from my voice as possible. "Please. Abigail?"

Abigail's still out of sight, but she answers my call and Candy jogs in the direction of her voice. The hum of summer fills my ears, too loud and too quiet all at once. For one horrible second, I can't see either of them, but then they come into view, arm in arm, Shine whipping at their heels and no longer wrapped around Abigail's ankles.

"Are you sure you didn't see him?" Abigail's saying when they climb over the fence. "Tall, skinny, white T-shirt? You didn't see anything?"

"Only cypress trees, which are all of those things minus the T-shirt," Candy answers with finality.

"A boy?" I ask, pulling them to the safety of the porch. "Did you recognize him?"

Candy becomes impassive.

I'm too eager. A tall, thin boy. Nathan? Phineas? "Abigail?"

Abigail takes her sweet time pulling her eyes from the swamp to look at me, and her gaze is a brick wall when she answers, "No, I didn't see anything."

I have two choices: pursue the truth with two people unwilling to entertain it. Or preserve the fragile friendships I have.

We study.

We spend the better part of four hours sprawled across my room with history notes and textbooks covering every available surface. Instead of grilled cheese sandwiches, we order a pizza from Mrs. Trish at the Flying J gas station. She installed a pizza oven and an automatic espresso machine last year in an attempt to add a touch of class. Of course, it's hard to be classy when you time baking a pizza by smoking a cigarette. We break when her daughter, Chrissy, arrives on a motorbike with the pizza in tow. If the grease weren't enough to turn my stomach, the idea that it was christened in smoke and exhaust is, but I take a piece to keep Candy from grousing. Which she does anyway when I only manage a few bites.

The rest of the evening passes as it should, with reviews

and quizzing and the occasional discussion of how we can possibly get to New Orleans more than once this summer. By the time they leave, the night almost feels normal. But when I return from walking them to the door, there's an unwelcome surprise in my room.

Lenora May stands in front of the full-length mirror on my closet door. She holds a sundress in either hand, scrutinizing each in turn. One is a subtle, pale yellow thing. The other is dramatic—white with red petals cascading from one shoulder to pool around the hemline.

"Which do you like best for the senior graduation party?" she asks, as though we're sisters. "The red is striking, but I think the yellow is more me, don't you?"

I'm helpless against the assault of memory. I think of the dozens of times I've seen her wear the yellow dress; she always manages to make it look new by adding different accessories. The red, though, is stunning with her dark hair and hugs her curves in the best way. Once, she wore it to church and when we came home, Mama gently suggested she never do it again. We'd laughed quietly in her bedroom over Mama's prudish sensibilities, and vowed to each wear bloodred lipstick next Sunday. We'd been grounded for the offense, but even that punishment had been worth the moment of horror on Mama's face when we hopped in the car. Laughter, admiration, love. All for Lenora May.

Every memory is a wound.

"I don't care," I say, seeking a memory of Phin singing the wrong words to "You Are Mine" to make me laugh. "Get out."

"All right. I'll go as soon as you tell me what you've done with my car."

"I didn't do anything with *your* car." This, at least, is so satisfying I can barely keep the grin from my face.

"Oh, Sterling, what did I do to upset you?" she asks with a sigh, draping both dresses across her arm.

I nearly choke on my answer. "Stop pretending! We both know you don't belong here. You're not my sister no matter what anyone says. I remember my brother and I'm not the only one."

I let the challenge lie between us. I'm not so afraid, so bewildered as I was last night. Maybe she's an all-powerful swamp demon capable of changing hundreds of minds to suit her purposes. Maybe I'm just a small girl from a small town with no chance of saving my brother. Or maybe not.

If I can remember Nathan, and Heath can remember Phin, then I'm convinced whatever has happened isn't permanent. We can change things. We only have to figure out how.

"I'm going to save him from whatever it is you've done and there's nothing you can do to change that so stop pretending you and I are anything more than strangers."

There's a shift in her then. She pulls her arms close to her belly and her mouth falls into a gentle frown. She looks smaller, surrounded by her dark curls.

"Okay, Sterling," she says, moving to the door. "I'll stop."

She's not my sister, I remind myself as the door whispers shut. Then, I hunt the floor for my pj's and try to banish the false guilt swelling in my chest.

She's so convincing. No matter how I rationalize, there's still a piece of me that wants to race after her and apologize, to tell her she should wear the red dress because it makes her look powerful and composed and because Mama would say yellow. Every time she speaks, my mind betrays me a little more, force-feeding me counterfeit memories of loving and hating my sister, and it's only because I'm as stubborn as my dad was mean that she hasn't erased Phin entirely. But how long will that last?

Settling into bed, I gaze through the open window. The swamp chitters and snaps, alive with more danger than I know how to name. I remind myself I'm not alone. I have Heath. And Abigail saw someone tonight. A boy. Maybe Phin. But having allies isn't the same as having answers, and there's only one surefire way to get those.

I fall asleep with one dreadful thought in my mind: if I want to save my brother, I'll have to follow him inside the swamp.

IN THE MORNING, THERE'S A note taped to the mirror of my dresser. The script is so pretentious and cursive, I can barely read it:

Need a ride?—L M

I overslept and everyone's up with something to say. Mama holds my face between her palms while I reassure her I'm fine, fine, fine. Darold heard I was driving around with "that Durham boy," and exerts parental authority under the guise of the law.

"You *know* that boy's troubled. I may not have had cause to pick him up in a while, but that doesn't mean he's changed his ways." He doesn't leave it there. "Drugs. Alcohol. Raving about the swamp. I don't like the thought of you getting mixed up with him."

"He just gave me a ride home," I say.

"That's not what I heard," Lenora May sings as she packs her bag. She's acting for Mama and Darold, pretending to needle at her little sister. I glare and she adds, "But who listens to rumors?"

"Rumors about Heath might not be far from the truth." Thankfully, Darold either missed Lenora May's point entirely or ignored it. He speaks in a way that leaves no room for argument, on the edge of condescension and caring. It's a trick all men of the South have to learn before they're accepted as one of the good ol' boys. "I think it's best if you find other ways home from now on."

I'm about to share exactly what I think is best for me when Lenora May cuts in, "Ready, Sterling? I'm leaving now, if you want a ride."

Some things are better left unsaid.

The Chevelle's parked exactly where it always is, wet with dew and streaked yellow with pollen.

"How'd you find it?" I ask, disappointed, but not surprised.

Lenora May casts a furtive glance at the swamp before answering. "I remember things the way you do, Sterling. I remember Dad—well, the Lillard House seemed like the only likely place. It's where I'd have taken it."

I'm startled by her honesty. And I can't help but be grateful that she stopped herself before intruding on my most painful memories of the man responsible for starting my life. This is becoming an all too familiar dance: treading lightly through the minefield of my memories, grasping at some, sidestepping others, and fleeing the ones that stick to me like burs.

Lenora May unlocks the doors and has the engine revving in two seconds. I hesitate, but I'd rather get answers from her than the swamp. I settle into the passenger seat and buckle up. Once again, she's in a sundress and sandals with a white cardigan thrown over her shoulders. In spite of the morning shade, she's covered her eyes with huge, polka-dotted sunglasses that make her skin seem as pale as the moon and her lips as red as the Chevelle. She takes turns at reckless speeds and, as soon as we're on the main drag of Sticks, accelerates to fifty in a thirty-five-mile-per-hour zone.

"You know school's the other way, right? And my *dad's* a deputy?" I resist the urge to grip the seat. Never let them see you squirm.

"He'd die a happy man to hear you say that, you know." Gear change. "Now, if you and I are going to stop pretending, I think we need to get a few things straight, don't you?"

The speedometer climbs.

"Okay," I say. "Let's start with what you did to my brother. I know he's in the swamp and you're not. I want to know how we fix it."

Her smile is pained. "I'm sorry, but there's no way. It'll be better for everyone if you forget he ever existed."

"Don't you dare tell me what's better for me." The speedometer climbs again. Wind whistles around the antenna, distressed. "Tell me how you did it."

"How about I tell you a story instead?" It's a rhetorical question. Her fingers tighten around the steering wheel. "It's about a brother and sister who loved each other very much, so much that when their father demanded the sister marry a cruel, wealthy man, they ran away. Into the swamp, where they knew they'd be safe."

The speedometer continues to climb. Beneath my feet the floor begins to rattle. She shifts again and we shoot forward so fast my head bounces against the seat. It's thrilling and terrifying, especially when I remember how little lived experience she has behind the wheel.

"And they were *safe*." The word becomes a curse the way she casts it. "They discovered the swamp would keep them safe forever if they wanted. But for that they had to become a part of the swamp and give up any chance of ever returning to the world outside."

Nothing about this story sounds familiar. It's not one of the Clary tales I've ever heard, though it would certainly fit among them.

"So, they did. They consumed enough of that wicked Wasting Shine to bind their souls to it and it made them immortal. It made their bodies as changeable as the swamp, but it also changed their hearts, and the longer they were left alone and isolated, the more twisted they became. Now, they steal the souls of anyone who strays too near because it feeds their own power, and they never let anyone go. *That* is what waits in the swamp. They never let anyone go."

"Except for you."

Faster.

The trees are a blur. My body begins to shiver like the board beneath my feet, thrumming in a wind I have no control over.

"That was luck and I'm *not* going back there. I can't live like that again. Not ever."

The turn in the road takes us both by surprise. We're going too fast. Lenora May shrieks. The tires squeal. The car skids onto soft dirt, fishtailing to a stop inches shy of a pine tree. One of Phin's precious hubcaps rolls down the street, and there's a hissing noise competing with the pounding of my heart. I leap out of the car and press my shaking hands into the dirt. My stomach constricts around the complete lack of food I gave it this morning. The other door opens and Lenora May's shaky laughter spills over my shoulders.

"Oh, Sterling!" she cries. "Don't be afraid! We're alive!" Her hands tug at my shoulders until I'm facing her. All I can see are her eyes, so green and exquisitely bright. "You've been so safe all your life. So safe you might as well be dead.

Phin did that, he kept you from *living*, but I won't. I promise you, I only want to live as fiercely as I can."

My hands are cold between her trembling fingers.

"That's what Phin should be doing!" I find the hubcap with my eyes. "You're ruining everything he loved! Why did you have to take his life?"

Her smile fades and the air seems to chill in its absence. "If it had been up to me, I wouldn't have. But the Shine required a trade—to let a life go, the swamp needed a life in return. I'm very sorry for him and for you, but he's stuck. Truly. And he wouldn't want you to stop living your life just because he's gone."

"He would come for me." As soon as I've said it I know the only false part of the statement is that Phin would have *already* come for me. It wouldn't matter how afraid he was or how many people warned him away, he'd have been over that fence in no time and he wouldn't have rested until he found me. "I'm going to find him."

"Don't. Please don't go into the swamp."

Any small doubt I had about going vanishes with those words. If there's one place I should be looking, it's where Lenora May tells me not to.

"I'm going to find him," I repeat.

Sadness tinged with fear creeps into Lenora May's face when she says, "Then I guess we'd better get to school."

I expect her to argue or shout or do something other

than go retrieve the runaway hubcap and toss it in the trunk. But she barely looks at me. She surveys the tires the same way Phin might, crouching by each one to inspect the tread. Then she drives us to the school parking lot in silence.

Before I leave, she catches my wrist. "Sterling, one thing," she says. Her eyes linger on the hunk of metal on my arm. "If I can ask one thing, that is."

"You can ask," I say, prepared to ignore anything that comes from that lying mouth.

"It's this: be careful. And if you do go after him, make sure you take that bracelet with you."

The only thing that gets me through exams is knowing I have a plan. It may not extend beyond "go into the swamp and find Phin," but it doesn't have to. I know he's there now, alive and stuck. Just because there are also terrible things doesn't mean I shouldn't try. Much as it pains me to take a lesson from anything Lenora May has said, one thing did ring true. All my life Phin has been the one to keep me safe. She meant it as a negative, but that's only because she's never had a brother like Phin. I won't feel safe again until he's back at home.

Heath texts before first bell, *i remember. phineas harlan saucier.*

I reply, *Nathan Payola.* Then a second message, *I have something to tell you.*

81

Without knowing it, he strengthened my resolve. Usually, the end of a school day would find me and Candy and Abigail in Candy's car, heading to her house, where no parents exist to bother us. Today, things fall apart, so naturally I don't even have to make excuses. Abigail looks exhausted and begs off for a nap, and Candy excuses herself with a smirk the second she spots Heath at my locker.

Heath stands up straight when he spots me, a soft smile releasing his scowl.

"She found the Chevelle," I report. "Next time we steal a car? Remind me to pick a hiding place Phin *didn't* know about."

"I was thinking we could take it down a few notches and try something sane like skydiving or gator hunting or watching a movie at my place." His grin is infectious. I can't believe this is the same Heath that's been skulking at the back of classrooms all year when he wasn't absent altogether. It's crushing to say no. Doing something as normal as watching a movie sounds better than just about anything, but Phin's waited long enough.

"I'm sorry, but I need to—" I stop myself before I lie, and instead tell the absolute truth. Everything Lenora May said to me this morning. With every word, Heath's smile dies a little more. "I know they're alive, Heath. Abigail saw someone yesterday. It had to have been one of them. And after

82

what Lenora May said, I have to go after Phin. Today. Right now."

Lockers slam and someone bumps Heath in their hurry to leave. He keeps his voice hushed, but tinny notes of terror slip in. "I don't think this is a good idea."

"I know it's not, but I don't see any other choice."

"Staying safe," he insists. "Staying *sane*. That's a good choice. I can't tell you how many times I've thought I heard Nathan's voice, or how many times I've woken from a dead sleep at the fence, ready to climb over. I'd probably be long gone, too, if Old Lady Clary hadn't wrapped this cord around my wrist and told me to be a good boy and stop talking about Nathan."

He holds up his wrist where that ratty leather cord still hangs. This close, I see it's three strands braided together with a silver medallion woven into the center. It's depressingly unsurprising to learn that Old Lady Clary's been hushing more people about the swamp than me.

He continues, "Abigail didn't see Phin or Nathan. This is what the swamp does! It fogs your brain until you can't remember what's real anymore and then it sucks you inside."

It's the word *fog* that does it. I suddenly remember Old Lady Clary telling me that the swamp had more than one kind of fog. She'd only had eyes for my bracelet.

"Heath! This is why we remember! It has to be!" I grab

his wrist and show him mine. "Whatever these charms are, they're keeping our heads on straight."

It makes too much sense not to be the truth. For whatever reason, Old Lady Clary made sure Heath had something that would keep his mind clear of the swamp's fog. Abigail didn't have one and that's why she claimed she hadn't seen anyone. Once it was over, she probably didn't remember it. I'm so certain about this I could explode, but there's one way to make sure.

"Have you ever, even for one minute, taken yours off?" I ask. "If you have and you still remember Nathan, then I'm wrong, but if you haven't, then it's enough of a correlation to be convincing."

Heath leans against a locker and closes his eyes, becoming motionless. There's a roughness to him that I've never bothered to notice. The constant creases around his eyes, the defensive hunch of his shoulders. It's as if even thinking about the swamp takes him to the brink of exhaustion.

"No," he says, opening his eyes. "I've never taken it off."

I'm right. I know I'm right about this, and Heath knows it, too.

But I see the argument building in his eyes, the year-deep fear of the swamp that's kept him quiet and alone. I can't let that same fear keep me away any longer, but there's no reason Heath has to come along. A year of missing his best friend has been torture enough. At the very least, I can protect him from having to go inside the place of his nightmares.

"But," he says like he's about to disappoint, "I didn't have it for days after the crash and I still remembered."

"Oh." My mind races for an answer, something— anything—that supports my crumbling theory about why we remember, but there's only Lenora May's strange warning.

"I'm not saying they're not related," he offers with no real hope in his voice. "But just because we remember them, doesn't mean they're alive."

"Well, *I'm* not going to give up that easily," I snap, and as soon as I've said them, the words taste bitter. "Oh, no, Heath, that's not what I meant."

He shakes his head as if to excuse the comment, but the distance he puts between us speaks more loudly. A shove would have done just as well to push him away.

"Yeah, I know. Don't worry about it," he says, but his eyes shift from mine. "Listen, I owe you a Coke, but I just remembered I'm supposed to go see Doc Payola in a few minutes."

"Maybe tomorrow?" I bite down on another apology. It's better if he doesn't stick around. At least not today.

"It's a date." He clears his throat and manages a rough smile. "A real one this time."

The school's a tomb when we leave. We climb into the

truck, and Heath revs the engine to take me home. The passenger side's a little cleaner than it was yesterday. The dash is as cluttered, but he's gone to some effort to make sure the seat's clear and there's room for my bag on the floor. Tomorrow, if all goes well, I'll be back in this truck, going on a long-overdue date with Heath Durham. I'll paint my nails and wear the tall leather boots that are too hot for this sort of weather, but make my legs look too long to pass up. We'll have a Coke and maybe watch a movie and be nothing but normal for a few hours.

But first, I'm going after Phin.

I WAIT FOR NIGHT.

It's been a long time since I had a reason to escape through my bedroom window. Before Dad left, Phin and I had it down to a science. We could descend the wall in less than a minute and be hidden in the woods outside the swamp in two. If we hadn't been so afraid, it might've been fun. Traipsing through the pines until they gave way to oaks, then hunting our way through to the ghostly columns of the old Lillard House. We'd stay there until we thought it was safe to return. Sometimes that was all night.

With Darold's spare switchblade in my boot and a flashlight in hand, I lean my stomach against the window frame and lower myself down the wall. My feet reach the roof of the porch more easily than they did when I was six and seven. I move carefully over the slanted surface to find the notches Phin cut into one of the porch's posts—the notches Lenora May frantically chipped out with an ax one afternoon when Dad was away—and climb to the ground.

Fireflies wink all around, mingling with the Wasting Shine and Mama's Christmas lights. Combined with this year's crop of gold doubloon and human skull Mardi Gras beads, it looks like a little pirate graveyard, a warning or a reminder that danger lies beyond this point.

I try to find a piece of whatever stupid courage Phin must have felt to propel him into the single greatest danger we've ever known. There was something so effortless, so thoughtless about the way he flung his legs over the rails and landed in a sprint. The key is not to think about it, but I can't clear my head. I keep hearing our angry words from that afternoon over and over.

It was such a stupid fight. One that started the minute Phin announced he was leaving for Tulane. It shouldn't have been that much of a surprise. He was as focused on that goal as he was on fixing up the Chevelle. His excitement was the only reason I'd ever thought seriously about college. Most of the good folk of Sticks consider it'd be faster to throw your money in a fire if you're that keen on wasting it, but then, most of the good folk of Sticks think the periodic table has something to do with birth control. More than once, Phin reminded me that it was possible to love a place and leave it, and he and I were destined for a life bigger than the whole of Sticks.

I believed him, but I didn't understand him. Not completely.

I could've completed his college applications for him and it still would've come as a surprise to hear he was leaving. But the real shock of the whole affair was realizing that meant I'd be left behind. That didn't happen in my brilliant brain until the acceptance letter arrived. And that was the first day I didn't finish my dinner.

We fought every time we spoke because I couldn't look at him without feeling resentful or abandoned. But Sunday was the first time he'd been driven to violence.

Then he was gone.

And it's my fault.

If I was afraid to live in a town without Phineas, I'm plain terrified of living in a world without him. With an unexpected combination of fear and guilt and recklessness, I set a foot on the bottom rung of the fence and rest my fingers on top. Shine licks at them. I jump back, clenching my hands to fists and glaring at the sinister coils.

The swamp continues to beckon.

I can do this.

"Phineas Harlan Saucier," I say to whatever might be listening. "I'm coming for my brother."

Placing my palms firmly on the top plank again, I climb the fence and land softly on the other side. The Shine threading the muddy ground shatters beneath my feet and shifts in a frenzied way. Phin's bracelet warms against my skin.

With a deep breath, I follow the path Phin might have left. Shine brightens the otherwise dark swamp, but it glitters incoherently, confusing my steps so I have to move slow and careful. Plants brush against my knees, vines slither over my shoulders, and I lose my balance more than once.

"Phineas!" I call quietly. Then again, louder, "Phineas!"

My feet sink in warm, thick water. Sweat is cold on my forehead. I turn around and see that the path I took is gone— gone and I don't know how I'll find my way again. When I stop moving, those glittering vines reach for me. They curl around my ankles and tickle my arms. I shake them off and run, but the next time I pause, they creep toward me, reach for me, curl around my cold fingers, and tug.

"Phin! Phineas! Phin, please!" I cry, splashing through water that nearly reaches my knees. The only response is the harsh shriek of some swamp animal, the *thump, thump, thump* of something falling or crawling or running.

And getting closer.

I freeze. I stop everything except my heart, and make myself as small and as quiet as possible. If Phin were here, he'd know what to do. *Oh, God, if Phin were here, I wouldn't be mindless with fear.* Whatever else is in this swamp, it's surely worse than a girl armed with a flashlight and switchblade.

Something stings my leg and I shriek loud enough to be heard by anything within a hundred miles. I crouch down until my butt hits the water, but it's too late. The thumping gets louder and faster. I'm fixing to run when a voice calls, "Hello? Is someone there?"

For a moment, I'm sure it's Phin. My smile's as wide as the Mississippi, but then he calls again, and his voice is familiar but not my brother's. It's a second before I spot him through the cypress trees, tall and broad and definitely not Phin.

"If you know what's good for you, you'll stop right there," I shout.

He takes a few more steps, coming around the trees with hands raised. He's not much older than me, dressed in jeans and a mud-splattered T-shirt, and I know exactly who he is.

"Nathan!" If I knew him better, I'd hug him, but I settle for climbing onto the same muddy path he's on. Simply standing in front of him is a victory.

"Thank Jesus, Sterling Saucier," he says with a sigh. His voice is raspy and he walks like his shoulders weigh two tons each. "I've been lost for hours. Please, tell me you know the way out of here."

Hours? With that one word my hope fizzles, but I decide not to burden him with the truth just yet. "Have you seen another boy around? Dark hair, blue eyes? My brother's lost, too."

He shakes his head. Everything about him is tense and alert. Even his T-shirt seems to hover above his body, ready to flee. "The only other things I've seen are the sort of things you don't want to see," he says with a nervous look around. "We ain't alone in here."

It's the way he pulls at his arm that makes me shudder. Shine snakes through the mud to my feet and his, glowing in streams of brown and black and yellow. Around us, the swamp is a smothering chorus. How did I ever hope to find Phin in this wild place?

"C'mon. If we keep the moon behind us, we should be able to find my backyard." I leave the invitation open and start to walk. When he joins me, I ask, "What's the last thing you remember, Nathan? Before you got lost?"

"Shh." He stops and holds up a hand, tilting his head a little to listen with wide eyes. When he returns his gaze to me, it's already miles away. "Run," he says.

Before I can ask why, something crashes through the swamp. Again, Nathan shouts for me to run and I do, hard on his heels. The noise gets closer. I try to run as fast as him, but every other step is a struggle. I stumble and slip and sink in deep mud. Soon, his figure is so far past me I only catch flashes of his white shirt.

"Wait! Help me, please!"

Every crash is closer than the one before. I risk a glance behind and see a patch of the dark night sky racing toward me. I see yellow eyes and a pale, gray face, and I hear my voice saying, "No, no, no!"

Nathan calls for me, once, twice.

Then a hand like tree bark grips my wrist, spinning me until I'm nose to nose with the pale-faced beast. His breath is a suffocating gust of rot and mud. His body curls over me like a punishing wave. I can see no way out. Nothing at all except the narrowed yellow of his eyes. Then, heat flushes my arm where he grips me. He recoils with a snarl and I'm on my feet again, flying through the swamp.

I don't look back. I don't see or hear Nathan and I don't dare call for him, so I run until I can't feel my legs and then I run some more.

Something pink flashes between the trees ahead, but I don't see it clearly until I stumble into a small grove on the edge of a wide pond. In the center of the clearing, with roots that crawl over the bank and spill into the pond, is a cherry tree in full bloom.

It's so unexpected that I stop.

My heartbeat is furious in my ears, but I can't look away. Gnarled branches reach in all directions, each a flurry of elegant pink blossoms surrounded by muck and mire. Shine twists through the ground in thick ropes; each of the long tendrils spirals away from the black roots.

Cautiously, I rest one hand on a low branch and listen, but there's no sound of the beast. *Did I lose him or is he simply toying with me? Does it matter?* Dipping beneath the heavy branches, I sit and resist the urge to panic.

I lost Nathan as soon as I'd found him and now I'm lost, too.

Little shining tendrils pull away from the roots of the tree to caress the tarnished silver on my wrist. I let them settle there and with my free hand brush my fingertips over a tendril that has the green-black sheen of mud. It feels delicate, but alive and real. Its edges are sticky and cling to my skin like cricket legs, gripping and releasing, pulling on me as I pull on it.

The air around me cools, and I have the sudden and fierce sensation of being watched. I spin and search the clearing, ready to run.

A figure lounges a few feet away, half hidden in shadows, but enough in the light that I can see it's a boy not much older than me. He rests an arm over the knee propped in front of him. It's an unbearably beautiful and commanding pose that's only accentuated by the strangely old-fashioned shirt he wears. His black hair sweeps away from his face as though pushed by a constant wind. But it's his eyes that pull my gaze: dark as mud and steady as rain. I can see the smile in them without having to find his lips.

"Sterling." His voice is a murky whisper.

"I know you?" I reach into the foggiest parts of my memory for a name and find none. If he's from Sticks, he's no one I've ever met, but if Lenora May's story was even partially true, there's no telling how many people are trapped in here. His clothes aren't from this century, which means he's probably been here for decades. Another victim the swamp claimed and the world forgot.

"No," he says. "But I've met your brother. I'm Fisher."

I spring to my feet and close the distance between us. "Phineas? Where is he? Is he okay? Please, take me to him."

It's only when he glances down that I realize not only have I tugged him to his feet, but I'm gripping both his hands. With an apology, I drop them and remove myself from his personal space.

"It's all right," he soothes. "I can understand and sympathize, but I don't think taking you to him is the best idea. He's . . . not quite himself these days."

"What do you mean?" A hum begins in my ears. Beetles and frogs and night birds provide a background chorus as shadows thicken.

Fisher stands close enough that he can speak low and be heard through the din. "He's trapped. Someone trapped him in order to free themselves, and his cage, well, it's not a pretty sight."

I can't tell if I'm furious or terrified. Probably both. "Lenora May. She appeared the day he went in, and everyone in town thinks she's always been there."

His expression darkens. "Lenora May," he says with so

much knowing behind it that all my questions fall flat. "I *knew* she was up to something. She's always up to something."

Vindication pushes me forward. "What's she done to Phin? If she's hurt him, I'll—"

Shine snaps around my neck and tightens a split second before Fisher's hand presses against my mouth. The shiver that assaults my spine tacks my feet to the ground. I'm suddenly six years old, hiding beneath my bed, keeping so still, so, so still.

"Don't. Don't threaten her." He releases me just as quickly, the tendril uncoils, but I can't swallow for the rock in my throat. "Forgive me, Sterling," he continues. "I don't mean to scare you, but this swamp listens. You must be careful what you say."

It's another minute before I can speak. He stands so close. I take in his dark hair and eyes, his pale skin, the strange cut of his clothing, the way the swamp seems to lean toward him. *Does it obey him or fear him?* I wonder. Or does he simply know how to protect unwitting souls from it? As my adrenaline wanes, I find I'm practically cozy with his presence.

"What are you?"

His smile is sad when he answers. "Once, I was a boy. Now, the swamp is my home. I'm as much a part of it as it is of me."

"A ghost?" This is the sort of question that should make me nervous. Any rational girl would be if she encountered a well-dressed, smooth-talking boy in the middle of the swamp. He paces the length of the clearing before answering, holding his hands behind him as though they might prevent him from thinking. The drape of his sleeves does little to hide the strength of his arms. All sorts of words spring to mind and none of them are the usual sort I'd use for boys my age. Like "poised" and "noble." Mud coats his shoes and the bottom six inches of his dark pants, but it doesn't detract from his bearing.

He comes to a stop by the cherry tree, one hand resting on its branches. "I'm not sure what you'd call me, but I suppose 'ghost' works well enough. I exist as a part of the swamp's magic. An extension of it, you could say. It keeps me alive, but only so long as I stay here."

"And that's what Lenora May was, too?"

"Yes," he says with more longing than I could unpack in a week. "It was not always the case. Long ago, she was a girl, like you, who wanted to be safe from a world that would decide her fate for her. She escaped by bonding herself to the magic of the swamp. It was a desperate choice."

I recognize the story. It's the same one Lenora May told in the car, only where she told it with anger, he tells it with something like sorrow. He holds his gaze away as he speaks.

"Over the years, her desperation turned into resentment and jealousy. She wanted to leave, but that was impossible, so she captured anyone unfortunate enough to find themselves in the swamp. She was so viciously resentful of anyone who lived a normal life. I can't count the number of souls she's trapped here. I believe you encountered a few tonight."

My terrifying flight through the swamp from that pale-faced beast is too close for comfort. What could anyone have done to deserve such a fate as that? I search the dark woods behind Fisher, and again I'm struck by the way even the Shine seems passive in his presence. There's no hint of concern about him and that serenity trickles into me until each of my nerves has calmed.

I ask, "One of them was—is—a friend. How can I free him?"

"Only Lenora May can free them, unfortunately."

His body is so still as he talks. I study the slender line of his nose, the curl of his dark hair. It's a combination I've become reluctantly familiar with.

"You're her brother," I say.

He nods. "And I love her, but she's become devious. She's been looking for ways to extend her reach beyond the boundaries of this little world. I'm afraid she'll not take kindly to the idea of you having found me."

He falls quiet, watching me for a long moment. I fight the urge to squirm under his gaze, but I'm utterly unable to look away. Finally, having reached some conclusion, he shakes his head. "No, she won't like this at all," he mutters, and plucks a blossom from the tree. Cupping it in his palms, he whispers through the gap in his thumbs. A glow seeps between his fingers, white and red and ochre.

"But I'm her brother and that means this is partly my fault. I will help you." He moves to my side once again. "If it's in my power, I'll help you free your brother and remove Lenora May from your home. Take this." He offers a small, perfectly formed cherry. "If you can slip this into her food, she'll be powerless against the pull of the swamp and will return. Once she's here, I should be able to reverse what she's done."

The cherry looks unremarkable in my hand. Small, red, and perishable. "How?"

"It is of this swamp and anyone who eats it will be irresistibly called to return." He seems amused at my skepticism and adds, "Where things come from *matters*."

I roll the fruit from side to side before dropping it into my pocket. It seems so simple, so easy. But it sure didn't seem very difficult for Lenora May to cross the fence in the first place and take what didn't belong to her. If it's true, then I'm one bite away from saving my brother's life and putting my own world back to normal. That's a chance I'll gladly take.

"Thank you." This could all end over breakfast. By tomorrow, Phin could be home where he belongs, cussing at his hair for being curly instead of straight. But he's been trapped for so long already. "Is he okay? Is he in pain?"

Fisher's smile is understanding and sympathetic. "I give

you my word, he's in no pain, only trapped. In his mind, this is like a very strange dream. Confusing and mysterious, but nothing painful. I imagine your experience has been more painful than his."

It's a comforting thought. For all the frustration I've experienced, it's been bearable. With a solution in my pocket, the burden I've carried for days feels lighter than ever. So long as Phin is safe and not in pain, I can focus on what needs to be done.

"How do I find you again?" I ask, thinking of the pale-faced beast. "For that matter, how do I get home?"

"It seems you have a knack for navigating the swamp already." Shine sharpens his smile. "Don't fear. Your way home will be clear and as for finding me again, all you need do, my brave girl, is say my name. And I will find you."

PART TWO

With howls and groans and pleading, dear,
The swamp will call you near,
Beware the songs it sings to you,
Beware the things you hear.

PRETENDING IS THE SORT OF lying I learned from my mama when I was six years old. When there's a bear living inside your house and he's got a tendency to get spitting mad, you don't tell anyone about it. You pretend it's normal. You ignore the spitting as best you can and clean up after. And when that bear gets to swinging his big paws, you pretend you're the clumsy one. After all, mishaps are bound to happen when you aren't paying attention. There's always a little piece of truth stuck inside a good pretending.

Wednesday morning I pretend there's nothing wrong inside my house. I roll out of bed and take the first shower, dodging Lenora May on my way out of the bathroom. Mama has a hot breakfast on the table when I come downstairs. Grits, eggs, and sausage all grease-glossed and gleaming under the kitchen lights. I pile a thin layer of eggs on a piece of toast and eat as much as my anxious stomach will allow before declaring that I've got to meet Candy and Abigail for a last-minute cram session. Mama pretends not to notice what's left on my plate, but Darold clears his throat in a significant way.

At school, I try to keep my mind off how to get this little cherry into Lenora May's mouth and focus on exams instead. At lunch, I share the news of my upcoming Heath date with Candy and Abigail, who decide this means we need an after-school prep session. I don't argue and within fifteen minutes of the final bell, we're in my bedroom with every shirt I own draped around the room. A few are draped over Abigail, who, after plugging her iPod into my player and selecting something that sounds disturbingly like Country/Electronica, immediately climbed into my bed and shut her eyes.

"What's wrong with you, anyway, Beale?" Candy rips away the shirt covering Abigail's face and tosses it in the discard pile. Apparently, I won't be wearing pink. "You're infecting me with your yawns and I think it has a detrimental effect on my brain. If I got anything lower than an A minus on that history exam, it's your fault."

Abigail's eyelids don't even flutter, but she lifts a choice finger, elegantly telling Candy how little she cares.

"Have you been studying late? Are you worried about

your grades?" I ask. It seems unlikely. We all like good grades, and getting them is a condition of staying on the volleyball team in the fall, but Abigail's never been one to stress.

"Or," Candy says, lowering the tank top she was considering with no love in her eyes, "is everything okay at home?"

Her family—even her twin sister, Valerie—hasn't been the most accepting, but they've never been cruel. Unless you consider private weekly meetings with the pastor cruel. They might be. Abigail never wants to share details.

"I'm fine," she says, kicking the shirts off her legs to sit. "Everything's fine, I'm not sleeping so well. That one." She points at a pale yellow top with a faded Darwin fish in the center. Phin gave it to me for my birthday three years ago.

"Jean shorts, black boots, red for the nails." Candy tosses me a bottle of nail polish, red as the cherry in my pocket. "Boom. That's teamwork."

Abigail naps through the rest of the session. The music blares and Candy and I don't lower our voices a smidge, but Abigail's fast asleep. She doesn't even stir when Lenora May stops by with a steaming plate of fresh pastries and settles on the ground next to us like she's done it a hundred times before.

"Feels like I haven't baked in ages," she says, clearly delighted with herself. "But last night, I dreamed of these tarts I had when I was a kid and it was all I could think about today. So, I found a recipe and I baked."

She kneels so primly with the platter on her hands and her gingham-print skirt pooled around her knees, she should be on the cover of a magazine. People do not naturally look like paintings without trying, but everything about her seems so irritatingly effortless. Even the tarts she baked on a whim are perfectly square with dollops of red at the center. Candy eats two in the time it takes me to convince myself to take one. It's remarkable how easy it was for her to waltz into my bedroom and get Candy to eat something when I've been racking my brain all day for a similar scheme. The bloodred center of the tart gleams, a perfect hiding place for a cherry.

"What did you use for the filling?"

"Some of Mama's old preserves." We lock eyes. "Strawberry. Try it."

It occurs to me this could be a trap. Fisher said she was devious. She could be trying to banish me to the swamp the same way I'm trying—and failing—to banish her. If I hadn't gone in and met Fisher, I'd be helpless right now.

"Can't." I put the tart down on the plate. "I'm allergic to strawberries. I'm surprised you forgot."

She looks disappointed, but also indifferent when she shrugs. "I'll try something different next time. Cherries, maybe. Is she okay?" Her eyes lift to Abigail. She's rolled to her side, giving us a clear view of the dark circles beneath her eyes. "She looks a little ill."

"She's not sleeping well," Candy supplies between bites of

steaming tart. "These are supergood, May. If I could bake, or if I'd ever wanted to bake, you'd be my queen."

I could kiss Candy for giving me the idea.

"I wish I could try them. When do you think you'll make another batch? Maybe I could help?"

Skepticism locks both of their faces in the same position for different reasons.

"Glad to see you're taking an interest in food again," Candy gets in a dig.

I'm not about to have another fight about food. Lenora May considers me for a moment, unsure, but unwilling to break in front of Candy. My smile is relentless. Finally, she yields and suggests, "Tomorrow after school?"

"Perfect," I say, knowing that was one of the finest pretendings of my life.

I tell Mama that I'm going to Candy's for another study session. She never complains about studying during finals and gives me a ten p.m. curfew. Darold's got the swing shift, but he's surely infected Mama with his anti-Durham campaign. As long as I'm back by ten, they'll never know the difference.

It's dusk when Heath texts to say he's parked down the road where Mama won't see. The sky's a dusty blue, the crickets are hard at their work, and the swamp's full of Shine straining at the fence. A coat of fresh pollen has settled on the Chevelle and there's a fuzzy peach hanging from the rearview—something Phin would never allow. I ignore it as best I can. I've got a plan that will solve all of that tomorrow. Tonight, I'm on a date that's one year overdue.

We drive with the windows down, the warm breeze kissing our cheeks. There's nothing like early summer evenings in Sticks when the air's as warm as bathwater and everything's vibrant with singing. It's like the whole world's happy to be alive. Heath takes us away from town, along the side road until it curves at the river.

"The Lillard House?" I ask.

"I have a surprise for you."

It becomes full dark when the truck passes beneath the oak trees. The row echoes with the chirping of frogs and beetles. Up in the canopy, Spanish moss floats lazily on the air, the tails of a hundred ghosts. The Lillard House glows with collected moonlight, all cold and pale but for one window that winks golden.

Heath's acting like the cat that got the cream when he pulls me up the steps. With one gentle tug, he unhinges the lock and gives the front door a shove. It swings inward with a long, slow whine.

"After you," he says with a half bow.

"What did you do, Heath Durham?"

Inside, the hallway is dim and vast. A set of dusty footprints leads the way.

"It's as close to a bank heist as I could get," he explains.

"But that lock really did take ten minutes and a smartphone. Who knew lock picking would be harder than stealing a car?"

"I believe this is called 'breaking and entering,'" I tease.

Two steps into the hallway, the ceiling catapults up, making way for a grand staircase that wraps the walls in two directions. Heath's old footprints don't go up either side, but lead straight between them, deeper into the house.

"Would that make it better than or equal to a bank heist in the grand scheme of things? I don't want us slipping down the criminal chain."

"Definitely better," I say.

The footprints move off to the left, through a doorway that's fancier than anything in my house. The scene inside makes me stop.

"Oh, Heath, it's beautiful."

Candles light the room, perched on the long mantel of a fireplace and on the ground in glass cups and tin cans. In the center is a red, flannel blanket with tattered edges and one corner shredded to bits. Two bottles of Coke stand at one end and right beside them is a stack of Styrofoam containers. In the air is the telltale scent of something deep fried. A Miss Bonnie's specialty made more palatable by the dust tickling my nose.

"I hope you like catfish." He wasn't nervous before, but now he plucks at the cord on his wrist. This, I discover, is all it takes to make me nervous. I grasp his fingers and pull them away from the only concrete thing tying him to the swamp.

"As long as there's tartar sauce, I'm good with just about anything."

We settle onto the blanket and break into the food. My stomach emits a strange, shrill noise and I realize I haven't eaten anything of substance since breakfast. It's probably embarrassing how quickly I eat the first piece of fried fish, but when I look up, Heath's on the edge of a laugh.

"Never thought I'd meet anyone who likes catfish as much as I do."

"I don't," I say, surprised at the grease on my fingers.

"Could've fooled me."

I give myself a minute and a swig of Coke to make sure I'm not about to be sick. It's been a few weeks since I've eaten so much in one sitting, and overwhelming my system with fish and grease might create problems. But two minutes later, my stomach shrieks again and I reach for a second piece.

I'm doing it all wrong. Dating is about getting to know the person you're with and here I am chowing down like a stray dog. As though he's somehow connected to my thoughts, Heath laughs and reminds me to chew between bites. I throw a hush puppy at him. It thumps against his shoulder and roles away, collecting dust on its cornmeal shell.

"The life and death of a hush puppy." He shakes his head,

mournful. "I've got to admit," Heath proceeds cautiously, "it's a relief to see you eating. You've—uh—well, you've gotten pretty thin recently. I was getting worried."

The candlelight can't cover the hint of a blush in his cheeks. I work hard not to mirror it, but I can't ignore that he's been paying such close attention.

"It's stupid," I admit, toying with another hush puppy. "But have you ever gotten so caught up in a fear that it affects what you do every single day?"

"I've got an idea what that's like."

"I've never been able to rely on anyone like I rely on Phin. When we were little, our dad would hit us. Phin always protected me and he's been the one sure thing in my life ever since. I wasn't ready for him to go away. The thought of living anywhere without him, well, it scared the shit out of me. It—it was like I was shrinking."

"I understand. Before Old Lady Clary brought me that charm, I didn't want to leave the house. Seeing those swamp lights was terrifying. They reminded me of everything I'd lost that night. I wasn't just afraid of the swamp, I was afraid of living."

"But it got better?" I reach for his wrist and trace the leather band. "With this?"

"It got easier," he corrects. "This helped, I guess, but it didn't get better until two days ago."

I meet his eyes while the rest of me explodes.

"Sweet Pete, you aren't one for subtlety, Heath Durham."

"Says the girl who asked me to steal a car."

Our laughter travels through the hollow rooms. Through one tall window, I see the swamp, glowing dimly at the bottom of the hill, and remember what brought us here in the first place. It wasn't some long-lost romance. It was just loss.

"Heath." I close the Styrofoam box and wipe my fingers on my shorts. "I went into the swamp last night."

I have the sense that I could set my watch by the fifteen seconds it takes Heath to react. It's as if when he experiences an emotion, he sifts it through some filter before letting it appear on his face. He does this the same way he does anything, with practiced calm. So when he says, "You are crazy." I know it's fairly serious.

"And I saw Nathan," I continue. "I spoke to him. He's alive. Trapped, but alive. And I met someone who says he can help."

There's no way to keep it short. I tell him everything about last night and my plan for getting the cherry into Lenora May's mouth. By the end of it, I'm on my feet with excitement.

"It's going to work. I know it is and as soon as it does, we'll figure out a way to save Nathan, too. I'm sure Fisher will help us."

"You really trust him? How do you know he's not just as bad as she is?"

"I—" I stop. Can I trust anything that comes from the swamp? "I think he feels responsible in some way because she's his sister, and as horrible as she's become, he still loves her. So, I trust him enough to try this. What can it hurt?"

"Okay, but a cherry?" He holds the fruit between his thumb and forefinger. After a whole day of riding in my pocket it looks as fresh as when Fisher created it. "Doesn't that seem a little flimsy to you? How could this possibly work?"

"Maybe it's flimsy." I remember my own reluctance and Fisher's response. "But maybe not. 'Where things come from matters.' That's what he said. We don't know much at all about how things work in the swamp, but it's true that the taste of things like honey and wine are affected by the area they come from, so it makes sense that a swamp cherry might have properties associated with whatever this swamp magic is."

"That makes a sort of sense," he says. "Not that you need my approval, but this sounds like as good a plan as any. I might actually be feeling hopeful right now."

The rest of the date passes too quickly. When the food's gone, we explore every room in the Lillard House, making up stories about the people who might have lived here when it was first built. It should be eerie, sneaking through cob-webbed doorways and into rooms as stuffy as coffins, but our stories keep any dark thoughts I might have at bay.

We're home by 9:58 p.m. sharp. Conveniently, Darold pulls his cruiser into the driveway at exactly that moment. Even though Heath stopped on the road, there's no way Darold didn't see me here, which means my cover's blown. Darold takes his sweet time shutting the car off and gathering his things. He's in no hurry to leave us alone out here.

"Piss," I mutter.

"Not my biggest fan," says Heath, watching as Darold pops the trunk and rummages around inside. I'd lay down money there's nothing in there but a spare pair of boots and an umbrella. "Guess I can't blame him."

"I guess not," I say, but part of me does. Part of me blames this whole town for being so willfully blind to something so powerful, Heath's parents for not believing him, and Old Lady Clary for keeping secrets. It isn't enough to say something's dangerous and leave it at that. Fear doesn't protect anyone. Fear only makes us more vulnerable when we should be finding ways to be strong.

And suddenly, I'm unbuckling and crawling across the seat. I take Heath's face in my hands. I smell mint on his breath and then I press my lips to his. Five seconds pass before his hands grip my waist, before he exhales and leans into the kiss. Five more pass before I remember to breathe and pull away.

In the dark of the cabin, Heath's face is in pieces. Moonlight catches on shards of his lips and eyes. I let my fingers stray into the shadow of his hair and am delighted when he shivers.

I say, "If we weren't already in so much trouble—"

He kisses me and I kiss him with laughter on my lips. This time we're brief and when we part, he whispers, "You're worth all the trouble in the world."

My steps are so light when I slide from the truck and walk into the house. It's only when the front door clunks shut behind me that I remember to look for Darold's disapproving face. But he's not in the living room with Mama and she merely glances at the clock to communicate my five-minute tardiness. Whatever Darold's reason for not telling Mama, I've got no urge to worry about it tonight. Nothing could mar this moment.

I take the stairs two at a time and race down the hall to find Lenora May, anxious to share—

I stop in the doorway of her empty room.

The feeling sours.

And now I'm angry all over again, at Lenora May for invading my house and my heart, and at myself for letting her. Guilt is a worm in my gut and even though I *know* it's not my fault, nothing can erase the fact that my instinct after sharing a beautiful first kiss with Heath was to tell my older sister.

I want to hate her so purely, but still a part of me resists.

From the bathroom, I hear the shower squeak off and I'm sick over how close I came to giving her a sincere moment. I hurry to my own room and rest my back against the closed door. Then, I find the cherry in my pocket and cradle it in my palm.

Tomorrow. By the end of tomorrow, I'll never think of her again and all my precious memories and thoughts will be safe again.

THERE'S A SONG MY GRANDPA Harlan used to sing. Hum, really. In the evenings when he'd sit on the rocker with his pipe burning sweet tobacco, he'd hum the same tune over and over. He said it was a gift song. No words, but full of promises. Someone had given it to him long ago and now he was giving it to us.

Phin and I would create a nest of quilts by his feet searching for shapes in the black pines until one or both of us fell asleep. We did that as often as Mama let us. In my memory, that was every night. I'd fall asleep cuddled up to Phin with sticky summer dew on my skin and Grandpa's lullaby in my head. Then I'd wake in my own bed with the previous night's dirt still between my toes.

I must've been dreaming of Grandpa because I wake with his song in my ears. But it's not Grandpa's voice I hear. It's Lenora May's, trilling down the hallway.

Suddenly, I'm so awake I could split wood. I leap from bed and charge to her room, where she's zipping a dress that looks curiously like one of Phin's plaid shirts.

"You can't have that!"

She stops her singing. "The dress? I think the zipper's broken." She tugs ineffectually on the little tab. "Can you see?"

"The song." I make no move to help her. "You can't have that song. Don't sing it. You can live in this house, you can drive Phin's car, but you can't have that song."

"Oh," she says, pressing a hand to her heart. "I—I'm so sorry, Sterling. I didn't mean to upset you." Sunlight fills her green eyes like tears. "Truly. I won't sing it again."

I don't know why I say it, but I thank her before locking myself in the bathroom.

On my way downstairs, there's a strangled sound coming from her room. Crying? I pause, unsure, but then I catch a hissed "damn zipper," and continue on my way.

Mama's in the laundry room, folding and muttering to herself. She calls good morning, but makes no mention of the night before. I guess Darold still hasn't reported on my evening activities. That's a small blessing. I'm not sure how I feel about it, but I know better than to look a gift horse in the mouth. I hurry on my way.

I swing by Clary General for coffee, wishing all the good ol' boys stationed in their rockers a good morning. Something's got them on the edges of their seats. All brows are furrowed, but they stop their agitating to give me a gruff welcome as I pass. Old Lady Clary's in her usual position behind the counter. She's smothering a set of sticky buns in her famous brown sugar glaze humming a little as she rocks back and forth on her feet.

"Still got that bracelet on?" she calls without looking over her shoulder. The floorboards cackle beneath her feet. "Mmm, child?"

"Yes, ma'am." Reflexively, I reach for the bracelet and run my fingers around the silver band, over the sharp rise and fall of the petals and leaves. "It helps me remember, doesn't it? The people everyone else forgets?"

Old Lady Clary freezes for a second. Then she picks up her tune again and shuffles to the other end of the workstation to rinse her hands. "Yes, shug, that's one of the things it does." My mind snags on the word *one*. "Some would say it's a curse, remembering," she says, returning to my end of the counter with the sort of smile on her face I can't help but reflect. "Just coffee today?"

The air tastes so good, my mouth waters. I can't help myself.

"And a sticky bun. Unless you'd like to tell me about any of the *other* things the bracelet does."

She takes my money and folds it away in her register, pretending she's not watching me from the corner of her eye. The register chimes and she hands over an extra-sticky sticky bun along with another of her smiles. This smile isn't as warm as the first. It pushes her eyebrows up, her cheeks out, her chin down. It's as if she's saying, *I know what you're up to.*

There's no more time for questions. The door opens and in tromp all the men from the front porch. They take their time, stomping on the mat and clustering around the doorway. Sheriff Felder is the first to break away.

"Miss Ida," he says, setting his coffee mug on the warped countertop. His expression is grim. "Mind if I take a look at the property line? We've had a few reports of vandalism at different points along the fence and I'd like to have a look around before I get going."

Old Lady Clary waves him through the back door. "Always welcome, Sheriff."

By the front, the men are grumbling. All of them wear similar expressions of concern and stand with hands on hips. Among them, I spot Darold. He's dressed in business casual: a gray polo shirt embroidered with the logo of the STICKS POLICE, and dark blue jeans tucked inside brown cowboy boots.

"Any word from the schools? How's the fence there?" one man asks. I can't tell which mustache moved the most, so there are about four possible speakers.

Darold stands tall among them. It's always strange to see him in town, to see who he is when he's not grinning at Mama or lounging in his recliner with a beer in hand. He doesn't slouch or study the ground. He keeps his shoulders back and his eyes steady on whatever's coming at him. But I guess he has to. There's more than one of those boys always looking for him to slip up.

"Nothing from the school yet," he says. All grumbling comes to a halt to make room for him. "But there was some damage along the fence at the side road, and Rhetta Chaisson says there were planks down on the far road, too."

My walk to Clary General this morning had been a quick one. I hadn't noticed anything wrong with the fence. Of course, my mind may have been a little too occupied with thoughts of kissing Heath to notice much of anything.

Mrs. Chaisson lives down where things start to look less like town and more like the national reserve. Though her road also runs alongside the swamp, we call it the "far road." We're the only two families with houses that butt right up against the swamp. Except for the Lillard House, a few businesses, and one of the schools, everything else keeps a healthy distance.

"Ain't good," Featherhead Fred barks, and more softly adds, "Bad omens."

"Now, Fred, it's bound to happen. The fence is getting up

there in age. This is probably the work of a couple rambunctious seniors pulling down planks to amuse themselves."

"But there was damage behind your house, too, ain't that right, Gatty?" Mr. Tilly, a dog lover who always has one or two pale-eyed Catahoula curs around him, asks. Like so many others, he looks to Darold for reassurance. "And you and Emma didn't hear anything?"

"Doesn't sound like rambunctious teens to me," another voice adds.

Theories start to fly. Someone suggests a squatter after wood for a new shack, someone suggests bears, and someone suggests poor Featherhead Fred's just trying to make trouble. They're all riled up about what's to be done and who's to blame. And they're talking circles around the swamp; every single one of them working hard to believe there's nothing unusual about it.

"Why's the fence so important, anyway?" I ask.

All eyes fall on me, each looking equally baffled.

It's Darold who finally speaks. "What kind of question is that? You know as well as anyone the fence is there for our protection. It was your granddaddy who built it."

It's no easy thing to challenge a pack of good ol' boys. They wear their truths and sureties like armor and it's probably foolish to think I'll be able to force them out of a habit as deeply entrenched as denial.

"Protection from what? It wouldn't do much against a

gator and it certainly wouldn't stop a bear worth its hide. So why's it there?"

The silence that falls is heavy. No one's willing to say it. They'd rather sit here and pretend we've got a squatter while people go missing.

"Our swamp is a dark place," Old Lady Clary hisses in my ear. I'd been too focused on the conversation by the door to notice her come forward. She stands at my shoulder, her soft body leaning into mine. Her breath is sweet and hot on my neck. "A wild place and no place for young girls like you to be treading. You can't trust what goes on there. Can't trust what you see, what you hear."

"How's that any different from the rest of town?" I declare loudly, crossing to the front door. All but Darold clear the way. "I'm going to be late."

He stares down his nose and doesn't move. We've never been close, but that's not entirely his fault. Phin and I weren't ready for another father figure when Mama first brought him home. We'd had all we could take between a violent dad and a dead-too-soon grandpa. But he's good to Mama and that's as much as we could ask for. It almost doesn't matter what he is to me.

Almost.

"Excuse me," I say.

"Need a ride?" he asks. "I'm headed that way, and you and I have something to talk about."

So this is how it goes. He knows I lied and went out with Heath and, in return for not telling Mama, I'm supposed to let him treat me like a daughter.

"No offense, *Darold*, but the last thing I need is a deputy escort to school."

It's pitch perfect and all the old boys laugh me right through the door. They've probably already forgotten my troublesome questions about the fence.

Because that's what they're good at.

Candy finds me in two seconds flat. Either she was stalking my locker or she had a system of spies in place to tell her when I arrived. Both are likely.

"Also, why are you suddenly so against using your cell phone?" she asks as though we were in the middle of a conversation. "I—" She stops dead, her eyes locked to the half-eaten sticky bun in my hand.

"I'm not." I shove my coffee into her hands and open my locker.

"I beg to differ," she volleys, wisely choosing not to comment on the pastry. "Where is it? Right now. Where is it?"

It takes me a minute to fish my phone from the depths of my bag. I hold it up for Candy to see that the sound was switched off. Pressing the MENU button, I'm surprised to find I've missed ten text messages from Candy, three from Abigail, and one from Heath. The last sends an abrupt and rousing current through my body. I'm suddenly desperate to flip through the messages to his, but I'm too slow. Candy snatches the phone from my hands.

"Ooh, la la, what's this?" she teases, pushing my coffee mug into my hands. "A message from Heath? Post steamy, illicit date? What could it possibly say? It's a best friend's job to screen, right?"

"Candy, don't!" I protest, but she's too much in the spirit of things to relent.

Her fingers move over the screen until she finds what she's looking for. I brace myself for the worst.

"Well, that was underwhelming," she announces, handing the phone over. "What does this even mean?"

Not sure what to expect anymore, I look at the screen where Heath's message glows. It's only three words, but they mean the world: *i remember u*.

"Nothing," I say to Candy. To Heath, I respond with four words of my own: *i remember u, too*.

The day crawls by. I finish my French exam in half the allotted time, and my chem exam just as quickly. I wish I could put my head down and sleep like Abigail, but I'm too focused on how to get the single cherry into a tart for Lenora May. Over and over, I practice slicing the cherry in my mind, pitting it, and setting the halves in a mug. When her back is turned, I'll place them in a tart and pinch the corners so I know which it is. Then it's as simple as handing her *that* tart. There's so much room for error I couldn't fit it all inside Noah's Ark.

But it's all I've got.

Things go smoothly enough at first. On the drive home, we stop by the Winn-Dixie where Lenora May grabs peach preserves and I buy a small bag of cherries.

"My favorite." She snatches a cherry straight from the bag and I thank Fisher for knowing his sister so well.

At home, she puts on an oddly appealing mix of Mumford & Sons, Grateful Dead, and Phish. There's no one else home, so we turn it up until the clock on the wall gives an occasional shiver. And then she's dancing. She twirls on bare feet, her long curls dripping behind her. She gathers the flour and butter, the rolling pin and the pastry cutter, and lays them on the counter. Every step is part of her dance.

I've never been much for dancing. Moving without a specific purpose makes me feel awkward and vulnerable. On a volleyball court, every movement is calculated and predictable. One thing leads to another in this reactive choreography. But dancing is another story entirely, and Lenora May will bounce around to anything without a care in the world. Some small part of me has always envied that about her.

She sings and spins, and I can't help but laugh. Then her eyes are on me and her smile is brilliant. She pulls my arms and twirls me around the way she's done so many times before.

"I dare you not to feel this music in your soul, Sterling." She two-steps around me, pushing my arms into the appropriate form. "Music is where we sing our hearts for others to hear."

"I scream more than sing, really," I say, somewhat satisfied that she doesn't already know this about me.

She counters, "Then scream your heart out, Sterling."

By the time we've got the dough prepped and rolled flat, the filling mixed and chilling, I'm totally caught up in the dance, singing at the top of my lungs.

Lenora May demonstrates how to cut and fold the pastry. She's deft with the butter knife and forgiving of mistakes in a way that reminds me of the first time I tried waxing her eyebrows. The experiment ended in the phrase "It'll grow back," but I'd felt horrible for weeks. Luckily, the dough recovers faster and when I hold up my first, perfectly folded pastry, she rewards me with a sprinkle of flour on my hair.

"Now, you're a bona fide pâtissier." She holds up a defensive hand, but she's laughing too hard to plea for mercy.

"What's the plural of pâtissier?" I ask, tossing flour into her curls.

"Pâtissiers, of course!"

"When is there ever an 'of course' with French?"

"*Les verbes doivent s'accorder avec leur sujet*," she cries, invoking Madam and her relentless claim that "verbs must agree with their subjects."

When the timer buzzes, we load fresh tarts on a tray, swapping them for the baked batch, and prepping more. Slipping the cherry into a tart is almost too easy. There's absolutely no hint of suspicion about her and she doesn't blink when I pinch one tart into the rough shape of a cherry blossom. We work this way, side by side, for a full forty-five minutes. In the end we have fifty-two bite-sized tarts, half filled with peach preserves, half with a bit of semisweet chocolate and fresh cherries.

"This one's for me, right? The May flower?" She repeats the corny joke I told while molding the dough. The tart sits lightly on her palm. It looks more like a sloppy fleur-de-lis than a flower.

This startles me. Before we started, I'd been focused. Tense. Nothing but the embodiment of a plan to expel her from my life. But over the course of the afternoon I relaxed, becoming the Sterling who has a vibrant older sister and begrudgingly loves to dance. The plan—the tart—faded far into the background. I'd nearly forgotten it since putting it in the oven, nearly forgot that she was the enemy.

She brings it to her mouth and blows the steam away, cooing for the cherry to cool quickly and not burn her tongue.

It was that easy: she picked the one I told her was special. *How will it happen?* I wonder. *Will she take one bite and go running into the swamp? Will she wail like a siren? Tear at her hair and transform into something horrid and ugly?* I remember at least one of Old Lady Clary's swamp stories about a woman who roamed the swamp in a white dress, forever looking for small children to lure beyond the fence. Is that what Lenora May will do? Lure others? Am I trading Phin's life for that of the strangers Lenora May will harm next? Or will Fisher be able to help her remember who she was before?

There are so many unknowns and potential consequences. I try to tell myself I'm only responsible for Phin. There's something about that thought that doesn't settle well. I shift on my feet, but the feeling remains, stuck somewhere between my diaphragm and my ribs.

Then the thought I never expected to have: *Should I stop her?*

But it's too late.

She bites into the tart. Her reaction is immediate. Her eyes open wide and she drops it to the floor. One hand flies to her mouth, the other reaches for the faucet, for water. She rinses her mouth again and again, spitting into the sink, and when her eyes return to me, they're full of hurt.

"Sterling?" She asks so much with just my name.

I don't have any answers. My guts knot together and I feel sick, sick, sick.

"No," Lenora May mutters, stooping to collect the tart from the floor. It leaves a dark smear behind. "No, I'm not going back there. I can't. And you, Sterling, you stay away from me."

She gives me one final look before rushing through the door. The color of her eyes is obscured by tears. The screen door slaps its frame three times, and I hear her scream her heart out at the swamp.

I KILL THE MUSIC AND stand in the middle of the living room. Outside, Lenora May's gone quiet. All I hear is the *tick-tick-tick* of the clock on the wall. I wait for her face to reappear so I can understand this feeling in my gut. I think if I saw her, I'd know if it was anger or fear or guilt. But she doesn't return. The Chevelle revs and violently growls away.

My hands shake when I reach for my phone. Without even thinking, I dial Candy's number. She answers on the first ring.

"*Hola*, chéri."

Now, I'm not sure what I should say, what I *can* say. I should have called Heath. He would understand and it would be so easy to lay this frustrating, emotional quagmire at his feet, but that's not what I need right now.

"Saucier?" she asks when I'm quiet too long.

"Can you come get me?"

"Shit, are you okay? I'm coming."

She hangs up without waiting for an answer. I barely have time to pull on my boots and leave a note for Mama before Candy's honking her horn.

"What's all over you?" She turns the radio off as I climb into the passenger seat. The AC is set to arctic. "What's happened?"

It's a good question. I'm not entirely sure of the answer. My plan happened. Exquisitely, but something else happened, too, and I'm not comfortable with what that was.

Candy tugs at my hair, dusting the white powder from her fingertips with equal levels of concern and horror. Sunset makes her blonde hair shine orange.

"It's nothing. Flour. I had a fight with Lenora May and she took off. I . . . need to find her."

She doesn't press, but I have the sense that she gleans more than enough. It's as difficult to hide from her as it is from a military drone. "Lucky for you," she says, "I've got a good idea where she might be."

We turn up Candy's road and zip past rows of one-story brick houses on lots too big for a push mower. The Pickens residence is skirted by millions of blooming fuchsia and hot pink azaleas, and stone sculptures of everything from frogs to strange bird-gods peek through bushes. After a few miles, the houses give way to piney woods, and the road gets narrow and dark. There's an old bicycle reflector nailed to a tree, marking the barely-there road that leads to the track. It's only wide enough for one car and thankfully it's only a half mile long. If you meet someone coming the opposite direction, you either practice being pigheaded, or you practice driving in reverse. It's early enough that we don't have to do either. We drive straight to where the track's already buzzing with test runs.

Thursday night at the racetrack is a typical hangout in Sticks, but it's only special during finals week and Mardi Gras. That's when absolutely everyone goes. Candy actually likes the cars, or so she says, but except for Phin's, I couldn't give a fig about them. I like the track because it's dark and loud and exciting. This is exactly where Phin would be, so there's more than a good chance Candy's right and this is where Lenora May is, too.

A few reconstituted telephone poles surround the track, each supporting powerful floodlights. There's seating in the shape of a short stack of rusty bleachers that barely stretch the length of the track. Cars are parked sporadically around the western bend, all of their noses lit up and pointing inward. Dust and moths float in and out of the streams of light, lazy and frantic.

Candy parks a short distance from the field. She stopped

parking with everyone else the day Mitch Lome lost control of his car and slid into the cluster of trucks at the bend.

She asks, "You gonna tell me what the fight was about? Or am I just here for emotional support?"

I pause before answering. She's always been the sort of friend I could call in the middle of the night. No matter what the problem was, I could count on Candy to break things down to their simplest parts and give me a plan of action. She's decisive even if she's not always compassionate. That's why it was my first instinct to call her, and also why I shouldn't have.

"This is about your supposed brother, isn't it?"

She's also not forgetful.

But I can't bring myself to make this easier by lying. "Yes. And my intruder sister. I know it's not your fault that you can't see what's really happening, but think about it, Candy. She and I are nothing alike. I doubt she knows a volleyball from a basketball and the only dresses I own are somewhere in the darkest corner of my closet. She doesn't even look like me!"

Candy's shrug is obstinate. "Not all siblings look alike and it's totally normal for sisters to behave differently. But." She presses one hand to my shoulder the way people do when they're trying to stop a conversation. "You're my friend and so I support you in having a different view of reality, no matter how strange."

"Gee. Thanks."

This is a useless battle. Nothing will shake Candace Pickens away from a truth. Nothing except a charm. I think of Heath's bracelet and where he got it. Next chance I have, I'll get another from Old Lady Clary somehow and force it on Candy's wrist.

The crowd is nearly full when we leave the car, the air charged with growling engines and anticipation. I don't know what the stakes are tonight, but that doesn't really matter. I follow Candy into the stands where most of our friends have gathered. The air smells like cigarettes and beer and exhaust. I don't like it, but there's something comforting about the combination: at least it hasn't changed.

"Do you see the Chevelle?" I say into Candy's ear.

Candy squints over the crowd. "Nope, but I spy Quentin Stokes over there with my cousins. Rumor has it he's planning to make a move tonight."

The first set of cars moves onto the track and everyone cheers. I recognize Cody's yellow Charger, a green Mustang I think belongs to Jeremiah Rae, and the other two cars are familiar but I can't recall faces to go with them. Only in a place like Sticks are cars more easily recognizable than people.

A skinny blonde with melon boobs walks in front of the cars to catcalls and whistles. Her long legs flash in their headlights as she passes, a not-so-narrow strip of her hips and belly exposed beneath the knot of her shirt. She raises a black-and-white-checkered flag. Engines rev. The air thrums with static and stillness, this sense of waiting and wanting. I feel it echoed in my bones, humming through my blood.

She brings her arm down and everything screams into motion: the cars, the people, the air around. Gradually, the noise settles to something less intense. I scan the crowd again and this time I get lucky.

Lenora May's not in the stands, but in the light of the trucks on the field past the track. She has her arms raised and she spins in a cloud of dust. Her mouth is open and joyful, her head tilting up to the sky, her dark curls swaying behind her. Like earlier in the kitchen except now she moves in a slower, languid way. More eyes than mine have found her there. She doesn't notice. She spins and spins, pretty as a star and just as rare. She's standing not twenty yards away, but she's lost in the sky above.

I don't know that I'll ever be so brave. To stand in front of a crowd and take a moment that's only for me. Lenora May doesn't care that she's in the dirt or that she'll have to wash her dress three times to get rid of the stubborn smells that follow you home from the track, and not caring makes her both vulnerable and beautiful.

She stops spinning suddenly, turns toward the headlights, and disappears between two of the trucks. I feel a surge of panic. Is it possible the swamp prepared her for everything that comes with being a pretty girl in Sticks?

"I see her. I'll be right back," I tell Candy and pick my way down the stairs, careful to avoid kicking over bottles or stepping on hands.

My eyes don't adjust quickly. The light on the track makes the dark field harder to navigate. Shadowy figures slouch against tailgates. Cigarettes wink like red fireflies. And bottles of gold and clear liquor catch stray bits of moonlight. I pass the first two trucks, turning down three offers to pull from random flasks. There's a little bit of everything happening here, drinking, smoking, kissing, and more, all of it smothered in the roar of engines and a cheering crowd. It makes the night feel darker and smaller than in the stands.

I glance at each figure long enough to determine it's not Lenora May. There's a group of people clustered in the bed of the fourth truck, lounging and laughing and sharing drinks. A few of the laughs sound familiar, including Lenora May's. I edge to the tailgate for a closer look and spot her smashed between a boy and girl. I can't see either well enough to recognize them, but the boy has his arm draped over Lenora May's shoulders in a way that makes me bristle.

"Lenora May, can I talk to you for a second?"

Her voice is cloudy when she responds, "I'd rather not."

Someone snickers, but I don't move. There's one surefire

way to annoy a sibling and that's to stand around their friends while being young.

It only takes a minute before she speaks again. "Oh, fine, Sterling, fine."

Her voice is weary but she climbs awkwardly to her feet. Somehow she manages to keep her skirt down, but it's only luck preventing this entire truck from sneaking a peek where they shouldn't. I raise my hand to help, but she refuses. The smell of alcohol and smoke scoot with her, and we make our way a short distance from the den of iniquity, far enough that the racetrack is more of a buzz than a constant roar.

I wait until we've stopped to ask, "You're drinking?"

Nearly everyone at Sticks High does or has, but it doesn't seem ladylike enough for sweet and pristine Lenora May.

"Sterling," she says with a bleak laugh. "You aren't really going to talk to me about drinking, are you? I may not be your brother, but I'd be surprised if you were to tell me you'd had even a sip in all your sixteen years."

I don't drink. The smell of alcohol is loaded with too many bad memories. Phin made the same choice and it was harder for him because if there's one thing bad boys are supposed to do around here, it's drink. Many of the fights Phin found himself in were with guys who'd had too much. They were always the worst. *A man on fire*, Phin would say, *feels no other pain*. It was a lesson we learned well from our dad.

Lenora May has the same memories. I know she does because in all my memories of running from home, she's there running with me. But if I needed any additional proof that she's not really a part of my family, it's the languor in her speech.

Still, the hurt in her eyes when she bit into that tart was real.

"I didn't come here to talk about drinking. I came for answers. I want to know what you want."

"What I want?" She turns in a circle, throwing her arms wide and her head back, crowing at the sky. "I want to be reckless! Sterling, I want to drink until my head swims, I want to dance and laugh—do you know how long it's been since I laughed like you and I did today? I don't!"

She stops twirling, sways a little, and takes my hands in hers. Her cheeks are flushed, her smile both delirious and innocent.

"I've found *life* again." She gives my hands a small shake for emphasis. "All the things I gave up without intending to, I have them again. I have a home, a sister, and friends. I can bake and scream and run. All the things the swamp took from me. And I'm not giving them up. I can't give them up, Sterling. Please, don't ask me to."

All her laughter is gone, and I can see she's trembling on the verge of tears. I'm torn between sympathy and rage. This life she's loving is not her own, but she's holding on to it tightly. She loves this life as fiercely as she fears losing it.

I know something about living in that kind of fear. I know something about taking the good moments as they come because you never know what the next will contain.

"But why my family? Why Phineas? Why are you doing this to us?"

"It isn't about you! I know you won't believe me, but I'm not your enemy." She clutches at her chest. Frustration twists her features into something less pretty. "But, fine. You want answers. I'll give you some. You want to know why it happened this way? Because Phineas *wanted* it to. When he ran into the swamp, he *wanted* to disappear and never come back. He was tired of struggling, tired of being angry and afraid. He was running away, Sterling. Away from you."

Her words hit me like a truck and I stumble backward.

"Oh," she says, immediately regretful. "Oh, Sterling, I'm sorry. I shouldn't have said that."

I evade her grasp. Was it really my fault? I can't think about it. I can only hold on to this numb feeling for so long, and I don't want to be here right now.

Distantly, I hear myself saying, "Be careful, okay? Don't go anywhere alone." Sister or not, there's a long list of bad things that can happen at the track and I wouldn't wish them on anyone.

Her smile is strange and her voice quiet when she says, "Thank you."

Cheers rise from the track. One by one, the first cars stop racing. There are shouts and whoops, horns honking and guns firing as race night goes about business as usual.

I find Candy in the stands. I sit next to her and without a word she takes my hand in hers. For the rest of the night, I watch the cars go round and round the track until I can't hear the thoughts in my own head.

MAMA SAYS IT WAS GRANDPA Harlan who liberated us from Dad. Gave the last of his good health to getting rid of him. But I know different. Grandpa Harlan played a part, but he wouldn't have had a leg to stand on if Phin hadn't spent every minute of his waking life defying Dad. Sometimes in little ways. Emptying the chamber of his shotgun and hiding the shells behind the dictionary on the bookshelf. Sometimes in bigger ways. Shouting at him and taking the blows meant for me or Mom. I don't remember a time when he wasn't shielding me from one thing or another. He wasn't the sort to run away from anything.

Right?

I toss in bed. Lenora May's words are sticky and insidious. I try to recall the scene from Sunday morning. Though it was only a short time ago, it feels muddy and fluid, partly obscured by a memory of fighting with Lenora May over a pair of sandals I'd borrowed without asking. Beneath all that, Phin's there, giving me the bracelet, looking crestfallen when I didn't love it, and furious when I accused him of not caring what happened to me. I search each moment for some hint that Lenora May is wrong and I'm not the reason he left, but it feels possible.

It's also possible that she was being spiteful. Her motives are far from trustworthy, but I don't feel like I know anything anymore. Five days ago, I knew she was the devil incarnate and the only way to banish her was to follow Fisher's advice. Today? I can't quash the part of me that wants to slide into her bed like I did when we were kids and tell her I'm sorry for not trusting her.

I know what Phin would say. "Trust yourself, Sass. When things get tough, you get tough right back and always, always trust yourself. And me," he'd add with a grin.

If only it was so easy.

Too frustrated to sit still any longer, I send a predawn text to Heath, which takes five minutes to type, delete, retype, repeat. But finally, I send, *u up?*

Though the clock reads 5:13 a.m., his response is immediate—*what's wrong?*—and has an effect on my breathing I didn't expect.

My next five texts sound more frantic than I mean them to be, which is why he arrives at my house before the sun has risen high enough to mark its territory. Fog is wet in the air when I run down the gravel drive and climb into his truck. The cabin smells like coffee.

"Yum," I say, happy to see two Styrofoam cups tucked into the holders beneath the radio.

"Isn't that a second-date sort of comment?" Heath asks, his eyes uncharacteristically bright. His smile makes me bold.

"Not when you look like that," I say. Far too quickly. Heat rushes to my cheeks as I consider how true the comment is. We haven't seen each other since the kiss and he's looking unbearably sexy. He slouches in his seat with one hand on the wheel, not appearing at all like he rushed to get here, but the water dripping from his hair tells a different story.

Heath's laugh merges with the rumble of the engine. We drive through the middle of town, and beyond to where we're surrounded by kudzu-covered pines. Sunrise is a narrow strip above the gray road, a streaky puddle of orange and pink and blue.

I tell Heath everything that happened last night. Through it all he remains quiet, with his eyes focused straight ahead. By the time I finish, I realize he's already turned us around. A quick glance at the clock tells me we've got under twenty minutes before the bell announces our final day of sophomore year.

"I don't know what to believe anymore," I add. "Yesterday, I had what I needed to fix this and today I've messed it all up. And some cursed piece of me is *glad* it didn't work. She's not my sister. I know that, but I don't want to hurt her and that makes me so mad."

Again, Heath is quiet. Giving me the space I need not to lose it right here in his truck. I don't want to cry, so I grit my teeth and stare at the passing trees until my eyes don't burn. So much of this is my fault. Phin's trapped because I drove him away, because I didn't stop him, because I messed up and Lenora May didn't eat the cherry.

I nurse my coffee but no matter how much I drink, my hands and feet feel cold.

"I feel crazy."

"You're not crazy at all," he answers quickly. The truck takes a turn with a little more oomph than necessary. "Don't let anyone convince you you're anything but sane."

"They convinced you." I remember our conversation from the hallway, when he told me Old Lady Clary gave him the bracelet and told him to stop talking about Nathan. "What happened?"

He parks in the student lot with a clear view of the swamp at the bottom of the hill. Sunlight splashes over the tops of cypress trees, leeching the Shine of its eerie light.

Heath watches it, too, but his shoulders are tense and his fingers grip the wheel. There's no mistaking the fear he feels.

His motions and reactions are so quiet, so private, it's as if I'm witnessing something I shouldn't.

"After Nathan disappeared," he begins, "whenever I got close to the swamp, without even meaning to, I would wind up at the fence. I'd be out for a run or walking between classes, and I'd turn toward the swamp like it was where I meant to go all along."

I shudder. In all my recent obsession with the swamp, I've never felt out of control.

"One night, I dreamed of going to look for Nathan. It was so real. I could feel the humidity. I woke up halfway over the fence, right down there." He points, but doesn't really look. "It happened a couple of times. My parents would call the sheriff, I'd get picked up, and they'd ask me what I was doing. It took me too long to learn that Old Lady Clary was right and talking about Nathan was a bad idea. I thought I was losing my freaking mind. So did my parents."

I remember how readily Mama reached for her phone to call Doc Payola. If I hadn't found Heath so soon, I might have kept fighting at home, too. And that would've led me down the same troubled path.

"I think antidepressants were the first thing my parents thought of. Doc Payola agreed to try it. I didn't want to believe I was crazy, so I fought them over it. But the same day Old Lady Clary gave me this charm, she told me to take the pills."

Heath finishes his coffee in one gulp. "She told me that I'd been infected with Shine because I'd swallowed swamp water the night of the crash, and there was nothing to be done about it. Then she slapped this around my wrist and told me the pills would help dull my new swamp sense or whatever."

He reaches to pop the glove compartment, where a host of orange bottles rattle like snakes. "Now, I always feel like I'm a little bit crazy, but . . . I don't care as much. That swamp still glows like an army of demons hides inside, but as long as I don't look at it, I can sort of forget. I guess that's not the most heroic way of handling things, but it works."

All the rumors about Heath being a stoner or an alcoholic make sense now. His eyes have been glazed because he *has* been drugged, but it was the only way he saw to save his sanity. I can't imagine what I would have done without him. He's been doing this completely alone for more than a year. No wonder he disappeared after last summer. I barely made it a day before breaking down in the cafeteria.

"I took them until the day you told me you were going after your brother and made me feel like a coward."

"I never meant to make you feel that," I say, closing the glove compartment. "I think what you've done is very brave. Choosing not to take them."

Heath's laugh is rough, self-deprecating. "Giving up on pills isn't brave. Going into the swamp after my friend would've been brave. I never did that. *You* did that."

It's a compliment, but given his self-criticism it's too awkward to accept. Instead, I say, "You can't blame yourself."

"No, I know. What I'm really trying to say is that I still believe you, Sterling. Nothing is going to change that, I swear to you. I'll do everything I can to help you find your brother and bring him home. Don't you believe he meant for this to happen. I don't. Lenora May doesn't know what she's talking about."

Something surges up from my belly, through my lungs, and makes my heart thump five times faster. I push myself across the bucket seat and wrap my arms around Heath.

"Thank you," I say against his neck. "I don't know how to make that sound as big as I mean it to be, but thank you, Heath. Thank you for believing me."

Heath's hands are warm and flat against my shoulder blades, his chin pressed against the bare skin of my shoulder. I feel small and secure in his arms with my hip balanced against his thigh. This is different from the kiss. That felt chaotic and delirious and like something beginning. This is the opposite. Together we are solid and smart and somehow not new at all.

All around, the parking lot is filled with students who have more energy than they know what to do with and we're creating a target. The first "whoop!" is distant. So far away that there's a chance it wasn't directed at us, but a second and third follow before the truck heaves like a ship in a storm. Heath's arms become a vise around me as the truck lurches. We rock back and forth to the sounds of cheering and jeering and pounding against the sides of the truck. Heath keeps his arms locked around my waist but even so, my head knocks against the window.

"You're doin' it wrong, Durham!" someone cries. I recognize the drawl of one of the Wawheece boys. Typical. "Get this truck rockin'!"

There are more than a few of them circling like vultures. Each one adds another crude comment, hollering at the top of their lungs.

When it stops, Heath is through the door, squaring shoulders with one of the Wawheece brothers. With three boys fanned behind their leader, these are bad odds for Heath.

I climb out on the other side, where the other Wawheece brother waits, grinning at me like he's invited me to kiss his boots. It's the sort of look that makes me feel small and rotten inside, and it takes every bit of stubborn I've got not to slink away. This is the brother that shaves his head. The other keeps his hair long and ratted—a perfect habitat for fleas. One of the boys is Lamont, the other Riley, but I can't tell which is which. They're basically a two-headed entity with one brain between them and even that brain is challenged on a good day.

"What're you looking at?" I spit.

I've never had trouble with this gang. They've always had enough sense not to mess with Phin or his friends. But No Hair doesn't back down. His eyes rake over me like I'm fair game. I feel another layer of Phin's protection melt away. As far as the Wawheece boys are concerned, I'm just another girl who should fear or revere them.

On the other side of the truck, Flea Bit and his three minions are goading Heath. The jabs they throw are loud enough for me to hear. Heath's response is quiet. He keeps his eyes fixed on Flea Bit's face. Judging by the way the three lackeys glance at their leader, whatever he's said makes them nervous.

"What did you say?" Flea Bit pushes his nose into Heath's face. He's taller, broader across the shoulders, and I'd be willing to bet he fights dirtier, too.

No Hair blocks my path to Heath with a filthy leer. From the school, the warning bell rings. Everything else is quiet.

Heath's arms are tense, but he doesn't retreat when he answers, "I could say it again, but I don't think you'll understand it any better a second time."

Heath must have seen the punch coming, but he doesn't move to defend himself, doesn't try to counterattack the way Phin might've. He stands there and lets Flea Bit's fist crash into his face.

It's enough to distract my captor. I dart around the truck, diving straight into the mess of flailing limbs and cuss-crazed boys. Heath's trying not to get pinned, but someone has his arm pressed against the truck. They're about to give him a real beating.

"Stop it!" I scream, inserting myself between them in time to catch a fist with my ribs.

All my air leaves in a rush. My lungs refuse to work. I hear my name and see Heath's face flush red as he gives Flea Bit a hard shove in the chest. Flea Bit hits the ground and so do I.

I can't breathe. Panic rises. Again I try and fail to draw a breath. The world is loud in my ears.

"Take it easy," Heath says, his hands so warm on my cold, cold skin. "Relax, relax, you're okay."

He continues to murmur in my ear, stroking my shoulders with deliberate calm. I smell the clean rosemary-and-mint scent of his soap, and that's when my lungs remember what they're for; as they slowly open, pain stabs my side.

The boys are gone. Scared off because they hit a girl. It's only me and Heath and a few fussy mockingbirds in the parking lot.

"Our first fight," I say, and immediately regret laughing.

Heath's cheek is mottled pink and white with a little blossom of blood near his eye. It doesn't seem to bother him. While I hunch over my bruises, he smiles through his.

"I thought that was more of a fourth- or fifth-date sort of thing."

It's the second time he's said "date" today like it's no big thing. Given the circumstances, I suppose it isn't really. Still, I feel slightly breathless again.

The pain in my side eases slowly. I remember this sensation too well—the shock of pain that spears your entire body. Maybe it wouldn't have happened if Phin still existed. But if it hadn't happened, I wouldn't know that instead of running away from a fight, I dove straight into one.

Heath keeps a hand beneath my elbow as we climb to our feet. The movement encourages the pain. Sitting through a day of school isn't going to be easy, but it'll be worse for Heath. There'll be no hiding what he's been up to. At least exams are over and all we have to do is pick classes for next year.

Ducking to investigate the damage in the rearview mirror, Heath dabs at the blood with his fingers. They leave rusty smears on his pale jeans and he frowns. It's a look that says his mama won't be happy about that stain.

The final bell blares overhead. We're officially late.

"At least we'll get to add tardy to our list of criminal achievements," I say.

"It's worth it." Heath pulls me near, falling into one of his somber expressions. "Sterling Saucier," he says.

"Heath Durham."

His eyes narrow in a smile. Sunlight shines through them, illuminating too many rings of brown and brass to count. He bends closer.

"May I kiss you?" he asks.

I close the gap between us, press my lips to his, and forget everything else except this feeling. The world has never been so small. It's all in the space between us, all in the press of his hand in my hair, all in the tang of blood on his lips.

We part. Breathless, laughing, and shaking with adrenaline.

"Yes," I say, and he leans in to kiss me again.

THE LAST DAY OF SCHOOL is too pointless to bear. I make it halfway to class before deciding to ditch. Heath is right. I'm not crazy. There's no way Phin wants to be stuck in the swamp for the rest of his life. I've messed things up. First with Phin and then with Lenora May. And now I've got to fix them. I'm done relying on other people telling me where Phin is or what Phin wants. I'm going to see him for myself.

The trip home isn't comfortable. My ribs hurt at first, but the more I move, the better they feel, and soon enough I'm able to step into a careful jog. A few cars pass, but I don't get nervous until I see a police cruiser stopped on the road ahead. I stick to the tree line on the opposite side, but as I get closer, I see it's Sheriff Felder and a few other boys. They're all huddled by the fence with their backs to me. Must be more damage.

When I reach the house, Mama's Corolla is in the driveway. I drop my bag and change my shoes at the screened porch, making sure to keep quiet. My hands shake as I pull the bootlaces tight over my calves, a combination of adrenaline and exhaustion. As soon as I've double knotted them, I'm off and over the fence.

In the full light of day, the Shine is faint. Ghostly tendrils reach for the bracelet, warming my skin as they wrap loosely around my wrist. It's not aggressive, but I remember the way one of these seemingly gentle vines gripped my neck a few nights ago. I brush them away and they reach again. No matter how violently I swat at them, they float to my wrist and snuggle up to my bracelet.

Fisher said I had a knack for navigating the swamp. Mostly, I think I have a knack for not dying in it, but I consider what he meant. The only thing I did on my first trip over the fence was say my brother's name. Is that what he meant?

"Phineas Harlan Saucier," I say.

Shine begins to weave together, forming a trail. I move quickly, all too aware that there are beasts in this swamp and my last encounter with one was nothing short of terrifying. Shine leads me on a mostly dry path through tall foxtail plants, past a squatting juniper bush, and into the grove where the magnificent cherry tree spreads its limbs like wings. Each blossom full and open to catch the sunlight.

"Thank you," I say because giving thanks is polite no matter who, or what, you're giving it to.

I catch a bit of Shine between cupped palms, so I can whisper to it as Fisher did. I say, "Show me Phineas," and then for good measure, "please."

The lights fly from my hand, skating over the pond and hovering there. Something flips in the water—a quick, quiet sound. I almost miss it, but turn to see ripples drifting toward the edges of the pond. In the center, something has broken the surface and it's moving, pushing ripples ahead of ripples.

I crouch, pressing my knuckles into the spongy ground. Whatever it is, it's not a snake or a gator, but it's round like a turtle. It stops a few feet away. I stare at it a bit longer and, with a start, I realize it's not a turtle.

It's a head.

Eyes, big and blue and human, lift above the water. Dark hair slicks over the crown. The skin around the eyes looks as rough as tree bark and as dirty green as hanging moss. But the eyes looking at me are more familiar than my own.

"Oh, God, Phineas." I lean forward, not caring that my hands and knees are covered in mud. I only care that those are my brother's eyes.

At his name, he lifts his whole head from the water and I gasp at the way it both is and isn't Phin's face. His once-smooth skin is scaled, with lips pulled into a hard grin. Teeth peek from beneath them, eggshell white and sharp: a gator's grin. The edges of his once-firm nose are soft, smeared down his cheeks, making his nostrils overly large and dark. An airy, hissing sound drifts from his horrible mouth.

"Phin, oh, God. Oh, my God, is that really you?" Panic pushes my voice into a high, thin pitch. I'm not in control of it or my breath, which huffs unevenly in my ears.

Phin blinks slowly, drifting closer in an eerily graceful way.

"Phin? Can you speak? It's me, Sterling. Your sister, Sterling Annabel Saucier. I steal your magazines and sit on your car, never eat the candy you give me, and I'm constantly pissing you off. You sang me songs after Dad left when I couldn't sleep, and last year you got a tattoo that Mama doesn't know about. She'd skin you alive if she did. Can you hear me, Phin? Please, say something!"

"I'm hungry," he says, a sound that seems to crawl from his throat. It's devoid of the warmth Phin's voice should have, all mud and gravel. He reaches with webbed hands, each finger tipped with a sharp, black claw.

Not my brother, I think, *a trick*.

I pull back so abruptly that I slip. My balance gone, I skid down the muddy bank, hitting the water as I topple over. I see the rictus of my brother's face inches from my own. Claws grip my arm, fear grips my heart, and I have a second to wonder if the town will forget me when I die here.

Suddenly, there's a tug at my waist. I'm pulled backward, crushed against a body that's warm as the swamp air.

"Sterling?" Fisher's voice is in my ear, his hands biting into my waist. "Are you all right?"

"*That's* his cage?" I struggle in his arms. "*That's* what she did to him? Phin!"

I slip again before my feet find solid ground. I twist against Fisher's grip, scanning the pond for the creature with my brother's face. He's several feet away, submerged in brine, watching me with shallow eyes.

Fisher catches my chin in his hands, dipping his head to look into my eyes with such intensity that I freeze.

"Are you all right?" he repeats.

I shouldn't wish that the answer was no, but there's something about his unwavering concern that makes me want to fall into him.

"Yes," I say, pulling away before my cheeks tell my secrets. "I'm fine."

"No," Fisher says quietly with a stern shake of his head. His eyes have fallen from my face and he lifts my right arm gently. "You're bleeding."

Two gashes streak my forearm. One deep, one not. Both bright with blood dripping to the ground. Phin's claws must be every bit as sharp as they look. Now that I've seen the wounds, I feel them. A stinging pain crackles through my arm and sends a vicious tremor down my spine.

"That's going to need stitches," I say, beginning to feel fuzzy. "Big ones."

The more I study the cuts, the less I feel like that arm belongs to me. It looks like a painting. Something isolated and disconnected from the rest of me. I think of Doc Payola's office and how there's no chance I'll be able to hide this from Mama and Darold. *What will I say? Freak accident in the bleachers? I fell against an angry box cutter?* As ridiculous as they sound, anything will be easier to swallow than "attacked by a gatorboy in the swamp." I can imagine Mama's bug-eyed expression when I tell her, and I begin to laugh.

"Hmm." Fisher's frown becomes disapproving.

For some reason, that tickles me even more. Each laugh leads to another, carried forward with its own delightful momentum. "I'm sorry," I say. "It's just, I'm gonna be in so much trouble."

"Perhaps not," he says.

Holding my arm steady in one hand, Fisher extends the other. As if called, a single frond of Shine drapes itself over his palm. He pinches the light between his fingers, detaching it as easily as if it were made of Play-Doh or clay. His fingers skim over the top of my bracelet. Blood has fallen into the hollow spaces, leaving the silver bouquet looking like ghastly red roses. He dwells on the band as if he can't decide if he's going to remove it. Then he presses the bit of Shine against my deepest cut, does the same with the second wound, and lays his hand over both for a brief second.

A growing warmth seeps through my arm, sinking into my bones. It's followed by a wave of nausea that crests in my belly. I'm dizzy. The air is thick and suffocating with the hot scent of mud. My palms and feet tingle for a moment. When it passes, Fisher has one hand against my neck, the other around my waist, supporting me.

He says, "Forgive me, I've forgotten that the sensation can be disorienting. It should pass quickly."

My belly feels full as the Mississippi after a storm. Gradually, my head clears enough that I can stand on my own. The skin on my arm has knitted itself together, leaving two pale pink lines behind. The stinging pain is entirely gone. In fact, even the soreness in my ribs has vanished. When I look up, the Shine is bright and crisp. Fisher's hands fall away and I move from beneath the everblooming cherry tree.

"What was that? I feel so awake," I say, staring at the trunk of a large cypress tree growing in the pond. Dozens of its strange skinny knees push up through the water like wooden straws and between each is woven an intricate web of Shine in pale grays and greens. I never would've seen it before.

"That was the magic of the swamp. And you are more awake now than you have ever been."

With Shine still thrumming against my skin, pieces of understanding click into place.

I reach for the ground, and Shine rises to my fingers as

it did to Fisher's. Effortlessly. Instinctively. The small tendril shimmers with energy. This Shine—this magic—can do so much more than steal my brother and implant a false sister. It can heal and transform.

Lenora May said she knew the things Phineas did, that Shine worked by using what was already there. It hadn't created her history, it had given her Phin's. People didn't forget Phin so much as they remembered someone else. And just now, it hadn't erased my wound, it had bridged a gap, leaving a scar behind.

It all makes sense except for one thing.

"Why do most people forget?" I turn again to Fisher, who stands near. Watching. It's startling to find his attention so squarely on me, but I won't be deterred so close to the truth. "When people go missing why do we forget them? And how?"

"I'm afraid that is more than I can answer; however, I assume it is a matter of self-preservation. When the swamp pulls someone inside, it pulls in all of them, even the pieces others carry. Like memories. That way, no one starts looking at it sideways."

It seems to me that's the only way people look at the swamp, but I get what he means. If anyone suspected the swamp had a mind of its own, they'd try to fill it or drain it or otherwise destroy it. As much as I hate that my brother is trapped here, I somehow can't wish the swamp away.

"Likewise," he continues, "when Lenora May broke

away from the swamp, she did it with great force. In a sense, she exploded through a barrier that sent her life flying into the town."

"Like a dirty bomb," I say. "Like shrapnel."

"Precisely. And just as damaging."

"Has it always been like this?" I study the way Shine courses through the ground, a chaotic, dense system of roots. If my grandpa knew about it, then it's been here at least as long as I've been alive: a secret wrapped inside a secret.

"Since before Lenora May and I were born." Fisher caresses a low branch of the everblooming cherry tree. "And that was a long time ago."

The implications are staggering. The Wasting Shine might have been here for hundreds of years, quietly growing in the center of the swamp. It's been here since before Grandpa Harlan built his fence, before the Clary women started telling stories, before Lenora May and Fisher became a part of it. How many lives might this swamp have touched and changed? How many others might be trapped inside it?

"Is it evil?" I ask, remembering the pale-faced beast.

It takes a moment for Fisher to answer. "No, it's not in its nature to be good or evil. It is a living thing. A plant capable of taking on the shape, the qualities, that you give it."

"What do you mean 'the qualities you give it'? How can anyone give a plant its qualities? It's either poisonous or it's not."

I can't tell if his hesitation is reluctance or frustration.

There's a little of both in the way he presses his palms together. Finally, he says, "In the same way some plants seek the sunlight, this magic will bend itself to your words so long as your intention is clear."

I consider how the Shine moved away from Candy, unwilling to be touched, and how it always seems to reach for me, for the bracelet I wear. Bending like flowers, but the metaphor doesn't work beyond that. "How about magnets? Shine is like any old piece of iron. It has potential, but it's not a magnet until you force all the electrons to move in the same direction. We're the ones aligning those electrons by telling it what to do?"

He smiles. "You're a surprising creature, Sterling. Electrons are beyond me, but it sounds correct. Every time we speak, we influence the world around us. The magic of the everblooming cherry is more susceptible to your will."

Rolling the little ball of Shine between my fingers, I think of clear water, running my hands beneath a faucet. "Clean," I say, and the little ball melts over my skin, clearing all the blood and muck away.

"I—" Fisher stops, his face goes blank. "That was quick."

"I've always been a fast learner," I say, feeling all over pleased with Fisher's shock. "Especially when something makes sense."

"Indeed," he answers.

It feels so easy. Pluck a piece of Shine like a berry and give it purpose. Easy and dangerous. And right in the center of Sticks. Maybe it's a good thing folks pretend not to notice. Maybe they're right to keep up the fence. Surely, if people knew there was power here, they'd come for it.

Phineas is only a distant bump in the water now. His blue eyes float on top, dull and wet as a gator's. From this distance, he could be anybody or anything, but I know what I saw in his face. I don't doubt that creature is Phineas.

I say, "He's not human anymore."

"He is and he isn't," Fisher answers, standing at the edge of the pond, eyes trained on Phin's shape. Cherry blossoms are dazzling behind his dark hair, glowing in a pink-and-ochre halo. Somehow, the pink is a perfect highlight to his restrained and defiant beauty. "I've seen it happen to many lost souls. So desperate to escape their human lives, the transformation occurs almost naturally."

I ignore how closely that resembles Lenora May's claim that Phin was running away. "But everyone doesn't change. I saw Nathan Payola the night I met you. He went missing more than a year ago, and he looked like always."

"That is true. She didn't change all of her victims. Only when it suited her. If it amused her to leave someone locked in the moment they became lost in the swamp, she'd let them roam. If she wanted to keep them close, to tie them to her will, she changed them into something more primal."

I try to make this vicious image of Lenora May match the

one I know, try to imagine her laughing at poor lost Nathan or gleefully transforming my brother into the twisted creature I just saw. It's a rough fit. The closest I come is this: a memory of the Lenora May wearing the grimmest smile I've ever seen as Deputy Darold cuffed our dad and hauled him away. That's as evil as my mind lets her be.

Phin's not visible anymore. Only a ghost of a trail remains through sticky duckweed. "Can it be reversed?"

"Without Lenora May to take his place the way he took hers, there is only one way." His tone keeps my hopes in check. "We would have to physically break his connection to the swamp, and that would kill him. I wish it weren't the case, but without Lenora May, I'm—I'm helpless."

Even with all that's happened, he loves her.

"The cherry didn't work," I admit. "And she knows I tried."

The change in him is subtle, but something falls through his face and shoulders, down to his toes. For a moment, I can't distinguish his feet from the muddy ground. It lasts only a second, here and gone so fast that I'm not sure if it was real.

"That is unfortunate," he says, each word precise.

"There must be another way. Maybe a way to free you both and Phineas and Nathan and anyone else trapped here."

His response is immediate, vicious in its passion. "No. There's no other way, Sterling, believe me. It's a waste of your time to even consider it. Lenora May and I belong here. It's the fate we chose together. Anything else is unacceptable."

"Okay, I get it." I take an involuntary step back.

"I didn't mean to frighten you. I'm just—I'm worried for you and your brother, and for anyone else Lenora May might harm. I'm afraid she's become a monster."

The trails Phin left in the algae have closed over themselves, erasing the evidence of his passing. Once again, the pond is a dish of sunlight and scum. Nothing moves here. Nothing changes.

"You think she's dangerous?"

"I think she's capable of anything," Fisher says, stooping to pull a coil of Shine into his hands. "We'll try it again, but this time, I'll show you how to make certain she eats the cherry."

Fisher picks another blossom, cups it between his palms, and speaks softly over it. A small flash of light escapes his fingers, and when he opens his hands, a new, perfect cherry rests on his palm.

"I won't be able to fool her again. She'll be expecting this." I try not to sound as hopeless as I feel, but I doubt Lenora May will take anything from me she didn't watch me harvest. We've lost the element of surprise, and that was all we had in the first place.

Worst of all, I'm not sure I *want* to trick her into doing something she very clearly doesn't want to do.

"Then you'll have to make her." It's his tone that gets my guts to grumbling. It's the sort of tone Candy might use when she's about to ask me to do something I probably shouldn't, like break curfew or bleach my hair.

"What do you want me to do?" I ask.

Fisher pulls Shine into his hands and begins to shape it. "Magic cannot be removed from the swamp unless it has been bound to a physical object. Anything from a cherry to a piece of clothing. Her comb perhaps. Or a bracelet like yours. It's tricky, but I suspect not for you."

His attempt at flattery does nothing to dislodge this sense of dread. Whatever he's about to tell me to do, I'm sure I won't like it.

Oblivious or indifferent, he continues, "When you infuse the object, simply give it a command as you did to clean your hands. And when Lenora May touches whatever it is, she will be compelled to follow that command: listen, eat, *obey*."

I flinch. There are words that have power. This is something every southerner knows: words used carelessly can get you run out of town or worse. Harmful, threatening, historically loaded words we all know and precious few of us say. *Obey* isn't one of the top five, but it scores high with families like mine, and if my hackles hadn't already been halfway to heaven before, they are now.

"So," Fisher continues, resigned and possibly amused. "Perhaps tonight, you might charm her fork, her spoon, her hairbrush, anything you feel sure she will touch. Whatever it is, be very clear with your intentions. Her desire to resist will be as strong as your desire to save your brother. Be forceful."

The thought of forcing my will on anyone is repugnant as a cup of chaw spit. But I nod. "Okay."

As if sensing my growing discomfort, he slides his hands down my arms. My skin warms and relaxes beneath his touch. Not a natural touch, I realize now, but one that's blended with Shine.

And then I suddenly jump. How many times has he touched me? If controlling someone is as easy as commanding Shine, who's to say he hasn't directed my thoughts? Has he been manipulating me the entire time? I scrub at my forearm.

"Sterling," he soothes, "remember she is a jealous and vengeful creature. This is the only way to save your brother."

I search the flat water for any sign of Phineas, but the swamp denies me even that small comfort. I nod, and sense more than see Fisher's smile. It's not one I can return. I take the cherry when he offers it again, and follow the shining path home.

WHILE I WAS IN THE swamp, the heat of the day rolled in beneath tall thunderclouds. They moved slowly, looking for a place to rest, and sat on top of Sticks like tired, fat dogs. Beneath them, the air is still and thick and smells like rain.

My yard isn't empty when I reach it. Heath stands three feet from the fence, hands on his hips, eyes studying Mama's collection of Mardi Gras beads and Christmas lights.

"Jezuz," he says when he spots me. "I had a feeling. You have a helluva time trusting people, don't you?"

"What does that mean?" I climb the fence, careful to keep from dripping mud on the top planks where Mama or Darold might spot it.

"I—I would've gone with you. That's what that means."

If the stutter weren't enough to give away his fear, the way he studiously avoids looking at the swamp for too long does. He's terrified of what's beyond the fence. It makes his offer a brave one, but not one I can accept. He sees the reason in my face and heaves a defeated sigh.

"What'd you find this time?"

"Phin," I say, and before he can react, "or what he's become. He's more gator than boy anymore. Fisher says it's Lenora May's doing."

We cross the yard, and Heath helps me balance as I carefully remove my filthy boots. It's a delicate process involving the edge of the brick steps and precisely applied pressure. The first one falls with a thud right into Mama's iris bed.

"You don't sound like you believe him." He switches hands so I can attack the next boot.

"I'm not sure anymore. He thinks I should try again except he wants me to be more aggressive this time. He wants me to force her." It sounds as distasteful as I thought it might.

The second boot leaves a thick smear on my calf, but doesn't break any flowers when it falls. I hold the cherry for him to see. It gleams red in the afternoon sun and just thinking of trying to trick Lenora May into eating it gives me pause.

All my memories are telling me Lenora May is a far cry from evil. I know they're not real, but knowing and believing aren't always the same and some part of me believes them.

She's here and Phin's not. That should be the end of it, but I keep hearing the gravity in her voice when she begged me to let her stay.

I assumed Fisher was a victim, but he doesn't seem concerned with his own freedom. I thought that was his sense of responsibility and honor, but now I'm not so sure. Would an honorable person ask me to force someone to do something against her will? I don't know who to trust and my gut's all twisted.

"Don't take this the wrong way, Heath, but we need help."

"No argument here, but where do we get it?"

"From the one girl in Sticks who's had all the swamp stories memorized since she was old enough to tell them."

As requested, Candy meets us on the porch of Clary General after school. She's dressed for the occasion, everything she's not allowed to wear during the regular year: too-short shorts, low-cut tank top, and cowboy boots. Even I can admit it's hot. Judging by the way Heath becomes suddenly fascinated with a couple of fighting mockingbirds in the yard, I'd say he agrees.

"Look at you delinquents," she says with a sly grin. "I convinced Mr. Tatum to give me your yearbook. You can thank me in Pixy Stix. Now, let's get inside. I don't want to burn unless I'm in a bikini."

"You're pretty close as is," I say.

"I know, right? Mrs. Gwaltney just about had kittens in front of everyone when she saw me. Which you'd know if you'd bothered to show for our very last day as underclass-women."

Heath falls into step behind me as we stomp up the front steps and into the cooler air of Clary General. As usual, it smells like pinewood and coffee with a hint of the scent I've only ever associated with camouflage hunting gear.

Candy snatches an armadillo purse from the shelves and models it saying, "I can't believe no one's ever bought me one of these. What girl doesn't want a purse made from the husk of an armadillo?" The one she's picked has red beads in place of eyes and a brass lock protruding from its chest.

"That's obscene," I say. "Put it down."

"Where's your pride, Saucier? That's fine Sticks' crafts-manship you're hating on. You won't find better in any other bayou town. What're we doing here anyway?"

"I've got some questions for Mrs. Clary and then I've got some questions for you, okay?"

With a shrug, she replaces the armadillo purse on the shelf next to a collection of gator feet then follows me through the store. We have to go out back to find Old Lady Clary where she and five other women are in the shade of pine trees.

Using a grill lighter, Old Lady Clary lights sticks of incense for Mrs. Tatum, who's looking unusually strained.

The other four women are dotted along the fence line, praying or whatever it is people do here with their candles and
incense and plates full of pie. Mama's always said it's best to
call it prayer and not think too hard on it. Before a few days
ago, I would have done just that. Now, though, I think it's
one more way in which Sticks buries the truth.

"Everyone's freaked about the fence," Candy informs us.
"There was all sorts of superstitious chatter about it at school
today."

We wait until Old Lady Clary is done, her long lighter
tucked away in the pocket of her red-and-white-striped
apron. She peers from beneath the wide brim of her floppy
hat, considering us the way a cat might consider three baby
mice. It's the sort of look that makes me regret needing to
deal with her, but there's no other way to get Candy's brain
on straight. With a small shake of her head, Old Lady Clary
shuffles our way, her steps hindered by the presence of hungry chickens in the yard.

"My, my, my," she says, humming her Ms like they're too
tasty to relinquish. "Don't you three look as serious as heart
attacks. Don't tell me, I can guess. Mm-hmm, my dears, I can
see you've been getting involved with the swamp. Clear as
the sun at noon. Well, let's go inside. Come on."

Already, I'm relieved. She brought it up first, which means
we won't have to convince her to talk about the thing no
one wants to talk about. Not that I anticipate getting much

from her, but there's only one thing I need.

We follow her to the register, where she perches on her wooden stool and busies herself with her ledger.

"I need another charm," I say, pressing my hands flat on the counter the way teachers do when they really mean something. "Like the one you gave Heath."

"Ma'am," Heath says in greeting.

Now, she looks up from her book and pulls the bifocals from her nose. "But dear, you already have one. And better than any I could make, I promise you. Yours has got more power than I've ever had access to. One of mine'd be a waste."

Her openness is a small victory; one that fills me with hope. She's confirmed it: these bracelets have power.

"It's not for me." I glance in Candy's direction. She's not paying a whit of attention. It seems the seven-day candle collection was messy enough to demand her expertise. By the time she's done, they'll be alphabetized and arranged by color.

"What does she need one for?" She leans in to speak more softly. "Has she been in the swamp? Eaten something like this fool boy here?" She gives Heath a meaningful look.

"Eaten anything? No. I just need her to remember."

She shakes her head. "Sorry, shug, I don't give charms to anyone that wants them. Only folks that *need* them. Like this boy did. Anyone foolish enough to swallow a piece of the swamp risks going mad unless they got a charm to keep their brains clear. But if she don't need one, it's safer that she don't have one—if she don't already remember those that've gone, she'll be happier remaining that way."

Without meaning to, she's filled in more gaps than I could've hoped for. Why Heath started to go mad, why he stopped, why we are the ones to remember. It's all there.

"I know how to work the Shine. So, please, ma'am, sell me a charm or tell me what words you use to make them and I'll do it myself."

Her eyebrows shoot up at that. "It's not a good idea to go messing in that business, and I'm pretty sure I shouldn't be helping you to do it."

She folds her arms across her chest and fixes us with an impassive look. *How does this woman manage to infuriate me so?* I shouldn't have bluffed. I've got no idea how to make a charm. And I don't even want to think about how many things could go wrong if I pick the wrong words.

"Mrs. Clary, ma'am." Heath leans forward with his arms on the counter. It makes his shoulders look broad and sturdy—authoritative. "With all due respect, you might be right and we should stay away from the swamp, but if we don't get help from you, we'll get it from someone, some*where* else. It's up to you, really, how we go about it."

He puts words together so easily. I can hear exactly how he's plucking at her adult sensibilities to get the answer we want. I couldn't have done it, but Heath makes it all sound so easy and logical. Then, before my very eyes, Old Lady Clary transforms from stubborn old woman into something more austere. Still, her mouth is a tight, unbending line.

"You know I've been over the fence already," I say, pushing Heath's groundwork a little further. "I saw him, Mrs. Clary. I saw my brother and what he's become. . . . I can't leave him there. No matter what you say, I'm going to try to save him, and I need all the help I can get."

"Every bit as stubborn as your granddaddy," she mutters before taking a long drink of her water. "All right, I'll give you one, but you'd better be sure. Not everyone can hang on to multiple realities if you know what I mean, and this town's got all the Featherhead Fred it can take."

If there's anyone capable of dealing with this sort of confusion, it's Candy. "Yes, ma'am, I'm sure."

At that, she ducks beneath the counter and rummages around in hidden drawers, muttering to herself the whole time. It's enough to capture Candy's attention. She makes big, baffled eyes at me, but I shrug. The good thing about being old is that you can get away with a lot of crazy without people making too big a fuss. Candy only rolls her eyes to let me know her patience has worn thin and joins us at the register.

Finally, Old Lady Clary reappears and presses a woven leather circle into my hand. It's not the prettiest thing, but it'll have to do. I reach for my money, but she clucks her tongue.

"Not this time, shug. You hold on to your money and promise me you kids'll be careful."

"Yes, ma'am, we promise," I say hurriedly. "C'mon, Candy."

Before I can step away from the counter, the same wave of nausea I felt when Fisher bound Shine into my wounds crashes over me, and my vision clouds. I lean forward—I can see how firmly my hand presses against the counter, but can't feel it—and then it's gone.

A rushing ocean fills my ears and there's a tickle in my nose. Behind the waves are voices, cresting and falling, reaching for me, trying to tease me from the surge. It seems a long time til they punch through, but I'm content to stay in this fuzzy place, this cotton ball space where I'm not hot or cold, just quiet.

"I think she's waking up." The voice is suddenly clear and very close.

I open my eyes. The world is a smear, and something pinches my waist.

"Pull it together, Saucier. C'mon, wake up!"

"I think I should give her mother a call," says another voice.

My feet are on the ground. The pinching at my middle is a hand holding me upright.

"No, look at that, her eyes are open. Poor thing's been working too hard lately."

Little by little, my vision clears. Candy's got me through the front door and the heat of the sun revives me a little. I see my legs moving down the stairs before I feel them. Once the fuzz starts to clear, it leaves quickly, and I realize I must've started to faint.

"Don't slow down now, Sterling. We've got you." Heath's voice clears more of the fog.

I started to faint and Heath caught me.

"Say good-bye to Old Lady Bat-brain unless you want her calling your mama." Candy hooks one arm through mine, lending her strength and momentum.

I dredge up enough energy to call my farewell and toss a smile over my shoulder. Then we're in Candy's car. I rest my head against the seat and close my eyes, but Candy's having none of it. She punches the side of the headrest, making my brain collide with my eyes.

"Candy!"

I've never heard Heath's voice at that volume. Candy's face is rigid. I know why, but I don't have any apologies for her.

"What. The. Hell," she says. "Have you eaten anything today? Anything at all? Because I don't think you have."

"Just leave it alone," I say. I'm not about to explain that I had a dose of Shine that's kept me going as well as any meal. The ironic truth is that ever since that night in the Lillard

House, I've been eating better than I have in months.

"That's a no. And no, I won't just leave it alone, Saucier. You *fainted* because you, I dunno, exist. This has gone too far and it's time you faced it. You need a damn hamburger. I'm buying. That means it's a gift, and etiquette says you can't refuse a gift."

"I'm not doing this on purpose, Candy!" My throat is so tight I can hardly speak. "This was totally out of my control!"

"I don't believe you," she returns, unrelenting. When Candy gets her nose in something, she can be as ruthless as a turkey buzzard. Pick, pick, picking until the bones are clean. "I don't believe that you get to this point—*fainting*—unintentionally. I don't believe that you don't have control. And I'm not going to let you believe that, either."

I can't explain anything to her until I get that charm on her wrist and reintroduce her to reality. And I *need* to talk to her about it. I'm tired of this wall between us. I'm going to knock it right the hell down.

"Okay," I say even as she noses the car into one of the stalls at Sonic. "Get me a damn hamburger. And in return, I get to give you a gift you can't refuse."

I display the bracelet. The charm in this one is a ceramic tile pressed with some saint's face. Basic, but not anywhere near Candy's style.

"Seriously? You are cruel, Saucier." She snatches the bracelet, fixing it around her wrist as she places an order for three hamburger meals.

From the backseat, Heath squeezes my shoulder. I don't know what I expected. There was no flash of light, no immediate sense of knowing that came over me when I put my own bracelet on. I just watched Phin go in, never forgot him, and started seeing the Shine all at once.

It was different for Heath and Old Lady Clary. They didn't watch Phin cross the fence. I had to say his name before they remembered. But they were capable of remembering. That's what these charms do: make us capable of seeing how Shine has changed reality.

As we eat, I watch Candy carefully, waiting for some sign that the charm's done its work. I demolish the burger and pass the fries to Heath. Candy doesn't protest. She only eats a handful of her own fries before also donating to the same cause.

"Thank you," she says, collecting all the bits of trash from my lap.

Unlike Heath's car, Candy's comes with rules. One of those being that the person who leaves garbage behind shall lick her tires clean. It's a sign of how concerned she's become that she let us sit inside while we ate something with more grease than a banana.

"So what do you want to do on this our day of exoneration from the sophomoredom?" She waves at a yellow truckload of screaming former seniors pulling into a slot three spaces down. "That is, before we round up the girls to crash whatever party my cousins are hosting at the trailer. We can make an allowance for you, of course, Heath. Just this once. Because you're pretty."

"That's very thoughtful," he says, clearly amused at the way Candy directs the world.

"One more time." My gut cramps. I wish I hadn't eaten quite so much. "His name is Phineas Harlan Saucier."

"You've got to be kidding me. You're both in on this madness?"

"It's not madness," Heath replies quickly, winning a scoff from Candy.

"Just say it, Candy. Just once. Phineas Harlan Saucier."

She repeats his name and I wait for the memories to unlock or return or do whatever it is they do. I wait for that surprised shake of her head, the vaguely confused look in her eye as she reconciles what she knows with what she knew, but it doesn't come. She looks at me with that same expectant expression.

"There. I said it. Can we move on?"

It didn't work. *Why didn't it work? Did Old Lady Clary give me a bad charm? Did she do it on purpose? Why would she do such a thing?* She wouldn't. That's the answer. She wouldn't bother with sabotage; it just didn't work.

My phone buzzes three times in quick succession with a message from Lenora May. All it says is, *It's time we talked. Meet me at home.*

"Yeah," I say, uncertain how I should be feeling in this moment. "We can move on."

PHIN SAYS THERE ARE TWO ways you can tell a person's lying. First, they start talking, and second, they stop. It's the sort of perspective you develop when the town you live in is built on secrets.

All it takes to divert Candy is the suggestion that Heath and I have intimate plans for the afternoon. She drops us at Heath's truck and we heed Lenora May's beckoning message, returning home to find her waiting at the kitchen table.

Her face is desperately honest and she clutches a folded piece of paper close to her chest. Its edges are tattered, the creases so worn they might fall apart in her hands. Her eyes move to Heath briefly.

"He knows," I say.

"I saw your boots," she says finally. "You went into the swamp again. And I know you've met Fisher and he's the one who gave you that cherry. I know you won't stop trying and also that you don't believe I'm not the enemy. But maybe you'll believe someone else."

With some reluctance, she offers the paper. It whispers between her fingers as I take it. I don't understand the pain I see in her eyes, but I do know it's real. Whatever is written on this page is as dear to her as my brother is to me.

The date in the upper-right corner is July 10, 1997. The paper looks much older than that, as if it's been opened and refolded a thousand times. The small handwriting is as neat as it is jagged.

My Sweet May,
    I've entrusted this letter to Ida Clary, who has been a friend to us both these many years though you have never met her. I have no reason to believe you will ever read this. But I have hope.
    It's been thirty-eight years since I saw you last. I am an old man, May, and do not have much time left. I don't know how to tell you of all that has passed. But I must tell you one thing, and that is the story of what happened the night I abandoned you in the

heart of that jealous swamp.

It plagues me to think that you're still waiting there beneath our eternal cherry tree, and even more to imagine what you must think of me. I did come for you, as promised, and with a way to extract you from that cursed Wasting Shine, but it was your brother I found. He threatened to kill you if I ever dared enter the swamp again.

Heaven help me, I believed him.

I left with the intention of finding another way to save you, but the swamp was different after that night. It began to move, to shift, and expand—closer and closer to town, as if wanting to consume it. And as it grew, it took people, our friends and our family. Ida and myself were the only two in town to remember those who disappeared—my eyes remain open thanks to your bracelet, my love, which I have carried every day of my life—and so it was up to us to protect our town.

We built a fence of Canadian pine to keep the swamp at bay—Ida knew the only way to contain the Shine was to create a powerful barrier of our own. My only regret is that *the fence kept me from you, too. I couldn't risk your life by crossing it and I couldn't ask anyone else to do that for me. There were good and bad reasons for this, but the very core of the matter is this: I left you there and I am more sorry than I will ever properly express.*

If you find this letter in your hands one day, I hope that you will forgive me for not loving you as well as I should.

Love,

Harlan

Harlan. Grandpa.

Pieces of the past suddenly begin to fall into place. If you ask Mama, the swamp is the reason Grandma left Grandpa. Even surrounded by family, he could never extricate himself from it. If he wasn't sitting on the porch, watching the swamp with eyes as narrow as pumpkin seeds, then he was walking the perimeter. He called this "fence walking." Mama called it "obsession and a sad one at that." A man who'd built so many of the beautiful old houses of Sticks shouldn't be obsessed with something as simple and mundane as a fence. But now I know. He wasn't obsessed, he was in love. It's so tragic I almost can't bear it.

"Okay, I'm listening," I say, sliding into a chair.

With a cautious glance to the window, she clears her throat delicately and begins, "My name is Lenora May Lillard and I was born here in Concordia Parish in 1845."

She gives that a moment to sink in, which is good because Heath is on his feet and I'm not far behind.

"Lillard?" I ask. I know that name. "As in *the* Lillard family? No. That's not possible."

"I'm afraid it is. I grew up in Oak Point Manor—that's what we called it then, now you know it as the Lillard House—and for most of my life I was happy. People didn't fear the swamp so much then. There were stories, of course, and Mrs. Clary had all the best ones, but they weren't all these tales of madness and despair. There were good ones, too. The Clarys were even known to go into the swamp to collect remedies that could cure nearly anything."

"How is this even possible?" Heath's fingers rest on my shoulder.

"It shouldn't be," I say, looking again at the letter in my hands.

I guess she could have faked it, but the paper's old as time and there's no mistaking my Grandpa's handwriting. I recognize it from old plans for this house, the ones Mama had framed after he died. They've been hanging in our dining room for years and years. That, combined with recent events make it possible, even probable, she's telling the truth.

I think of what the Lillard House must have looked like

with a fresh coat of paint and big, lazy rocking chairs lining the porches. Before the years weighed down the floorboards and a thousand storms battered the walls, it must have been impossibly beautiful set against the dark oaks. Lenora May makes all sorts of sense when I picture her there, orbited by crinoline and layered skirts.

So does Fisher.

Heath slumps into his seat, boneless as a sack of potatoes, and Lenora May takes that as a sign to continue.

"Before I explain what happened, I have to tell you that we loved the swamp very much as children. It was our secret hideaway and it was a *good* place." A frown flashes across her lips almost too quickly to see. "Fisher was good, too. He only ever wanted to keep me safe."

I know what she's not saying. "You're afraid of him?"

Her response is in her hesitation. I think of the easy way Fisher moves through the swamp, the way Shine seems to lean into him like he's the sun, and how I felt at the end of our conversation today. Lenora May's fear is quiet, but it's serious as summer and it resonates with something I already knew.

Taking a shallow breath, she continues, "Fisher was friends with Elijah Clary, Mrs. Clary's son. From him, Fisher learned how to construct a charm and manipulate Shine.

"When the war came on, my father decided it was prudent for me to marry immediately. He chose a man with a brutal reputation. I couldn't bear it and, on top of this, Papa was sending Fisher away to fight for the Confederacy. We had no time to waste. We decided to escape into the swamp and not return until enough time had passed that we could choose our own destinies."

"So you stayed and turned into what? Ghosts? Demons?" I ask.

"No, there was more to it than that. From Elijah, Fisher also knew how to redirect Shine into things—tangible items: a bracelet, a gris-gris, a piece of food. Or our bodies." She becomes very still for a second. "He was sure it would keep us safe. That by merging our lives—our bodies and souls— with Shine, we'd be safe from the evils of the world. And I trusted him. We went to the pond, built a fire of oleander and sumac, and breathed the smoke until we were well and truly poisoned."

"Jezuz," Heath mutters. "You killed yourselves."

"Yes and no. As we lay dying, we swallowed cherry blossoms. We took their magic into our bodies and, in return, it threaded our veins with power. We became a part of the swamp and it was wonderful because there was nothing to fear. The swamp gave us everything we needed—food, shelter, warmth, protection." She smiles a soft, sad smile.

"It was amazing. We could spend days learning how the water moved from pond to pond, or seeing which of us could find the smallest spiderweb. And the Shine! We could do so much. We were powerful, and I was happy for so many years.

"Eventually, though, I grew weary of that life. I asked Fisher if we could go, as we'd planned, but he refused. When I tried to leave anyway, he became furious. He told me I would die if I left—the cost of having such perfect protection from the swamp was that we were bound to it. Forever. I think he knew it before we ran into the swamp and didn't say." She shudders at the memory. "So, I stayed with him because my only other choice was to die."

"I'm sorry," I say, swept up in her sadness.

"Jackass," Heath adds. And then, "Sorry."

"How did you meet my grandfather?"

A smile opens across her face. "Many years later, a young man stumbled into the grove of the cherry tree. He was a little drunk and a little lost and very overwhelmed by seeing Shine for the first time." She laughs. "When you're drunk, Shine is very bright and dizzying. But even so, he was sweet."

Her smile is the truest kind. Though her cheeks flush with embarrassment and she presses a hand to one side of her face, she cannot contain it. Watching her remember something so good calls up a sudden fluttering in my lungs.

"I wanted to see him again, but people do not often see Shine without help, as you know. To make sure he would find me, I told him to drink alcohol moderately until he saw the glow of Shine. To ensure he'd remember me, I gave him something else."

She shifts to sit cross-legged in her chair. In profile, she's a decade older with years of battle and hardship behind her. Her chin is raised, but her eyes are sad; she's a queen of wild things, and no stranger to sacrifice.

She says, "I'm glad it's still here. Your wrists are so slender, yet strong. The silver enhances that quality."

I'm slow to realize what she's been telling me: that this bracelet was hers once upon a time, and that she gave it to the man she cared for so he could return to her. It sounds like a fairy tale or like one of the more romantic stories from the Clary collection.

"So what happened?" I press.

"He returned. Every night for a week. Oh, he always looked so dashing in his fedora. He never dressed appropriately for the swamp. He insisted that the only way to visit a lady was in dress pants and shoes. Somehow, there wouldn't be a bit of mud on those pants. I don't know how he did it! Determination, I suppose. And every single time, he brought me flowers. Honeysuckle and lilac blossoms."

She pauses. Lost in some memory she doesn't share. Slowly, her smile fades. Her story has become dark even before she speaks another word.

"He said he'd found a way to free me. One of Ida's stories

had given him what he thought was the secret of the swamp and all I needed to do was wait. So I waited, and while I did, I made a terrible mistake: I told Fisher I was leaving." In spite of the warmth, she hugs her arms, rubbing her hands up and down, shoulder to elbow. And then her words tumble out.

"He was furious. He accused me of abandoning him, of not appreciating what we had, of being reckless and foolish to think Harlan would be any different from the man our father had intended for me. I'd never seen him so angry. He changed. I felt the Shine running toward him, channeling through him. I couldn't stop it. He shifted the course of all the Shine in the swamp so he controlled it.

"I thought he would kill me, but what he did was worse. He changed me. Twisted my bones so I could hear them snap and shift. My skin hardened, my teeth became sharp, and my nails grew thick and black. It felt like it took days. And when the pain finally faded, Fisher was there, holding Harlan's pin-striped fedora."

Tears shimmer in Lenora May's eyes. My own throat is tight and my toes squeeze together. I can guess at the rest of this story, but stopping her now seems like denying someone the final rhyme of a sonnet.

"'Lenora May,' he said, '*never* do this again. It's my job to keep you safe and that's what I'll do, no matter the cost.'" Her words are frail, stilted, and defiant. "I thought Harlan was dead and my brother a murderer. That day, I promised myself that I would find a way to get out. For Harlan. For myself."

"Sweet Pete, you could've been my grandmother." It's a staggering thought, and I spend a minute trying to figure how old Lenora May is or if it even matters. Old enough to have been my grandmother, and probably old enough to have been my grandfather's grandmother. Yet, here she sits, looking as young as Phin.

Heath drops his head into his hands. Lenora May shrugs, and all I can do is laugh. It's a strange moment of camaraderie.

"Tell me what happened to Phin," I say finally.

"I don't really know. That's the truth. I swear it. When Phineas came to the pond that morning, he was distressed. He looked so much like your grandfather that I reached for him. I've wanted to be free of the swamp for such a long time, and sometimes the Shine listens. When Phin knelt at the pond, he wanted to get away as badly as I did, and the Shine answered: we swapped places."

"So you're saying he's trapped exactly like you were?"

Lenora May nods in response. "Bound to the swamp with his life and stuck in the prison of a body Fisher created."

Heath releases a long "Jeeeezuz," but I don't let any of the encroaching despair take hold.

"But Grandpa Harlan thought he had a fix. What was it?"

I prepare myself for some impossible thing. He didn't free her, after all. If he had, we wouldn't be here right now, plotting how to save Phineas.

"Peaches," she says with a vague smile. "He said that where things came from mattered, and if I could eat something that hadn't come from the swamp or anywhere near it, I'd be free."

"Peaches?" That can't be the real answer. There's no way it's as simple as eating a peach. "There has to be more to it. Or maybe Grandpa was as cracked as everyone says."

Lenora May is shaking her head. "He wasn't. Shine is powerful, but it's not *all*-powerful. It has natural balances in the world like everything else. You just have to know what they are."

"Okay," I say, struggling to find the good in this, "but it seems flimsy."

"Like the cherry." Heath perks up, excited by the connection. "Makes sense. If eating something from inside the swamp can pull you into it, then eating something from the outside should do the opposite. Actually, this makes the cherry thing *less* flimsy."

It sounds as promising as anything else. If a cherry from that tree has the power to lure Lenora May inside the swamp against her will, then surely a peach from far away is as safe a bet as any. And I know the place to get it.

"It just so happens, Valerie Beale's family owns an orchard up north," I announce. "I can call her for directions and we'll have peaches by tomorrow."

Against my better judgment, I picture Phin's triumphant face as he leaps over the fence. Who knows? Maybe tomorrow we'll save him and Nathan and everything will go back to normal.

LEAVE IT TO A SMARTPHONE to forget a crucial phone number at a crucial moment. Valerie's number is nowhere to be found and I wonder if I've ever had it.

"I'll drive," Heath says, sensing my impatience.

We fly down the main drag of town. I give directions as we go. Valerie's family lives past the school where each lot is so heavily wooded it can barely be seen from the road. Not unlike mine. Heath speeds until I tell him to slow down. The Beale house is a modest two-story building with paint nearly as old as the town itself, and a collection of chairs from the sixties rusting on the front lawn. Five cars are parked to the side with their noses nudged into the woods. Most of them run, but never all at once. I spot Valerie's ancient Geo that's only safe for getting to and from school. Anything over thirty miles per hour and it'll shake you into a seizure.

Heath accompanies me to the front stoop. The door's had the same dingy wreath of fake flowers since I first visited in third grade. The flowers have been bleached to nothing by the sun, more fitted for a grave than a home with six people inside it. Above the door is a tarnished wrought-iron sign that reads, ABIDE IN HIM.

"Ominous," says Heath as he raps on the door.

"I believe the term is *reverent*." But he's right. The Beales are ambush religious. It's not that they are unusual for Sticks. Other than Candy, you'd be hard-pressed to find someone who didn't believe in God at least a little. The Beales are just militant. They won't get in your face right away, but wait until you've said something scandalous or sacrilegious or scientific. I learned a long time ago to watch my mouth in this house. "Maybe go easy on 'Jezuz' while we're here."

"Noted," Heath says, more to the sign than me.

The one sharp reprimand I'd received from the Beale parents had been over the topic of evolution, and that had been enough for me. Afterward, Abigail apologized for her parents in a whisper.

"Wait." I suck in a breath. "Heath," I say, reaching for his arm to stop him from knocking. The fog in my mind lifts a bit more, revealing a vast history I'd misplaced. "Heath, it wasn't Valerie."

"What?" he asks, concern bending his voice.

"Abigail. They were—are—twins," I say, tugging him away from the door. There's a reason I didn't have Valerie's number. We've never been close. Teammates on the volleyball court, sure, but friends? That was only ever Abigail. I know what this means. It's becoming sickeningly familiar. "Get in the car. Hurry."

I can't believe it's happened again. To Abigail. And just when I thought I'd started to understand.

"What was she doing near the swamp?" I slam the door so hard Heath's iPod dives off the dash. "Why does this keep happening? And how do we stop it? Heath. We have to stop it or it'll keep happening."

He steers us onto the main road with all the composure we have between us. It's only by his speed that I can tell he's agitated at all. I wish I could adopt some of his calm, but I think I missed the boat on that one. You have to be born with that sort of thing. And if Heath is as solid and dependable as his truck, then I'm a dirt bike, not much use for anything other than extreme terrain.

"Fisher said it was Lenora May. She was the one pulling people into the swamp, but how can she do that from here? She can't, right? She's not doing this." I feel the world spinning away from me. The truth is right before me, making me feel all kinds of foolish. "It's him. It has to be Fisher, right? God! How can you be so calm?"

"I'm not." He glances over. "I'm really not, Sterling. I'm freaking the shit out in here, but there's only one thing we can do about it."

I thought it would make me feel better to know he was as upset as me.

I was wrong.

"Hurry," I urge.

The only thing we can do right now is get our hands on some peaches and hope to high heaven they do the trick. I don't want to think about what happens if they don't. But no matter how hard I try not to, those thoughts sneak in, slippery as snakes. I picture a life without Phin, a life of never hearing him yell at me for something stupid I've done, of never visiting him at Tulane, of never telling him I was going to college to be every bit as brilliant as he always said I'd be. The town blurs through my tears until all I see are flashes of color: brown and orange, green and gray, blue and red, blue and red, blue and red.

"Shit," Heath hisses, pulling over to the side of the road. "It's your stepdad."

I see him through the rear window, fixing his hat in place. He takes a second to jot Heath's license plate number in his little notebook, then inspects the meager contents of the truck bed. It's five full minutes before he saunters to the window with a twist in his eye.

"Heath," he says in his most authoritative of voices. "Sterling." But he saved the bulk of his disapproval for me.

"I know I was speeding, sir," says Heath, offering his license and registration without being asked. "I apologize. It won't happen again."

"No, I 'spect it won't."

He could let him go. We couldn't have been going that fast. I know for a fact the sheriff's not big on unnecessary fines when they can be avoided, but Darold starts writing a ticket.

"Darold, please, can't you just give him a warning?"

Darold doesn't break his stride to answer. "Sterling, go wait in the car, please."

I sit utterly still. Stunned.

This is not the way things are supposed to go. Darold never tells me what to do. We're polite to each other, but the deepest conversation we ever had was when he first came into Mama's life and told me he wouldn't try to replace my dad. I told him that if he'd said anything other than that I'd have pulled every one of his teeth while he slept. He laughed, and that was that. He's never tried to be anything other than the guy who loves my mama, but he's breaking the rules. Again.

"Sterling." Darold stops writing and looks at me. "Go wait in the car."

"Fine."

I slam the door and go sit in the musty air of his cruiser while he intimidates Heath. I twist all the dials I can find, set the heat to maximum so the next time he turns it on he gets a real treat, then put my feet on his otherwise spotless dash. It feels like ages before he opens the door and slides in. Heath signals and drives away like he knows we're watching, or like he knows Darold is waiting for him to make another mistake. Darold lets him get ahead before following.

Neither of us speaks. It isn't until he's driven back to the house and parked in the driveway that he gets his words together. They're exactly what I expected.

"I want you to steer clear of that boy," he says.

"*Heath*," I all but shout, "is my friend and I won't stay away from him."

"He's careless and troubled and you *will* stay away. This is for your own good."

"Will I?" I slam the door of the cruiser and head for the house. "Good luck with that. Shouldn't you be doing something useful like repairing the fence and ignoring what's on the other side? Do me a favor and stick to that."

That struck gold. He flinches under the accusation.

"You know there's something wrong with the swamp," I press, thinking of the conversation I overheard between him and Sheriff Felder the day Phin went missing. "Why won't you say it? Heath isn't the problem, the swamp is!"

"I know the swamp's dangerous, Sterling, don't you think I know that!" His shout is an eruption. "That's exactly why I want you to stay away from him. He's more mixed up with that place than anyone and I don't want you anywhere near it!" He swipes his hat against his thigh, squinting at the sun. "Please, do as I ask."

"No!" Anger weakens my voice, but not my resolve. "I won't. Not unless you know something about him I don't. And don't think just because you didn't tell Mama about my date I *owe* you anything!"

"Sterling, I swear to God!"

"You swear what, Dad?!"

I stop. He does, too, and for a moment, we stare at each other in surprise because for a moment, we changed.

He makes the first sound.

"I—" His mouth gapes like fish. "The point is I stopped a reckless boy for speeding today and you were with him. That's inexcusable. You're grounded. All weekend."

That does the trick. Resentment flares to life, pushing that awkward moment firmly to the side.

"Fine!" I shout, and go lock myself in my bedroom.

In the quiet that follows, my own words echo in my head: *You swear what, Dad?!* I've never used that word for Darold. I swore I never would. Not because he hasn't been good to us, but because I ground that word to dust the day Dad left.

It was tainted and ugly and never to be used.

But I did and even though I'm pissed as a rattlesnake in a tin can, I can't help but be glad. The swamp's taken my brother and one of my best friends, but in some twisted way it's given me the dad I didn't know I was ready for.

DINNER COMES WITH A HEALTHY portion of tension. Mama, of course, supports Darold's edict that I be grounded for the entire weekend. But when she says, "What are you thinking hanging with a boy like that?" I get right to my feet and say, "He's not a boy *like that*. He's my *friend*." Lenora May comes to my aid, defending Heath's honor in her eloquent way.

The clock *tick-tick-tick*s before Mama nods and flutters a hand like she didn't mean to suggest I shouldn't spend time with Heath. Darold doesn't press the issue. I think he can see there's a fight in my eye because instead he compliments me and Lenora May on our finely baked tarts. An awkward bit of praise to accept.

When dinner ends, I'm allowed to retreat to my room

without further discussion. Outside, the swamp's glowing bright again. All that Shine moving in its strange seaweed dance, skidding up to the fence and away, up to the fence and away. It's peaceful and hypnotic, but I think it's pretending to be sweet.

It's late when I finally catch Heath on the phone.

"I found a few options," he says, skipping the events of the afternoon and getting right to business. "The closest orchard is a few hours' drive, but at least we'd be able to pick our own peaches and know for sure where they came from."

He emails me an address and I load it on my ancient joke of a laptop. The website is as country as it could be, with every spare inch trussed up in gingham print and dancing berries. The name POP'S PEACHES AND PRETTY FINE PRODUCE curves over the top like a rainbow. Briefly, we discussed running into the Winn-Dixie for a bag of apples or kiwis or something else that definitely didn't come from Sticks, but decided that nothing magical ever came out of a Winn-Dixie, and if we only have one shot at this, we'd better be sure no one had touched the fruit but us. Peaches seemed a fine tribute to Grandpa Harlan's original effort.

Pop's Peaches is in one of the northern parishes, a solid two-and-a-half-hour drive away, and not near any of Louisiana's swampy lands.

"This looks perfect."

"When should I pick you up?" he asks.

"Are you sure you can go? I don't want to get you into any more trouble."

There's a pause and I'm sure he's going to say no. He probably should say no. I'll be the equivalent of a wanted criminal when I sneak out of my house tomorrow.

"I'm in trouble, Sterling. *We* are in trouble." I can hear blankets rustle as he gets up to pace. "I know this is hard for you, but stop thinking I'm going to disappear. Please, trust that I'm here. I'm not going to run away when things get hard. I'm going to meet you tomorrow, get those peaches, and then I'm going inside the swamp with you to help find your brother and Nathan."

"Heath," I say, remorseful and grateful all at once.

Our relationship started backward, with all the important things coming first and all the silly, inconsequential details shrouded in mystery. I don't even know if he has a favorite color or what he likes in his coffee. Everything I know about Heath I've gathered by accident, from the floor of his truck or simply by existing in the same small town all our lives.

Maybe it's easier to not know the little things. They're what hurt the most when they're gone. What does it matter that Phin loves old cars and painted that '68 Chevelle red because it's my favorite color? It doesn't matter a damn, but looking at that car in the driveway is a knife in the stomach: the guts of my relationship with Phin all cut open and rotting in the sun. I don't want to feel this way about someone else. I don't want to get so close that losing them means losing a piece of myself. But I ask anyway.

"What's your favorite color?"

He makes a noise of confusion.

"It's important. I mean, not really, but I need to know because I know all of these really serious things about you and none of the little things. So what's your favorite color? Food? Sport?"

He takes a quick second to think. "It used to be orange, but this week it's blue. I can eat twice my weight in catfish. I think you probably knew that one. And baseball, which is also probably obvious. You?"

"Red, broccoli, and volleyball. Okay," I say, breathing a little easier. "It says the orchard opens at ten, but my parents won't be gone until nine so be here at nine thirty. I mean, be down the street. Just in case. And I'm paying for gas."

He laughs, but agrees, and before we hang up asks, "What I said before, do you believe me?"

I don't know why I hesitate. I've trusted Heath with so much. Why is it so hard to believe he'd want to help me? I know he does, but I can't say the words.

"Sure," I say, and then, "Good night."

My parents don't disappoint. Darold's off promptly by eight and Mama comes to check on me once before leaving to meet Mrs. Tilly. I lock my door and slip through the window.

If anyone beats me home this afternoon, hopefully they'll assume I'm enjoying my internment with a nap. Or that I'm just being willful.

Heath and I pass the first hour in silence, both of us lost in our own heads, sipping the coffee Heath so kindly thought to provide. As a rule, I try not to trust facial expressions before coffee, but I find myself analyzing every movement his face makes. Is he upset about yesterday? Did he even notice my lack of commitment? Is he irritated at being on the road this early on his first day of summer? I decide to check and lift his coffee to my lips for an unfortunate taste.

"Why bother with the coffee at all?" I ask, rushing to sip my own, mercifully unadulterated cup as Heath breaks into a laugh. "Lord. May as well drink straight-up milk and sugar."

I wear a disgusted face when Heath laughs again, but make a note should I ever have occasion to dress his coffee for him.

We take Highway 15 straight up Louisiana's side, slowing for towns with more churches than houses and more liquor stores than churches, all of them bigger than Sticks thanks to the highway. Fields open and close around copses of old oak trees and miles of pine saplings drowning in kudzu vines. The farther north we get, the more the land rolls and relents to being tamed. It's early yet for most crops, but cotton and soybeans and corn are already reaching up in thirsty green.

To find Pop's Peaches we have to turn off the main roads. I spend the second hour directing Heath down a series of increasingly smaller streets. The Ford heaves in all directions, proving there's nothing like a country road to test the willpower of a seat belt. By the end, the truck looks like something the dirt road hacked up.

We pull into a small haphazard lot and park in front of a sign proclaiming, POP'S PEACHES ARE PRETTY FINE! PICK YOUR OWN, THEY'RE ALL DIVINE! There's a single-story brick house squatting in a field to the right. To the left, is a produce stand made to look like a traditional red barn with dusty, white trim all the way around. Behind the barn, peach trees run away in neat rows.

The only person around is the barely twelve-year-old boy watching the shop from a nearby tree fort. He races to greet us with a curious "Y'all here for peaches?"

When we say that we are, he carefully explains that there's not much ready for picking, but we're welcome to try. Thanking him, we grab a basket and follow the bright green arrows leading to the trees with the ripest fruit. Up close, the trees aren't as tall as they appeared from the car. They're low, bushy things with long, scratchy branches. But even if they're not much to look at, the air in the orchard smells green and sweet as syrup.

It takes ten minutes to reach the first tree with a blue ribbon marking it as prime for picking. By that time, my legs and arms are so full of itches it demands all my willpower to keep from scratching.

Peaches cluster around each of the unruly branches, every one yellow or pink as a sunset. I leave the paler fruit alone and reach for one that's turned so dark, pink doesn't describe it. Neither does red—it's a between color that makes my mouth water. I give it a firm twist, and it releases with a sigh.

"Looks perfect," Heath says, holding branches wide to keep them from assaulting me.

I bring the fruit to my nose and inhale. "It smells so good."

Again, the branches shiver. I hear the *snap* as the tree releases another peach. Following my lead, Heath inhales the scent of the fruit he's holding. His eyes close for a moment and he smiles.

"Yeah," he says in agreement.

And with that smile still on his lips, he takes a bite. Juice runs down his chin, dripping onto his shirt and the grass below. He laughs and I do, too. The scent of peach saturates the air.

It's too much to resist. I take a bite and am consumed by the taste of spring-sweet peach. Juices spill down my fingers and chin. I take another bite and another until I've eaten the entire thing.

Heath watches me, licking juice from his fingers. Sunlight seems to burn away the last vestiges of the Heath of last year, the boy in the back of the classroom with dull, blank eyes. But more than that, he stands with his shoulders back and his chin higher than his collarbone.

"You've changed, you know," I say.

His expression is quizzical and I realize how strange that must sound coming from me, the girl who's really only known him for a week. It's so little time we could still count it in hours—168. Hardly long enough to judge changes in character, but then, how long do transformations really take?

The Heath of last week kept his truths hidden and never would've found himself in a fight with the Brothers Wawheece. This week, he's been by my side when no one else knew how to be and he's taken physical punishment for it.

"I know you don't think you've been brave, but that's not the way I see it."

"It's probably that I'm not drugged anymore. That's why I seem different." One shoulder climbs into a half shrug as he speaks, shielding himself from the compliment. "Everything else I've done because you were brave first."

It's almost painful to watch how neatly he sheds any suggestion that he's behaved admirably.

"You're dead wrong. Shall I tell you why?"

My tone startles a smile from him, as sweet as the peaches around us.

"I'll take that as a yes," I say, climbing out of the knee-high grass and resting my hands on his chest. "It's because I was too stupid to know what I was risking when this all started. I was angry and scared and rash when I made a scene in the cafeteria. But you'd been living with this for a *year*. You knew what you were risking when you shared your secret with me. That's real bravery, Heath Durham. Knowing the risks and taking them anyway."

"I hope you're listening to yourself," he says, catching my elbows to keep me from dodging his words. "Because you've changed, too." I fight the urge to squirm as he continues, "You may have been afraid when this started, but I couldn't have done any of this without your example."

There's a feeling in my chest, a lightness I don't know what to do with, but it's expanding like a balloon and I'm afraid it'll crack me open.

But Heath isn't done. "And Sterling," he says, hands still secure at my elbows. "I should probably tell you that I'm about to be brave again."

He's become so serious, so confident in this sun-drenched field that I whisper, "Oh?"

He nods and pulls me close to speak against my lips. "I'm going to fall for you."

When he kisses me, there is no world beneath my feet. There's only Heath's hands on my arms, his lips on mine, and the vibrant taste of peaches. This kiss is different from the others. It's fast and bruising, one diving headlong into the next, stirring a wildness in me I've never felt. It's hungry and substantial, and all the things I didn't know I wanted to say to Heath.

This kiss is a confession.

When we fall to the ground I only notice the brief absence of his mouth from mine, but then it's back and I lose myself in the press of Heath's body, in the demanding pressure in my chest.

The sound of a tractor passing uncomfortably near makes us part and we lay there, our heads in the tall grass beneath the peach tree, our hands twined between us while we catch our breath. For minutes, I listen as the rumble of the tractor is slowly replaced by the more intimate sounds of the orchard, the quiet hiss of leaves in a breeze, the first chitter of afternoon bugs, the faraway bark of a dog. My mind is quiet by comparison, reluctantly returning from the rush of that kiss.

Between the branches, the sky is a piercing blue. The peaches stand out against it in bold colors. They look defiant and secure, but I know it wouldn't take much effort at all to pluck them or for a strong wind to knock them from their perches.

"They're just peaches." Face-to-face with the small fruit, I'm less convinced of our plan. "How can we possibly think this will work?"

Heath's answer is almost flippant. "Tell that to Eve. Fruit is power. Or, well, technically in her case it was knowledge, but the gist is the same. It all depends on which tree you take it from."

Where things come from matters. Fisher said it, Lenora May said it, and now Heath's all but said it. I think of the cherry that was meant to pull Lenora May back to the swamp, of the bracelets that let us remember, of the single, paltry cherry tree in the center of a vast swamp.

I think of eight-year-old Phin staring down our callous father. Phin may have been the one to get hurt, but in the end it was Dad who went away. All because one little boy stood up.

I'm ready to admit that small, unexpected things can have big power.

"Okay, Heath," I say. "I believe you."

We leave Pop's Peaches with a basketful of fruit and a reminder from the boy that July's a better time for picking. The basket cost an extra two bucks, but neither of us thought to bring one along. With my belly full of peaches, I consider it a fine deal. If this works and saves Phin, it'll be an even finer one. If it doesn't work, having twenty-six dollars to my name will be the least of my worries.

The drive home feels fast. There's an easiness between us that wasn't there before, but also a peaceful sort of tension that urges me to sit close enough to press my leg to his. We spend the first bit developing a plan, which involves both of us going home for the evening, then meeting up at midnight to go into the swamp. From there, we'll find Phin, Nathan, and Abigail, feed them all peaches, and all return for celebration and pizza. As long as we move quickly, we should be able to do the whole thing without attracting Fisher's attention.

I decide not to imagine how difficult it'll be to feed gatorPhin a peach. That's a problem we'll have to solve when we're facing it.

For the rest of the drive, I play a wide selection from Heath's iPod in a quest to discover his favorite song. He has the expected array of country, a little rap, some pop. It's the classical that takes me by surprise. Bach, Beethoven, Chopin, Debussy, I play them all and watch as he relaxes into them. Before I know it, we're pulling off the highway and onto the main road of Sticks where half the cars we see are parked at Miss Bonnie's for an early dinner. The other half are milling around the gas station and Clary General Store. I recognize several faces at the pumps, boys from school filling the tanks of their pet cars for another night at the track.

When Heath turns down the side road, I see there are more than the usual work crews about tonight. I almost missed them because the pines are darker than the sky above, and the swamp isn't glowing as brightly as it was yesterday, but a few of the men are dressed in hunting orange and that's what caught my eye.

They're in the ditch by the fence, repairing fallen rails. Scattered over a full half mile, each of them is scowling and doing his best not to look worried. It isn't working. It's clear that even they know something's unquiet in our little swamp.

Heath slows as we pass. "I think I see your stepdad. Better not speed."

I slouch in my seat to avoid getting caught, but not before I spot Darold in the midst of the chaos, a sheriff's star pinned to the brim of his hat. "I swear he polishes that star five times a day. You'd think he hadn't been sheriff for the past five years."

Except he hasn't.

The fog lifts like a curtain, revealing Darold's life as a deputy, not as sheriff.

"Heath?" I ask, but Heath's already nodding.

"I remember," he says. "Sheriff Felder. That makes four people the swamp's taken."

We don't stop. Neither of us wants to hear how the swamp has rewritten history to obliterate Sheriff Felder.

It's enough to know that it's happened.

I SLIP INTO MY ROOM as easily as I escaped it. My door's still locked and sounds of the TV float up the stairs. Mama records her shows and plays them all at once while she cleans house on Saturdays. I'd usually do my list of chores at the same time, but she doesn't mind when I do them, just that they get done. I'm not in deeper trouble, yet.

With more than six hours to midnight, I've got time. I change into a tank and knit shorts already splashed with bleach, wrap my hair in a bun, and go to tackle the bathroom. Once all the nastiness of a dirty toilet is behind me, the rest of the work always seems downright enjoyable. It's not the truth, but there's power in perspective.

I've cleared half the counter of toiletries before I notice

the scent of lemons and how squeaky clean everything looks. The bathroom's spotless. I check the hallway hamper to find it, too, is clear of the week's dirty clothes. Mine and Lenora May's. One by one, I discover that every one of my chores has been finished for me.

Lenora May's in her room, curled on the bed with a book between her hands. It's one of her horror novels, which she's been reading far longer than Mama knows. She used to sneak them from Aunt Mina's house and read them on the floor of her closet to avoid discovery. Even when they scared her to tears, she kept reading them because the thrill was too good to pass up.

Now, her eyes are wide and she flips the page eagerly, as though afraid someone will come along and steal the book before she can finish. I suppose it's a valid fear after living in the swamp for so long. I'm not book crazy, but even I can't imagine what life without my favorite novels would be like.

I say, "You did my chores."

She jumps at the sound of my voice, pressing her book to her chest. "I thought you might need the extra time," she says after a few calming breaths. "I figured you'd gone for peaches and, after last night, I didn't want Mama giving you any extra trouble."

"You didn't have to, but thanks."

"You didn't have to listen to me." She gets up and follows me down the hall to my room. "It means a lot that you did."

All the evidence has swung firmly in her favor, but there's one thing that should have clued me in earlier.

"The song you were humming that morning was my grandpa's," I say, feeling a sudden swell of kindness. "It means you weren't lying. You knew him well enough that he shared that with you. And he wouldn't have given it to just anyone, so he must have trusted you."

Her smile is so soft and so sad. "That's not entirely true," she says. "*I* gave it to *him*."

A sticky breeze oozes through my open window, kissing my cheeks and fingertips. My stunned silence is broken by the sound of the screen door smacking against the frame and a cacophony of chimes.

Together, Lenora May and I lean across the bed, pressing our hands to the windowsill. Mama stands below us with a wicker basket perched on her hip. I recognize the basket—it's been haunting the garage for the better part of a decade. The wicker is dry and splitting in places, but it has a wide bowl and a handle that's tall enough to loop over her shoulder.

She cuts a quick path through the grass to one end of the fence. Reaching into her basket, she fusses with a clanging mess for a minute before a single wind chime emerges. She hangs it on the post, adding it to the collection of Mardi Gras beads, and moves down the fence to the next one. At each post she disentangles and hangs another chime, seven in all. When she's done, she surveys her backwoods burglar alarm with cautious satisfaction.

"Guess they're really spooked," I say, watching Mama hurry toward the house with the empty basket in hand. She casts two glances over her shoulder before going inside.

"Darold got a call this morning. The fence is falling apart all over town," Lenora May says in a voice soft as a shadow.

"It took Abigail. And the sheriff," I report. "Maybe more, I don't know."

"Not 'it,'" she says sharply. "Fisher."

She's right. I know that now. Even if Grandpa's letter didn't damn Fisher, he's the one inside the swamp. He said himself Shine couldn't be taken beyond the fence without help, and I haven't seen Lenora May get close enough to that fence to spit over it. Fisher's the one luring people—*my* people—into the swamp.

Lenora May's stuck inside a frown when I look at her again. All her limbs are pulled in tight to her body. She looks tense and alarmed. I have the urge to place my hand on her shoulder, to comfort her. Is that desire my own? Or the result of false memories?

It doesn't matter.

Before I can do anything, she unfolds herself and pushes away from the bed. "He's reminding me that he's more powerful than I'll ever be and he'll never let me go. He'll keep doing this until I return to him," she says, heavy with dread. "I'm still not free."

Dad used to tell Mama he hurt us because he loved us too much. She'd sit in her rocker and he'd kneel at her feet with tears in his eyes and lies on his lips. She'd stroke his hair and tell him it was all okay because we loved him, too. And I hated her for it.

But looking at Lenora May now, I see an echo of Mama in her face. It's the look of a person who can't see anything but the horror directly ahead of them. She's trapped, just as Mama was trapped, because her cage is so convincing.

Again, I speak before I think. "You will be," I promise. And I know I believe it.

AFTER MIDNIGHT, I'M ALONE ON the front porch of the Lillard House, straining my ears for any sign of Heath's truck. I sit pressed against the door, my knees drawn close because, even though it's dark, I feel far too exposed.

It's every bit as hot as it was this afternoon. The clouds that were spotty earlier have become a solid blue-gray sheet aglow with moonlight, trapping all the heat and stale air beneath it. I'd give anything for a breeze right now. It's so quiet, every move I make is enough noise to wake the dead.

A twig snaps. I wait for the rumble of Heath's truck to follow, but it's dark as a dog's nose beneath the oaks. He should've met me forty minutes ago and he hasn't answered a single text. I open his contact info on my phone and pause with my thumb over the CALL button. There's a chance a call this late will get him into a big pot of trouble, and he's already got enough of that. I think I shouldn't, but then I remember the sheriff's star on Darold's hat and mash the button. It rings once, then goes straight to voice mail.

Heath's voice is sluggish and uninterested. "It's Heath. Leave a message. Or not."

Hanging up is my first instinct, but before I do, I change my mind. "Hey, Heath, it's Sterling. I'm at the Lillard House. It's late and I don't know where you are. If you get this in the next ten minutes, call me. If not, well . . . call me."

I console myself with the fact that if the swamp had him, it would've taken his number the way it took Abigail's. But if the swamp doesn't have him, then where is he?

Ten more minutes pass. Two more phone calls and on the last I don't bother leaving a message. A slew of other horrible possibilities rush through my mind, car accidents, heart attacks, falling down the stairs. No matter how I try not to, I picture Heath covered in blood at the wheel of a destroyed car. And then I purge that image with the memory of his lips on mine. There could be any number of reasons Heath isn't here.

The bucket of peaches we dropped off earlier sits next to me. We left them, hidden from view, hanging from an oak branch. At least the plan didn't involve Heath keeping them. I've waited so long and they smell so good my stomach rumbles. I eat one and toss the pit into the trees.

Five more minutes. I spend them trying to balance my phone on my knee. There's only so much waiting a girl can do before it gets pathetic, and it's been a full hour since Heath said he'd be here.

Selecting four peaches from the bucket, I drop them into one of Mama's canvas grocery bags, and pick a path down to the fence. It's slower going in the dark, but the clouds are full of gray light, which helps me avoid the tallest patches of grass. Along the way, I make plenty of noise to scare any snakes or raccoons or other toothy pieces of wilderness.

All the Wasting Shine is dim and distant. It says something about the state of my life that pale Shine is more concerning than bright Shine, but there's enough to follow, and that's all I need.

I climb the fence and drop to the other side. From this direction, the swamp is unfamiliar. I adjust the bag on my shoulder and move carefully, trying to get to a place where Shine is close enough to command. All I need is a path. My feet slide in the dark, and the farther I go, the farther the dancing lights recede.

Sweat slips between my shoulder blades. There's even less air in the swamp than there was outside of it. Every breath I take seems to condense in my lungs, each one shallower than the last. Something bites my arm and I swat, unsuccessfully, at what I hope is only a mosquito. All around me the swamp grows louder and louder. It croaks and snaps and rattles. It groans and gurgles and shrieks, and I can't help but conjure the thought of that pale-faced beast.

I shake my head. These are the sounds the swamp makes. *I'm not afraid of the swamp*, I remind myself. *Not anymore.*

"Show me the way to Phineas," I call.

Though all the Shine is still far from touching distance, it begins to braid a dim path. I run after it. Before I've gone very far, it disperses.

Again and again, I ask it to take me to my brother, but every time I move toward it, it's farther away than I think. By the time I stop trying, my phone says two a.m. I've been at it for an hour, the path I've walked has closed behind me, and each time I begin to make progress, the lights disperse. Just like the stories say.

Panic starts to build in my throat. This is what the Wasting Shine does: leads the unsuspecting victim in nonsense circles until they're too tired to continue. And I realize that it's not trying to help me; it's trying to keep me.

My phone is as helpless as I am. Repeatedly, it tries to find a signal and fails. I am truly on my own.

"Move, Saucier," I say. It helps to imagine Candy's scorn if she knew I was standing here, leaning against a tree like a damsel.

I pick a direction and walk with purpose. If I can keep to a straight line, I'll find the fence eventually and make my way home from there.

The brush climbs to my knees. I walk vigorously, stamping and shaking the undergrowth to make as much noise as possible. There are lots of biting creatures in the swamp, and I hope to all the sweet heavens they're afraid of my clamor.

After another twenty minutes, I stop again. This patch of swamp is as unfamiliar as every other and my legs are starting to wobble from trudging through mud. I shiver in my swamp-damp clothes. I could die here.

All it takes is one snakebite, one twisted ankle, one long series of wrong turns and no one will ever find my body because no one will be brave enough to look. And what good will that do Phin?

There's one person who can help, but my entire plan depends on avoiding his notice. Even Grandpa Harlan hadn't been willing to risk a second encounter with Fisher—had refused to cross the fence after it was built. Why hadn't I stopped to consider that before pelting into the swamp alone? And why hadn't Heath shown up like he promised? I'm lost and alone, with no Shine to guide me.

There's only one way out. What other choice do I have?

All you need do, my brave girl, is say my name.

I hesitate, hoping the Shine will change its mind and

brighten before me, but the swamp is unyielding.

"Fisher," I reluctantly say into the tangle of vines. "Fisher, please, if you can hear me, I'm lost."

Then I throw my peaches into the thick, lean against a sturdy gum tree to stop the tremor in my chest, and wait.

IT'S HARD TO TELL HOW much time passes inside the swamp. It feels like hours since I said Fisher's name, but my phone reports that it's only been minutes.

The night hugs me too close. My skin is too damp and my feet are too wet. Again and again, I tug them up from the sticky swamp floor, and again and again they slide beneath that hungry mud.

An owl screeches in a way that makes people lay broomsticks over their door frames and cross themselves, their kids, and their dogs. I jump half out of my skin and take a few uncertain steps. All the trees seem to have shifted, and the brush has closed tight over any footprints I might have left. My own throat begins to close in response. I could scream, but that wouldn't do me any good. I'm too far from anywhere to be heard.

Something darts through the brush two feet in front of me and I shriek. The tops of the tall plants quiver in its wake. My heart shakes like a cicada.

I take a moment to catch my breath. Heat presses down on me. My ponytail sticks to my neck, the bite on my arm stings and itches, begging me to scratch. Then, directly to my left, the plants begin to make a continuous shushing noise as leaves whisper against one another.

I get real still.

The noise continues. Something is moving slowly through the thick brush and it's coming toward me.

I peer into the dark. The swamp floor is obscured by lizard's tale plants, each with a pale, curling frond that wags like an admonishing finger. Their movement clearly marks the path of whatever is crawling toward me. It's big, but also lumbering and quiet, which are small comforts.

"Hey!" I shout, rustling the plants. Anything but a predator should run.

The whispering stops.

I try not to make a noise. I try not to move or take up space. I will my legs to look like gum tree trunks, for my sweat to smell like swamp mud, for whatever this thing is to go away.

"You're a little the worse for wear, aren't you?" Fisher

speaks into my ear.

I jump. His breath teases my neck, warm and strong as Shine. I imagine it coiling around my throat, threatening.

"I got lost. Something's wrong with the swamp. All the Shine is fading. I couldn't follow it, I can barely see it anymore." I'm talking too quickly, revealing my nerves and my secrets, but with Fisher so close, I can't seem to stop.

Fisher lifts my chin and looks so long into my eyes I start to feel utterly transparent. His fingers are rough against my skin, just enough pressure to convince me to stay put. Even with Lenora May's story fresh in my mind, I search his coal-dark eyes for any sign of tenderness.

The smile in them is unforgiving.

Finally, he speaks, keeping his mouth dangerously close to mine. "The Shine is here. It's you that's changed."

I pull my chin from his fingertips. "I haven't. I'm the same Sterling I was." But even as I say it, I know it's not true. I have changed since I was last in the swamp. I'm a brave new Sterling with an ill-conceived plan to save the brother I drove away.

"Not quite." He extends an arm, and Shine fills his hand. He pulls it into threads with quick, practiced movements. "Clean," he says, draping the web over my shoulders.

Shine slides down my arms, over my belly, and around my legs. It warms and pulls all the sweat and mud from my skin. Its embrace is divine. I close my eyes and soak in the refresh-

230

ing warmth for as long as it lasts.

"That's better," Fisher says. "Now, I think we'd better talk about these."

He holds a peach. Bruised and slightly muddy, it's clearly one of the four I threw into the swamp however long ago.

"Phin said he was hungry," I say, hoping I sound convincing and not conniving. "Peaches are his favorite."

Fisher's eyes go narrow and shadowed, making my skin prickle with cold. It's a look as dangerous as a cornered raccoon. "How thoughtful of you."

"Can you take me to him?" Acting casual under his gaze is a unique kind of torture. He doesn't relent even as I stand to put distance between us.

Fisher steps behind me, so near I feel the warmth of Shine through my shirt. The only thing I can hope to do is make him believe my intentions were innocent.

"Sterling," he says into my ear. "I think you're lying to me."

"I'm—I'm not lying." The truth is in my stutter.

Without another word, he grips my arms tightly and pulls me forward. We move through the swamp faster than should be possible. I see the pink blur of the cherry tree as he spins me around and shoves me against it. My head smacks the trunk painfully. Pink petals rain down around us.

"Do you think I don't know what you're up to?" he hisses. "Do you think I don't remember? That isn't a *snack*. It's your betrayal of me and your brother."

"No," I say, reaching for Shine. I feel the sticky threads. They warm in my hand, but slowly, so slowly. I can't grip.

Fisher grabs my wrist and slams it against the trunk. Pain crashes through my arm. All the glowing threads fall away, and I go as still as the tree behind me.

"No," he repeats as though searching for the meaning of the word, and then again, "No." He draws himself up and is suddenly calm. "Well, this is a disappointing turn of events, Sterling. I thought you understood that I could only help your brother return if you helped my sister do the same."

"She doesn't want to." I brace for a blow that doesn't come.

"I see," he says with the sort of calm that only ever precedes the very worst storm. "Then I'm afraid Phineas won't be leaving, either."

He whispers a word to the tree, and Shine folds itself over my body. I can't move. I can barely breathe.

"I will give you one last courtesy," Fisher says without looking at me. "A moment to say good-bye."

FISHER EXTENDS A HAND OVER the pond, and Shine gathers to draw Phineas up from beneath the surface. He rises until his neck is near Fisher's hand, his monstrous body bound and suspended by vines that stretch from cypress trees. Water drip, drip, drips from every part of him, falling soundlessly into the pond. His eyes are full of Shine.

"Please, Fisher, don't." I have nothing left but the truth. "I can't force Lenora May to do something she doesn't want to, but maybe you can leave the swamp, too. The peaches are from far away, they've never been close to this place, so there's a chance they could free you as well. You and Phineas and Nathan and Abigail and whoever else is trapped here."

Phin struggles, but Fisher remains very, very still. I can tell by the tension in his shoulders that he's working over what I said.

"Let us help you get away from here," I plead.

"Sterling." It's not only my name; it's a warning. He drops his hand and Phin falls with it. Water sloshes over the bank and onto Fisher's shoes. His face is solid when he turns to me—a rock wall with a humorless smile carved into it. "You already had a chance to help me, but you've let Lenora May pull you into her web."

I don't know how to respond. The only web I'm caught in at the moment is his and there's terror pinching my throat. Why did I ever think I could scamper into this swamp and do the thing Grandpa Harlan failed to do so many years ago? The only answer I have is that I'm as stubborn as I am stupid. Phin has suffered enough for those two things and now he could die for it. There's only one thing I can possibly say to stop it and it makes every bit of me cold.

I say it anyway.

"Let me take Phin's place. I'll stay here with you."

The swamp hushes. All I hear is the thrumming of my heart in my ears. Every second that passes could be my last. Fisher could kill me without warning. And he might. Anger and power emanate from him in menacing ripples.

Fisher's expression doesn't change, but the air around him trembles and blurs like I'm looking at him through murky water. He moves quickly, pushing his face too close to mine. I recoil, smelling moss and spice, but also rot. The dark, deathly smell of the swamp.

"Why do you care about him?" He shakes the branches of the cherry tree. "He's the one who ran away when he should have stayed to protect you. Yet you want to take his place." His voice has become a growl and it makes my insides shiver. "Very well, my brave girl."

All the bits of Fisher's face have become narrow, sharp as knives. His eyes glare darkly beneath his night-black hair. Now I see how dangerous he is, all the veneer of kindness stripped clean. I turn away, trying to escape his reach, but he leans forward and places his mouth on mine. There is no escaping him. His kiss is confident and fierce, yet repellant—dark as the swamp around us. Shine warms between our lips and inside my mouth. It quickly transforms into something more cutting.

Pain slices from my brain to my belly. I can barely keep my legs from giving beneath me. Tears slip over my cheeks, hot and fast. I swallow my cries and press my back firmly against the cherry tree as if I might find a way to fall inside it. Then I close my eyes and wait for this to end—hope that it will end—and fear that it won't.

My teeth slice my lip and blood slides over my tongue. The taste is a bright color in my mouth. I swallow it to keep me warm as all the heat is pulled from my bones, as my body tries to transform into something unnatural.

Then Fisher curses and pulls away. Gradually, the pain drains from my belly. I'm weak and empty and gasping. Looking down, I expect to find a body that's not my own, something twisted and malformed, half gator, half me. But I see my own hands, my own knees, no hint of gator green anywhere.

The swamp sings, but I feel no warmth. I feel only this whip of a lizard's tongue licking at my ribs where my heart should be.

Then I fall to the ground, a useless heap of muscle and bone.

Again, Fisher wrenches my head up. This time his fingers dig into the soft spot beneath my chin. His other hand squeezes my wrist. He frowns at the bracelet, but doesn't pry it off. When he speaks, his voice is distant. Detached. "We might've ended this tonight if not for that little charm."

Too late, I realize what's happened. Lenora May's bracelet is stronger than I knew. Somehow it kept Fisher from taking me in my brother's place, and he thinks I tricked him on purpose.

"No, I didn't—"

The swamp hisses and snaps.

"Ah," Fisher says, an alarmingly delighted smile on his face. "Just in time."

Nathan walks into the clearing. His yellow-brown skin is

dusty in the moonlight and he tugs nervously at his elbow.

He looks from Fisher to me and, in a voice that's been scratched to pieces, asks, "Do either of you know which way I go to find the road? I've been looking for hours."

No, I think, *you've been looking for a year.*

He looks frustrated and sad and a little scared. He scrubs a hand through his hair. It sticks up, adding three inches to his height.

"And my friend. I think he's somewhere in here, too. I've looked everywhere, but I can't find him. Have you seen a white guy in a Saints cap?"

"Sterling." Fisher isn't looking at me. His eyes are trained on Nathan. "I want you to understand that I'm being generous right now."

With that, he walks to Nathan and presses one hand to his chest. Nathan's eyes go wide and bright with Shine. His head tilts away. His mouth gapes, filled with light and then dark, releasing a final, quiet sigh. When he falls to the ground, all I can hear is my scream tearing a hole in the air.

His body is silent and motionless in the underbrush. Wide-soled shoes make a muddy V shape, looking for all the world like he fell practicing first position in ballet. I doubt ballet was ever his thing, but I'm staring at his shoes and it's all I can think. Long trails of Spanish moss dangle over his head. They should sway, but nothing moves. Not the moss, not his chest, and not me.

Nathan is dead. Nathan is dead and the world will never know it.

A cold fist closes around my lungs, my belly goes tight, and I think nothing will ever work the way it's supposed to again. I'll never draw another breath that isn't also a sob, I'll never open my eyes without tears because Nathan is dead.

I can't look away. Not even when Fisher closes in.

"You call that being generous?" I manage to ask.

"Isn't it obvious? I've spared your brother. Now, listen closely because my generosity only goes so far." Fisher grips my arms, hissing his words. I can feel the bruises reaching down to my bones. "Lenora May did me a favor when she left as she did. It was so explosive that she left a very slender crack behind. Your fence is weak and it won't be long before it's completely useless. If I don't have Lenora May by midnight tomorrow, I will kill someone you care about every day until she returns, and when I run out of people you know, I'll drain the life from Phineas and feed it to the swamp. Do you believe me?"

I believe him so hard my heart turns to granite, but I can't let him feel my fear. Instead, I nod. Once.

"I'm not sure that you do. What was the other name you mentioned?" he asks.

I shut my eyes over the tears and will him to forget I was

ever stupid enough to give him the name of my best friend.

It's a hopeless thought.

"Abigail, was it? Oh, Abigail?"

And as though she were waiting for his call, she steps into the clearing, as tall and beautiful as ever. Her eyes are tired and she looks infinitely confused.

"Sterling? Why haven't you called?" She crouches in front of me and wipes at my tears, ignoring Fisher as though he's invisible. "What's wrong?"

"Abigail, I'm so sorry," I say. "Please, don't kill her."

The confusion on Abigail's face defeats my heart, and in the next instant, Fisher covers her body in a weave of Shine.

She screams. Her body begins to jerk, to make wet, snapping noises, to whimper and gurgle as it reshapes itself. It happens slowly. Painfully. Her body transforms into a gruesome mash of human and alligator. It's exactly what he tried and failed to do to me. She gives one final shriek of pain, and I tremble, wondering why I hadn't thought to do anything to keep Abigail safe.

When it's done, she regards me with placid, yellow eyes. Like Phin, her face has been twisted into a wide rictus. Unlike Phin, she's nearly all gator. Her body squats low on short legs with long, black claws digging into the mud.

"Now do you believe me?" He carves each word with the precision of a scalpel.

"I believe you," I repeat, never looking away from Abigail's once-beautiful face.

"Good, because that was the last of my generosity. Next time, I *will* kill her." He releases me and brushes his hands down the front of his shirt. You'd never guess he'd just killed a boy. "Now, off you go."

Fisher instructs the Shine to lead me home. I stumble through the swamp in a daze, no thought in my mind other than to follow the lights. If I think of anything else, I'll dissolve right here in the muddy pools.

I see the fence and my house beyond, but I'm not connected to my body enough to feel my feet hit the ground or the knots of my boots between my fingers as I untie them. Somehow, I make it to my room without drawing attention. I keep my thoughts simple: shower first, then clean clothes, then bed.

But once I'm clean and alone in my room, the dam breaks.

Nathan died in front of my eyes, Abigail was transformed, Phin was strung up like a puppet, and I walked away with an ultimatum I can't fulfill. My plan didn't just fail, it destroyed a life.

I should text Heath, but I don't know if I should start with, "Are you alive?" or "I got your best friend killed." Irritation at his silence and guilt over Nathan aren't easily reconciled into a single text. Sometime around five, I manage to send, *call me. pls.*

There's no sleeping after that. The world is restless, adding its own grumblings to the noise in my head. It starts slowly, a soft rattling that's easy to dismiss, but soon Mama's wind chimes are singing up a storm and the rattling becomes a violent *bang, bang, bang!*

Lenora May slides into my room with her hands clasped together. She climbs onto the foot of my bed, tucking her feet beneath her to look through the window. Neither of us speaks. The fence shudders and cracks as it's hit again and again by an invisible force. It won't last long.

"Girls," Mama says, a shadowed figure in the doorway. Predawn light falls over her tired face and white bathrobe, washing her in blue. "Storm's moving in. Could be a big one, so we need to get some tape on the windows. I'm making a hot breakfast."

She's pretending it's not unusual for our entire household to rise before the sun, or for the fence to shake itself silly. The rest of Sticks'll be doing the same—pretending the swamp is only a swamp, all the while visiting Clary General to light sticks of incense and seven-day candles for protection. Well, I've had enough of pretending.

"It's not a storm, Mama."

Her fingers tighten on the door frame and she looks past me to the swamp. Wind slaps the chimes into a cacophony, and I think Mama's finally going to say something true. But then she meets my eyes and says, "Course it is. Duct tape's in the hall closet. Don't dawdle."

"Mama!" I cry. "It's not a storm! The swamp is angry and you know it. Why do you keep pretending there's nothing unusual about it? You know that's not true. Why else decorate the fence?"

"Because I hate it." Her answer's a whip, and she takes a moment to recover her composure. "I love this town and everyone in it, but that swamp drove my daddy to madness and my mama away." For a moment she looks devastated—years of loss and pain etched around her eyes and mouth.

"So you know it's different," Lenora May says, sounding gentle and wise. "You've always known."

Mama steps into the room and takes our hands in hers. "I know that the more power you give something, the more hold it has over you and it doesn't do anyone a lick of good to feed them stories of swamp demons and the like."

With those few words, everything my mother has ever done begins to make sense. This is a lesson she learned from Dad. Once he knew he could hurt her by hurting us, he became more and more violent. And once you tell people a thing has power, then it does. That's the power of belief.

"It's only a storm," she says, stroking her soft fingers down our cheeks. "It'll blow over soon enough."

I know she wants me to agree, but pretending doesn't make me feel strong anymore. I say, "I'm not afraid."

"Good girl," she answers, bending to kiss my forehead and then Lenora May's. Just before she leaves the room, she adds, "Remember to dress warm for church."

The fence planks groan. A sharp crack makes me and Lenora May jump together and draw away from the window as a board falls to the ground in two pieces. Farther away, something else pops like a gunshot. It's followed by another and another as all around the swamp, boards snap in two and hit the dirt.

Lenora May's expression is tight. "It's him."

"Yeah, it's Fisher."

My arms ache where he gripped them and I taste blood on my lip. I don't know how to tell her about his ultimatum. I don't know how to ask her to choose between that life and this. The thought makes me sick.

She turns to me with an inquisitive frown. "You're horrible with secrets, Sterling. What happened? Tell me what happened."

"He was like you said," I admit.

I tell her about last night. Not about Nathan. I can't bring myself to tell her before I tell Heath. But everything else comes pouring out until there's nothing left. Her presence is sympathetic and I'm surprised to find that I'm glad she's sitting here next to me right now. Even Candy wouldn't know how to relate. She hasn't got a frame of reference for something like this. And I'm damn glad about that.

Lenora May pulls the window shut, blocking the noise. She twists the latch with a sigh and says, "He wasn't always like this."

It's what Mama used to say. Early in the morning when Dad was sleeping off his affair with the bottle, she'd take me into the bathroom to brush my hair and kiss my bruises.

I never believed her, either.

As if reading my thoughts, Lenora May continues, "When we were young, he was my protector and somewhere along the way, he forgot what that meant." She laughs a humorless laugh. "It's strange to think of myself as older now than I was then. I look exactly the same, yet I've lived so many years. I should be wise by now. It's singularly cruel—I mean—it sucks that I'm not."

"Nice to see you're picking up our less-refined lingo."

She laughs again. It's such a delightful and proper sound that I sit up straighter. I should have a cup of tea in my hand to go with that laugh.

The smell of bacon and coffee wanders into the room and teases my stomach, which growls and gurgles like a wild animal. It's been ages since I was hungry for breakfast, but at least it's something to look forward to today. Maybe the last thing, because I have to find Heath to tell him what happened in his absence—that Nathan was alive last night until I got him killed.

"Lenora May," I say, remembering one last thing. "Do you know what's making the Shine fade all of a sudden?"

Her frown is delicate, landing on her features as lightly as a hummingbird. "What do you mean 'fade'?"

I had hoped Fisher wasn't telling the truth and it isn't my fault that the Shine has become nothing more than a dim nightlight. But Lenora May's face confirms it. There's nothing wrong with the swamp—it's something to do with me.

A few bits of sunlight splash over the pines. The swamp grows calm and quiet in its presence, allowing the irritated chirping of birds and the sizzle of bacon from downstairs to reach our ears. Lenora May studies me with a frown waiting in the wings. Whatever she's thinking, it makes her look haggard.

"You know not everyone sees the swamp the way we do," she begins, and I nod. "The Shine is always there, but it's not something we expect to see, so most people simply don't. It's easiest to see when our senses are heightened—when we're children or close to death, when we're drunk or traumatized or sick or mad or scared—or any other time we're not completely in our rational minds."

I say, "I thought that's what these charms were for," twisting the bracelet on my wrist, but even as I say it, I know it's wrong. The charms keep our minds clear of the swamp's fog, but Heath saw Shine before Old Lady Clary placed a charm on his wrist. And when I asked her for a charm for Candy, the first words from her mouth had contained the answer.

"They ate something. Heath and Abigail both ate something from inside the swamp," I say, thinking of the swamp water Heath swallowed and the blackberry Abigail picked. "That's why they started seeing Shine, why they were called to the swamp." I hadn't been there for Heath, but I'd completely missed the signs in Abigail—her reluctance to confirm she'd seen Nathan, her exhaustion from sleepless nights.

Lenora May nods. "Yes, eating something from inside the swamp creates an unbreakable connection to Shine—one that allows the person to see Shine and the effect it has on the world, but that also drives him to return to its source. For most, that call is irresistible—even more so if the thing they ate was something as powerful as that cherry Fisher gave you. Fighting it can drive them to madness. But it can be tempered with a basic charm like Heath's."

The charm helps him remember without losing his

mind. That's why Old Lady Clary was so insistent he wear it. I'd assumed mine was the same, but I was wrong. Mine does more than help me remember because Lenora May made it to be more than a charm. She made it for someone specific—Grandpa Harlan.

"Mine protects me," I say, studying the silver bouquet. I don't have to imagine what words I'd choose to protect someone I loved: *protect, shelter, defend.* And if even part of me feared the source, I'd add, *from Fisher.* "And it helps me remember because that's what you wanted for Grandpa Harlan. But I've never eaten anything from inside the swamp. Why can I see Shine at all? And what's wrong with me now?"

"I'm afraid there's nothing wrong with you, Sterling," Lenora May hedges, scooting to the edge of the bed and getting awkwardly to her feet. "In fact, it's more the opposite. A week ago, your body was starving. You were in such a strained state that you could easily see Shine. And recently you've, well, you've been eating well. It's a *good* thing, Sterling."

Of everything that's happened this week, this seems cruelest. And I did it to myself. I've stopped being so afraid and letting that fear direct my life. I ate catfish and hamburgers and peaches and felt so strong and certain, but the entire time, I was undercutting the one thing that gave me a fighting chance in the swamp.

"You're saying the only way to see and touch Shine is by making yourself weaker?" I ask, choking on the injustice of it.

She doesn't answer. The truth hangs between us like a pendulum.

The swamp always demands a price and this is one I can't pay.

CHURCH IS A LITTLE LIKE cheating when I'm grounded. Not only do I get to leave the house, but half the town shows up for Mass. Mama and Darold like to sit up close because a sheriff needs to be seen, but they don't require us to sit with them.

Lenora May immediately finds the friends I've seen her with at school. She hasn't said much since we spoke, and I can't blame her for wanting some distance. I'm left on my own. If things weren't so horrid right now, it'd be a coup, but as it is, I spend the service glued to Candy's side hunting for missing faces in the familiar crowd. Course, it's tough to tell who Fisher may have taken and who might be sleeping off last night's revelry in the backseat of their car.

For the past five months—ever since Liddy Jacob's wedding got out of hand and a fire took the First Baptist Church of Sticks—we've only had the one church. It's Catholic in the morning and Baptist in the afternoon. This morning, there's an unusually large number of Catholics to be found packed into the single-story house. Storms have a way of bringing people to prayer and this one's no exception.

Father O'Conner's in a fine spirit as a result. His cheeks go rosy and he does his best to match the highs and lows of the service to the sounds of wind howling around the steeple. Candy's unimpressed. She spends the storm-themed homily muttering about superstition and the dangers of small-town thinking. She's not wrong. Right after Mass, this is the same group of people that'll trot over to Clary General. It's too difficult to tease fear from faith, so they'll cover all their bases at once.

At the moment, prayer doesn't seem like such a bad option.

Too many things have gone wrong. Fisher is too powerful. Phineas is too stuck. Who knows where Heath is, and I'm running low on options. It would be so much easier if I'd forgotten from the start, if Phin had disappeared and I'd never noticed a damn thing.

If our places were reversed and I was the one stuck in the swamp, I know Phin would've found a way to save me. I'm not good at fighting. I've only ever been good at running far and fast, at aiming high and laying low. Phin's the fighter.

He fought his battles and mine and it worked.

Except it hadn't worked so well. Lenora May was right when she said Phin was running away. Giving me the bracelet was his way of saying it was time to take care of myself. Instead of meeting him halfway, I used his fears against him and made him think that if he left, I'd wither away to nothing.

All of this is my fault.

I tug at the bracelet circling my wrist, stretching the band wide enough to fall off. It would be so easy to leave this wretched hurting behind.

Tug.

It slips. A little more and I'll forget it all.

Tug.

I won't remember how horrible I was to my own brother, or that I got a boy killed, or that I didn't notice when my own best friend was struggling against the swamp. I'll forget Phineas and Nathan and Abigail and all this guilt riding my heart. I'll be a different person. I'll believe Lenora May is my sister, I'll believe the fence is there to protect me, and I might even believe I'm a decent person.

But I'd also forget the first time I made it all the way through the periodic table of elements and Phin crowed with pride, I'd forget the delight I felt when Heath took my hand that day in school, I'd forget sharing a single, nasty cigarette with Abigail in sixth grade and the coughing fit that followed, and I'd forget singing at the top of my lungs in the kitchen with Lenora May.

I squeeze the bracelet until the bands press tight to my skin. It holds all the most powerful pieces of me. I may have lost Phin, but I can't give up everything.

By the end of Mass, Candy's teased out the story of my incarceration and Heath's disappearance. Albeit with liberal edits. She's immediately defensive on my behalf that Heath would stand me up for our midnight rendezvous. When Mama catches me to say the church ladies need her help in the kitchen, that Darold's gone to tend to yet more damage on the fence, and Lenora May went home with a friend, Candy offers to give me a ride. Whenever there's a big storm rolling in, the church ladies create food by the boatload and divvy it up between those for whom getting out of their houses has become a challenge. Mama'll be busy for hours.

"Thanks, Candace," Mama says with a smile that's already exhausted. "But don't drag your feet, you hear? This storm's liable to hit any minute."

"Yes, ma'am," we say together.

We drive straight to Heath's. The Durham house isn't a landmark or anything, but a year ago, when Candy thought Heath and I would be an item, she did some fact checking to make sure he measured up. Her mind doesn't lose much and

I'm not surprised in the least that she knows exactly how to find his house.

We take two turns from the main road and head up a short hill. Every one of these houses has some combination of columns and brick or columns and wood or columns and columns that makes them look like mini-antebellum estates. They're all big enough to hold two of my house and they all look like they're posing for a camera. I know Heath's house by his truck parked in front, obstinately blocking the view of a row of begonia bushes.

"Now what?" I ask when Candy's car drifts to a stop.

"What sort of question is that? Now you ring the doorbell and ask for your lover while I sit here and pretend not to watch."

"I was afraid of that."

Behind the house, the sky is thick and gray. A warm wind slaps at me from either side as I make my way to the front door. There's no rain yet, but it's so dim that the porch lights glow daffodil yellow in their frosted sconces. The door is made of that thick beveled glass that tempts you to stare real hard to see through. I press the doorbell and take a polite step back.

After a minute, the door opens to a woman who looks like she's been pulled from a magazine spread on southern style. Her hair is swept back in a beautiful, smooth bun, and little teardrop pearls hang from her ears. Her perfume reaches me a fraction of a second before her rehearsed smile.

"Can I help you?" she asks, folding her arms so the tips of her nails make small impressions in her green silk blouse.

Wind ruffles my Sunday slacks, which are shabby compared to the perfect lines of her navy pants. Never in my life have I been so intimidated by a pair of pants.

"Yes, ma'am, Mrs. Durham?" I say, speaking up to be heard above the wind. "My name is Sterling Saucier and I'm here to see Heath, if he's home."

Her smile goes stale right there on her face. "Sterling. How very nice to finally meet you." She says "nice" in the normal way, but she means another word entirely. "Yes, Heath is home, but I'm afraid he's not available right now."

Wind buffets me again, holding me in place.

"Is he okay?" I can't think of what I might've done to make him ignore my calls, but something's not right here.

"How kind of you to ask," she says, and again her words only masquerade as polite. "I understand you're partially responsible for his decision to refuse medication. Do you know what happens to a person when they suddenly quit taking the medicine they've been on for a year?"

"N-no," I say as my heart begins to race. "I don't."

"That's right. You don't. I think it's probably best if you go now, don't you? Heath needs his rest." Her smile returns, but she doesn't even try to infuse it with sweetness. This is a dry, dismissive smile. "So nice of you to come by."

The door shuts in my face. Wind howls in my ears, reminding me of all the things I've lost today.

I don't know what I look like when I crawl into the car. Windblown and devastated, or just dumb. My whole body vibrates with the ringing sensation of having been slapped. Candy gives me a moment, then, before prodding for anything at all, she leans over and pulls me into a hug. Her kindness is my undoing and I cry into her shoulder for a minute or ten, I'm not sure.

"Tell me," she says, when I'm sitting with a tissue in my hands that's disintegrating as fast as my life.

"I can't tell you without talking about things you won't believe!" There's a spur of anger that quashes my tears flat.

But Candy does the thing she excels at more than anything else and revokes my anger before it's taken hold. She says, "Okay, then I'll believe you. Every single word you say to me right now, Sterling Saucier, I'll believe you. That's a best-friend promise."

My throat tightens and a fresh wash of tears slithers down my cheeks. "Damn it, Candy."

After another hug, she starts the car and begins to steer us down the long drive of the Durham house. I'm preparing to tell her everything from the minute Phin leapt over the fence to Mrs. Durham's cold smile as she closed the door in my face. But as we're turning off the driveway, something *thwumps* against the car.

Candy slams the brakes with an especially colorful curse. I don't see anything through the rear window but the trees whipping in the wind and a piece of the Durham house hidden behind them. Candy's halfway out of the car when the back door opens and we both shriek.

"Jezuz, you could kill a guy with that scream," says a voice I know.

"Heath!"

"You asshole," adds Candy, pointing a single finger with all the menace she can muster. "If you dinged my trunk—"

"I'll take care of it. Promise. I'm sorry." He's slightly winded from sprinting after us. "But you were almost gone and I can't take the truck or Mom'll know. Any other day of the year, it's the eyesore she hides in the garage, but now she's got the thing parked right where she can always see it. Please, drive me away from here."

Candy sighs and returns her attention to the road. "I'll put up with a lot for dramatic displays of romance, but I'm holding you to your word, Heath Durham."

"What happened?" I ask.

He leans forward, putting his face between the two front seats. It's a mark of how invested Candy is that she doesn't snap at him to buckle up like a sane person. He pauses before answering, eyes flicking from Candy to me with a question.

"It's okay," I assure him. "She's about to believe everything we say."

ON THE DRIVE, HEATH EXPLAINS that two days ago Doc Payola informed his parents that he'd been off his antidepression
medication for days.

They flipped. His mother was sure he'd relapse and repeat
the sleepwalking events of the previous summer, but Heath
stood fast, and Doc Payola admitted that if they hadn't seen
symptoms of withdrawal by now, they probably wouldn't.

"Things got a little extra complicated after the speeding ticket," he confesses. "Your stepdad took an interest and
came by to discuss it yesterday while we were gone. When I
got home, they took my phone and grounded me for a week.
And when I tried to meet you last night, well, things went
from bad to worse."

"And how did your mom come to blame Saucier for the sky being blue?" Candy's tone suggests the question's innocent, but I see the glint in her eye. She's following a scent, and if Heath's answer doesn't satisfy, she might dump him right here and tell him to march home.

Heath fidgets. I could save him, but I let the question stand.

He clears his throat and says, "I may have delivered an impassioned speech about having found someone who believed me when I said I wasn't crazy, and someone who supported me no matter what. And I may have said that person's name in the course of a shouting match with my parents. And that may have been a huge mistake."

"No," I say, "it wasn't."

I spend the rest of the drive cataloguing all the ways he's different from his mama. They may have the same gold tones in their eyes and skin, but Mrs. Durham manages to look sharp and cool where Heath looks like a summer day. Ten minutes later, we're gathered around my kitchen table with a pot of coffee between us, ready to put Candy's promise to the test.

The house is empty but for us. In spite of Mama's warning that we hurry home, Lenora May must be with her friends. This would be easier if she were here, but I try to imitate her calm, deliberate manner of explaining impossible things to Candy. She has a way of making this insanity sound like something that not only could happen, but has. When I say it, it sounds desperate. Heath helps, adding a bit here and there, lending even more credibility to my tale.

I finish with a condensed and severely edited version of the previous nights' events, sans ultimatum. I skip anything having to do with Nathan. Heath has to be the first to hear it. Even without that addition, I can feel tension rolling off his shoulders.

Candy sits through the whole thing, still as a rock. Her eyes don't leave my face, her fingers are flushed white from being pressed so tightly against her mouth, and even her hair seems to have become straighter in its ponytail. Without warning, she stands and walks to the sink, dumps her coffee, then disappears around the corner into the bathroom.

I share a nervous glance with Heath before refilling both our mugs. I like coffee so strong you could stand a spoon in it and this comes close. The cinnamon stick I threw into the grounds adds even more bite. I enjoy the hint of spice on my tongue, but Heath cools his mug with a liberal application of milk and sugar. By the time he's done, it's barely coffee anymore.

"Did that go well? I can't tell," says Heath, slurping at his coffee and hissing at the heat. "I don't know if you know this but Candy's . . . intimidating."

"That's why she's captain of the volleyball team. We win or lose most of our games before the first serve ever goes up simply based on her intimidation factor." I laugh at a memory of Candy facing off with a girl twice her size from Alexandria. Candy shook the girl's hand and said maybe three words. The poor girl shrank a whole foot in the exchange. "I think it went well. At least, better than the other times I've tried talking to her about this."

Just then, Candy reappears. She looks much the same as she did, but she sweeps her car keys from the table and snatches her purse.

"Don't go anywhere," she states, stalking to the door.

And then she's gone. We listen as the sounds of her car get farther and farther away and we're left with nothing but the *tick-tick-tick* of the clock on the wall, and the *tap-tap-tap* of Heath's foot.

I need to tell him, but I can't bring myself to speak. I stare at him so long and so hard that he finally cracks.

"Um, you wanna see a trick?" he asks with a playful grin.

Without waiting for an answer, he digs a quarter from his wallet and holds it for me to see. In a quick series of motions, he mimics swallowing it only to reveal it's still safely in his palm.

"Sneaky." I reach for the quarter to verify that it is, in fact, real. "And surprisingly useless. Where'd you learn that? Two minutes on a smartphone?"

"Nathan." The word is a blow. "He had uncles who were really into magic tricks and they taught him when he was a kid. He tried to teach me a few of the easier ones, but this is the only one that stuck. He used to say that I couldn't turn tricks if I were a New Orleans hooker."

His laugh is a short bark. I should laugh because it's funny and a good memory. I don't want him to think I'm so prudish I can't take a joke about a whore, but I can't laugh. It would be terrible to laugh and then tell him Nathan is dead as a direct result of something I did.

"Sorry," he adds when I'm quiet too long. "I'm pretty susceptible to caffeine since I quit taking those pills."

I don't want to tell him.

"Hey." He runs a thumb down my cheek. "What's wrong?"

I'm stuck in his sympathy. I don't want to shake it away. I want to go back to yesterday afternoon when everything was good and promising. I want to return to that dusky moment when we kissed and nothing else mattered.

"Heath, I have to tell you something."

I hate the words as soon as I've said them. Generic and cowardly, they do nothing to prepare him for what's coming next. Even I don't quite know. I try to imagine how I'd want to hear that my brother was dead.

And then I stop trying.

"I haven't told you everything that happened last night." I pause, waiting for a reaction, but aside from surprise, there's not much else. He has no reason to suspect the truth.

If I don't say it now, I never will. My throat begins to

close, as if it might stop this horrible confession. "Nathan's dead."

"What?" he asks, not because he didn't understand, but because he doesn't want to.

Swallowing hard, I continue. "Fisher was angry about the peaches. I don't even know how he found them, but he did and he *knew*. Everything happened the way I said except before Abigail, he called Nathan and—"The sight of Nathan's face as Fisher pulled the life from him is so clear in my mind. "I didn't think Fisher would kill him and I'm so sorry, Heath, because I should have known."

"How could you have known?" His voice is a faraway thing, all hollow and empty.

He moves to the living room, stares through the window. His eyes are dry as kindling, his body tranquil as a locust shell, clinging to the side of a tree.

I pull his hand into mine and clamp my teeth tight. I know how horrible soothing words can be. There's no making this better.

"You should've waited for me." His hand is cold in mine, and tense.

Arguing the point feels petty. "I know," I say. "I'm sorry."

"Did he say anything? How did it happen?" he asks.

Quietly. "He was searching for you." *His voice was hoarse from shouting.* "He didn't really seem to understand what had happened. I think he got stuck in that moment after the crash. For him, it was still that night. And then—"

I think of Phin's body hanging in the air. How easily it could have been him if Fisher had decided differently.

"And then, Fisher just—" I don't have to close my eyes to see it all again. Nathan's mouth frozen in a silent scream and full of light. "Fisher just took his life away. It was easy for him. Like blowing out a candle. Fisher's not even human. Maybe he used to be, but he's—oh, God, he's not anymore."

Suddenly, Heath's eyes are full and wet. He slumps next to me, knees crashing to the floor. I collapse with him. His shoulders shiver against mine.

This could be me—the only one left to bear the memory of an entire life. It might still be me and right now I'm sure that if I lose Phin I'll take this bracelet off and sink into ignorance.

I think of Nathan, of his long arms and his sharp shoulders. I think of what his face must have looked like when he smiled, long and round all at once. I think of how graceful his fingers must have been when he vanished a quarter. And I think of his toes pointing up at the sky, his body melting into the swamp. I think of missing him, and for a second I'm Heath, and I'm afraid I'll suffocate beneath this pressure on my chest.

Be brave, I think, grinding my teeth against the push of tears. "I'm sorry I can't remember all of him with you." The words barely manage to squeeze around the painful lump in my throat.

His heart breaks across his face like a wave, then recedes. I watch a tear pull pale sunlight down Heath's cheek as he stares through the window, resisting his sorrow, hands fisted against his thighs.

"Nathan loved the idea of the swamp. He used to say the South had so much soul even the land commanded respect." His laugh is a humorless flare, dying as quickly as it came, leaving us in a silence that isn't only silence. It's death and the swamp and Fisher.

I open my mouth, hoping the right words are somehow waiting inside, but there's only air. Words won't change that Heath is the only person in this entire world who can truly mourn Nathan.

Not even his parents will remember that he's gone.

Tears make Heath's face bright with sadness. "His favorite color was green, and I don't remember a time when he wasn't chewing on taffy or licorice or gum. He loved that stuff. Said it was his duty as the son of a doctor to eat the hell out of some sugar."

Knowing such a small and inconsequential thing about Nathan does it. Tears sneak in beneath my laughter and I'm crying before I have a chance to stop, but I'm laughing, too, and Heath smiles.

It takes a deep, shuddering breath to get myself sorted

again and when I do, I find Heath glowering. "What is it?" I ask, suddenly fearful.

"What about Phineas?" His voice is low and level and as serious as a hurricane. "Did Fisher hurt him, too?"

"No." I brush at my tears, but they don't want to quit. "But he will. He'll kill Phineas and then Abigail and Sheriff Felder and whoever else he can get his hands on, starting at midnight tonight unless—"

There's a soft sound behind us, a cry of alarm or distress and I turn to see Lenora May standing in the doorway with one delicate hand pressed against her throat.

"Unless I return to him," she finishes.

By the time Candy reappears with a bag of books and a bottle of vodka, we've migrated again to the kitchen table and sit studying the wood grain as though it contains powerful secrets. She takes no notice. She breezes in, pausing at one cabinet before retaking her seat at the table, where she plunks the bottle and four shot glasses between us with determination.

"Now, I need a little stupid in me if I'm gonna do more than pretend. And for your sake, I'm gonna try." She opens the bottle and pours. "You're welcome to have a little. Not that any of you need much more stupid. Hi, May. Lucky I grabbed four."

Candy takes her shot and makes quick work of it. Nodding, Lenora May pulls one of the overfull glasses toward her as though she's been handed a fine meal without silverware. I leave mine in the center of the table. I may not know what I'm going to do, but I do know I can't do it drunk. Heath merely holds the shot between his fingers as if its presence is comfort enough.

Candy pours another round for herself and pushes a pile of books across the table: her collection of Clary General's Tales of Sticks Swamp. "Okay. Now that I'm stupid, let's talk strategy."

"Strategy?" Lenora May sips her vodka, doing her best not to wrinkle her nose and failing. I don't know if she's aware how not in character this is for Candy, but I know it's huge. The last time Candy accepted anything without evidence as irrefutable as carbon dating was when Abigail told her she overheard Bennett Hob telling Matt Thurman he thought she was hotter than Miss Bonnie's jambalaya. And she only accepted that because in her eyes it was "believable enough."

"Yes, strategy." She pushes a book at each of us and pours herself a third smaller shot. I had no idea she could put so much away, but she's never done this sort of thing in front of me before. "If we're going to pretend or assume that all or some of these stories are true—and honestly, that's a bit of a stretch for me—then we might as well see how they all turned out in the end."

"I thought everyone ends up lost or stuck or dead? I can't

remember a single exception."

Candy's smile is a little looser. "Those were only in the most popular stories. It's not as scary when you don't get stuck, and who tells non-scary stories at sleepovers? Read."

I was never as obsessed with these as Candy. She liked them because she knew they couldn't be true, and I didn't care for them because I thought maybe they could be.

The collection is divided by supernatural category with two entire volumes each on ghosts, demons, and witches, and one devoted to strange sights and sounds like the Wasting Shine and the voices of long-lost lovers. Under Candy's now entirely vodka-fuzzy gaze, we each begin to read.

I crack *Ghosts*, volume 2 and skim the table of contents for anything that looks relevant. The book smells a little musty and like the cheap perfume Candy wore through junior high, so sweet it even smells pink.

Flipping the pages, I find each story begins with its own pen-and-ink drawing. The first is of a Civil War–era soldier looking travel worn and anxious standing at the edge of the swamp. Just inside the shadows, a woman extends her arms, trailing gossamer sleeves behind. It's surprisingly detailed. The woman even has a fashionable freckle beneath her left eye. The artist has signed their name in the gritty ground and though I can't decipher all of it, the last name is distinctly Clary.

I keep paging through my volume, looking for anything

that wants to leap up and smack my cheeks, but the illustrations are all for the stories I know: "The Boy Who Cries at Night," "Mad Mary Sweet," "The Hollow-Eyed Cur." Though the beast of one tale looks suspiciously like the pale-faced creature that chased me on my first trip inside, there's nothing else new in these books. Still, with only eleven hours to midnight, I keep looking.

Lenora May stands when the clock dings two. "This won't help us. Half of these were written before Fisher and I went in and changed everything, and the other half won't tell us anything we don't already know."

"Well, what do you suggest?" Candy asks, irritated that her books have been rejected.

"I don't know." Lenora May heaves a pretty sigh and pulls her hair away from her neck.

Candy reaches for the bottle again, not that she needs it. The charm I gave her is there, a testament to how incredibly stubborn she is in all things. Leave it to Candy to be the only person in Sticks immune to Shine.

Realization floods my mind. She's not simply immune.

"Are you drunk?" I ask. At three shots in, she should be.

"Tipsy," Candy corrects. "It's been an hour. I'm not *that* much of a lightweight."

"That should be good enough. C'mon." I know I'm onto something. I hope I'm onto something. *Please, let me be onto something.*

I tug Candy straight through the door. To my eye, the Shine is dim as dusk. I can barely distinguish it from the dark woods.

"What do you see?" I direct Candy's gaze to the swamp.

Lenora May clues into my line of questioning and leans in with interest. According to her, intoxication should allow Candy to see Shine easily.

"I see a swamp. Mud, trees, and not much else," she says, confirming my suspicions.

"Okay," I say, remembering something else. "Climb the fence."

Everyone protests at once, but I hold up my hands and say, "She'll be fine. Trust me. Candy, please."

"Is the swamp dangerous or isn't it, Saucier?" Candy grumbles, but she does as I ask and vaults the fence with more ease than I'd have expected in her state. "How's this? Or should I walk inside and eat a few bugs, too?"

Though it's dim, I see Shine bend away from her the same way it did when she and Abigail tried to convince me there was nothing to fear in the swamp. Individual threads weave toward her only to veer away before touching. She swings her arms and spins, sending Shine flying away from her in a frenzy. By stubbornness or something else I can't begin to fathom, Candy repels all the magic of the swamp so solidly she can't even see it.

"How is that even possible?" Heath asks.

"That's not even all."

Slipping Heath's grasp, I climb the fence and stand next to Candy. Light glimmers in my peripheral vision. Lenora May shifts as she watches the Shine close in around me.

"Shine's on me?" I ask. Their eyes confirm it. "Good. Now, watch."

Reaching out, I take Candy's hand. I don't need to be drunk or starving to know what happens, Heath and Lenora May drop a curse in unison, which confirms what I suspected: Candy can repel Shine from anything, any*one*, she touches.

"I've never seen anything like it," Lenora May says. "What does it mean?"

"It means we have a weapon," I say, feeling something like hope start to stir in my chest. "It means I'm going after them. Phin, Abigail, the sheriff. I'm going to bring them all home."

PART THREE

Beware of whom you trust, my sweet,
Beware the things you eat,
The swamp will tempt and torment you,
Or swallow you complete.

"This is very simple." Lenora May stands with her arms crossed over her chest, trying to look determined. "We have no idea if Candy's strong enough to withstand Fisher's magic."

For the sake of guaranteed privacy, we've moved our discussion to the Lillard House. The dusty floor in front of Lenora May reflects her worry in a path of footprints. She's always been a pacer.

"I can't let you take this risk. Any of you. Too many people have already suffered." Lenora May tries to keep her voice solid and steady, but it quivers noticeably. "I will return to Fisher and take Phin's place. I really don't understand why we're debating this point."

She wants us to take her at her word, but I remember how happy she's been in the past days. How free and excited she was to be living life like any other girl. And I've seen how longingly she gazes at the letter from Tulane announcing her acceptance and scholarship. To keep from confessing any of this, she paces with her eyes trained on the floor.

"Because," I say again, "we can't trust Fisher to do what he says. There's no telling what he'll do once he has you, but I'm willing to bet 'Free Phineas' isn't high on his list."

"That also seems simple," Candy states. "Can't trust a liar, a thief, or a swamp thing who's killed to make a point. That's always true in the stories. 'The Mud-Mouthed Woman' was a filthy liar. She'd say anything to get you into the swamp. Then she'd eat your feet so you couldn't ever leave."

"Jezuz," shoots Heath. "That's sick."

Candy shrugs and muses, "Seems like a decent tactic to me," winning a sharp look from Heath.

She may be a little drunk, but having Candy to back me up on this point might be the most miraculous thing that's happened in this town since Featherhead Fred wrestled the alligator that took up residence in the primary school playground. Though I didn't see that with my own eyes, the story is generally accepted to be fact, if slightly embellished here and there.

"But there's no other way!" Lenora May cries. "We don't know if those peaches will work or not and even if they will, there's no way to get close to Phin unless I'm in the picture."

"If there wasn't a possibility that the peaches would work, why did they make Fisher so angry? Besides, you *will* be in the picture." I'm not willing to give up, not when we have a possible solution and four brains between us. "You just won't be a sacrifice."

"A decoy," Heath murmurs. His voice is thick with emotion. He hasn't added much to the discussion. It's selfish, but I dare to hope he doesn't hate me completely.

I say, "Exactly. Lenora May can go to the fence and call Fisher. He's bound to come. Then all you have to do is keep him distracted long enough for me to get to Phineas, feed him—and whoever else I can find—a peach, and get everyone out."

Lenora May frowns, pretty as a posy, and kneels on the ground. She's tense, unwilling or unable to relax around this topic of conversation—her life, her future, her humanity—they're all at stake, so I can't blame her.

"I don't mean to be difficult, really I don't, but I doubt that I'll be enough of a distraction. Fisher is connected to every single thing in that swamp." She chews her bottom lip, searching for the best way to say what comes next. I'm afraid she's about to expose me and tell everyone I'm not seeing Shine the same way I was, but she's more concerned with Fisher. "He's not the same person he was when we entered because there is so little of him left that isn't blended with magic. I think that in some ways he *is* Shine. I don't see how I could possibly distract him enough on my own."

"Then you won't be alone," I say.

I look at Heath, hoping he'll catch my meaning. He does. And if it were a baseball, he'd have dropped it.

"No." Heath's voice is suddenly substantial again. With his hands braced on his thighs, his shoulders are boxy and formidable. "You can't keep doing this, Sterling."

"What?" I say, surprised by the anger in his voice. "Trying to save my brother?"

"Thinking you have to do it *alone*. Candy can stay with her." He nearly growls and takes my hand in his. "I'm going with you."

The urge to accept this offer and let him take care of me is so strong, but I have to be stronger. If I'd been stronger before, I'd have waited for him. We would have gone into the swamp together and things might be different now. I shake my head, squishing the needy part of myself like a beetle.

"No, I need Candy with me. She's the best shot we have at deflecting Fisher's magic, if it comes to that. And—" I hesitate. No one's going to like this part of the plan. "There's a good reason for you to stay with Lenora May."

The frown on his face relaxes into curiosity. "What?"

I squeeze his hand and swallow my sadness. "Nathan."

His expression goes slack as an old man's. But I don't have to say anything else. He nods, understanding so much when

I've said so little. I wonder if we'll understand each other this well when the swamp isn't what connects us, and for a moment I panic. *What happens when all this ends and we go back to a life that doesn't revolve around the swamp?* Because one way or another, this ends at midnight and that means something for me and Heath. I just don't know what it is.

He says, "You want me to convince Fisher that I'm a threat. That I'll do anything to get revenge for killing my friend. That I'll . . . that I'll hurt Lenora May." His eyes are as flat as his voice. "Okay. I can do that."

"That could work," Lenora May murmurs. "But it'll have to be convincing. He has to believe you really mean me harm."

"Fisher killed my best friend," Heath states, but his shoulders fall a little. "I can be convincing."

Lenora May leans in, resting a hand on his arm. Her eyes are focused on his, hard and insistent. "Good. Then hit me."

"What?" Heath jumps to his feet and backpedals.

I knew it was coming, but I didn't expect Lenora May would suggest it herself.

"Hit me," she repeats, climbing to her feet. She inches forward, careful not to spook Heath. "If he sees blood on my face, he won't be able to think straight, and Sterling and Candy will have more time to do what they need to."

Heath's fingers curl into a fist and for a moment I'm afraid he'll actually do it, but he shakes his head. "No, no way. I'm not hitting you. Hell, no. I'm not that sort of guy."

My relief is short lived. Lenora May turns to me next. "All right, then. You do it. Surely Phin has taught you to throw a decent punch."

It's true. Phin taught me to throw a punch without breaking my hand or spraining my wrist, but I've never done it for real. He looked so much like our dad when he was in the thick of a fight. The sight made my skin crawl.

She reads the hesitation on my face as clearly as if it were a stop sign. "Come on, Sterling. Hit me as hard as you wanted to a week ago, when all this started."

I may have relished the thought of knocking her into next week, but my arms fill with lead and won't be moved. If I tried to swing a fist right now, I'd probably have a better chance of tickling her than drawing blood.

"What would y'all do without me?" Candy quips, stepping in with her fists raised. "Ready, May?"

Before Lenora May can answer, Candy's fist connects with the side of her face. Lenora May yelps and when she raises her head again, there's blood falling from the corner of her mouth. She nods and Candy throws another punch, leaving a mottled bruise of red and white on Lenora May's cheekbone.

"Jezuz," Heath heaves.

Candy runs a thumb across Lenora May's mouth, pulling a blood smear down her chin. Then she grabs Heath by the wrist and dabs blood on his knuckles. Heath looks faint at the sight or the implication, and Candy smacks the side of his head.

"Nut up, Durham." She grips his shoulders and gives him a quick shake. It's the shake she uses on the court when someone's head isn't in the game. "Mean it or go home."

"I'm good, I'm good." Heath dances away from Candy, giving his head a shake of its own. "I can do this."

We have a plan. It might be a good one, it might be a bad one, but we don't have time to search for another.

"Sterling." Lenora May catches me before we leave the house behind. The bruise on her cheek is darkening nicely. There's no way Fisher will keep calm once he sees it. "What about you? Can you see again?"

This is the question I was hoping to avoid. Though none of us has eaten since church, I didn't skip breakfast and the Shine is still as dim as it was yesterday.

I pitch my voice low enough that Heath and Candy walking ahead won't hear. "Well enough."

Her brow creases. She doesn't believe me and probably shouldn't. She won't like my plan any more than she'd like to see me starve, but there are only two ways to get close enough to the Shine to use it: through weakness or strength. And I'm choosing strength.

"I have a plan," I say, producing the second cherry Fisher

gave me. "It'll work fast, right?"

For a second, Lenora May doesn't answer, but presses her bloody lips together. Then, she nods and says, "Oh, Sterling," in a whisper strained by emotion. "Would you listen if I told you you shouldn't?"

"No," I say with kindness.

"Then, whatever you do, keep that charm on you." And even as she tries to hide her concern with a smile, I see it in the corners of her mouth.

"I promise." I pocket the fruit and give the silver bracelet on my wrist a turn. I have everything I need to get this done.

She links her arm through mine. Before we left the house, she changed from her Sunday dress into something more suited for a rescue mission. She picked a gray canvas sundress with pockets over her thighs, a few oil stains here and there. I recognized the cloth as that of Phin's work pants and asked, "The swamp couldn't give you a pair of pants?" To which Lenora May responded, "Why? On a girl, they're the single greatest travesty of this century." And we'd shared a laugh.

She added black cowboy boots instead of sandals. Both seem pretty pointless to me, but nothing could be more Lenora May. As much as I've hated her this week, watching her boots cut through this tall grass makes me smile, and I realize that at some point, I stopped hating her altogether.

"Thank you," I say, squeezing her arm. "No matter what

happens, thank you for trying."

She's quiet for a moment before saying, "I'd do anything for my sister."

"Me, too."

Candy and Heath stop at the crest of the hill, where wild sweet William dances a blithe, blue path all the way to the fence. We join them and pause, our attention fixed on the way ahead.

"Phineas Harlan Saucier," I say quietly.

"Phineas Harlan Saucier," Heath repeats the name.

"Phineas Harlan Saucier," Lenora May adds, followed by Candy.

"Phineas Harlan Saucier," the three of them say together and I swallow hard.

I raise my voice with theirs and together we give his name to the air, to the ground, and the swamp that took him. "Phineas Harlan Saucier."

A crack of thunder shouts a response. Loud as an explosion. The earth rumbles beneath my feet. Ahead of us, the trees lean across the fence as if a great wind pushes against them. One look at my friends tells me they all know what I do: Fisher is waiting.

In unison, three cell phones start ringing. Candy, Lenora May, and I all reach for our pockets.

"It's Mama," Lenora May says, nervous.

"It's my dad. He's never home this early," Candy states.

"Darold," I add.

Heath's grin is slippery when he says, "Bet my parents wish they hadn't restricted cell privileges now."

Below, tree limbs whip in a furious wind that doesn't reach us. The clouds have swallowed the sun, and panic makes me cold.

I ball my fists for strength and clear the tension from my throat. "Let's go."

THE SWAMP GREETS US WITH a humid sigh.

By the time we reach the trees, they've quit their fury. Fresh pine needles litter the ground, torn down by the wind that abused them a moment before. Mockingbirds fill the silence, laughing and shrieking above, and from deep inside the swamp comes the hiss and clatter of beetles, the trill of frogs, the too-human cry of a loon.

As we planned, Heath and Lenora May approach the fence cautiously but do not cross it. Lenora May is preparing Heath, giving him all the information he'll need to get under Fisher's skin. Like any good southerner, she started with his middle name and branched out from there. Heath will need all the fodder he can get if he's going to keep Fisher at the fence.

I lead Candy away, through the pines along the fence until we can barely see the others. We need to be far enough that Fisher won't notice us waiting, but not so far that we can't see what's happening. Lenora May watches us with her hand twisted in the fabric of her skirt. When I'm satisfied with our position, I wave and she nods before slowly, slowly advancing toward the fence. Even from this distance, I feel her fear. She hesitates. It's impossible that I see her shiver, yet I feel it skitter down my own spine. So much of this plan rests on her willingness to get close and cuddly with her terror.

Cold sweat settles in between my shoulder blades. The swamp holds its breath, and finally, Lenora May drapes her arms over the top plank of the fence. Shine reaches for her. She lets its tendrils taste her skin before pulling her hands to safety.

Immediately, I hear Heath's voice call Fisher's name. It doesn't echo so much as hiss through the swamp, as if the leaves and vines and mosses pass the name along.

Fisher, Fisher, Fisher.

Minutes go by. Shine tries again and again to cross the fence and reach Lenora May, but it can't. Candy fidgets beside me, the ground snickering beneath her shoes. I jump when Heath's voice becomes a shout.

"Fisher Enoch Lillard! I have your sister, Lenora May, and I want to make a trade!"

Candy growls her approval and adds, "Sexy."

I bump her shoulder with mine. "Now is not the time."

Lenora May verifies my statement by leaping farther from the fence with a small shriek. Heath grips her shoulder and gives her a rough shake, fulfilling his role as her warden. That's the only sign I need. Fisher is there and we have no time to waste.

We slip between the planks of the fence and run as fast as we can. As soon as I think it's safe, I pause. I take the cherry from my pocket, place it in my mouth, and bite. It's tart and divine, every bit as perfect as it appeared. If Miss Bonnie got her hands on a bowl of cherries like these, she'd kill half the town with a pie so exquisite they'd swear off food for the rest of time. It's gone too quickly and I drop the pit.

The effect is immediate and similar to when Fisher commanded his magic to heal me. Nausea sweeps up from my belly, dizziness washes down from my head so furiously that I stagger. Candy catches my arm. The feeling passes and I give her a confident nod. When I open my eyes, Shine is as bright as it's ever been. Maybe brighter. I pluck a bit of it as Fisher taught me, and roll the wisp of magic into a ball between my palms.

"Take us to the cherry tree," I whisper over the glowing ball while Candy looks on skeptically. To her, I probably look like Featherhead Fred, talking to nothing.

The light flies from my hands, flitting through the trees

and Spanish moss. I follow it as Candy comes behind with the bag of peaches over her shoulder, and together we run. Candy's not the squeamish type, but even she squeals when our legs sink to the shins in dark water.

"Hurry, Candy, please," I urge.

"I'm not lingering because I *like* it, Saucier," she snaps, but she hefts her feet through the slick mud.

We run and run. At some point, I realize I'm no longer following the Shine I commanded, but a feeling in my gut that seems to say, *This way!* We run until pink flashes bright between the tree trunks, and we break into the clearing of the cherry tree.

"This is it," I say needlessly because Candy's already reaching into her bag of peaches. Even here, so far inside the swamp, Shine pulls away from Candy. It won't or can't rest on her for too long.

"Where is he?" she asks.

Kneeling at the water's edge, I dip my hand into the murky pool and stir it around. The water is warm and thick between my fingers. Little bits of duckweed stick to my skin and I can't see more than two inches beneath the surface. With discomfort I recall my first encounter with gatorPhin.

"Phineas?" I call not too loudly. Only the frogs respond. "Phineas!" Shouting makes me feel bold, purposeful, and ridiculously exposed. "Please, Phin, you must come."

Every second feels like it could be the last. If Fisher isn't fooled by Heath and Lenora May's ruse, it won't take him long to suss out what I'm up to. When that happens, he'll be on me faster than I can say boo and I don't think he'll be inclined to mercy.

This is my only chance.

"Phin, please, it's me, Sterling, and I've come to take you home." I stir my hand in the water again, and again watch the ripples relax and go stagnant.

"Any other ideas?" Candy asks when more precious minutes have passed.

I want there to be another, better idea. I want to tell her that I have a plan B. But I shake my head and speak past the tightness in my chest. "He has to do this part."

Shine warms in the mud beneath my hand. It glimmers darkly in black, brown, and ochre, and I pull a small bit into my hands. I imagine Fisher growing impatient with Heath and turning his attention to the swamp. I imagine the expression on his face as he tilts his head, as if listening, while he feels me tugging on this web of Shine. And I imagine how like a spider he'll move, so much faster than I ever could, straight to the place where I'm struggling to make my brother see me.

Focus, I think, taking a long, slow breath and turning all my thoughts to Phineas.

Phineas crying in the dark when he thought I couldn't hear. Phineas sweating over his chemistry homework. Phineas smiling and happy because he got the engine in the Chevelle to turn over. Phineas red-faced and spitting mad with a beautiful purple bruise on his jawbone from a fight after school. Recalcitrant Phineas driving Mama and Darold up one wall and down another. Shy and embarrassed Phineas two years ago, admitting he had a girlfriend for the first time. Proud Phineas showing off his new tattoo.

Phineas home. Phineas home. Phineas home.

Candy grips my shoulder.

"What is that?" She points to a place where ripples have begun to slide toward us. Their progress is slow and patient and unmistakable and, just behind them, are eyes. "Alligator? It looks like a gator. Shit, if it is, run in zigzags, remember?"

It's possible that it really is a gator, a possibility I probably should have considered before now. I try to ignore the thought as Candy repeats the lessons every child in Sticks learns about fighting an alligator—go for the eyes, the ears, the nostrils, and if you have to, the valve behind the tongue, but mostly run like your britches are on fire.

Finally, he's close enough I can see the tortured blue of his eyes and the slick black of the hair on his head. "It's him," I say, relaxing a bit. "It's Phineas."

"Whatever you say," she says, pressing a peach to my shoulder and backing away.

That she can see him at all tells me something else about the puzzle that is Candy's strange ability—that she'll see whatever makes the most sense to see. In this case, a gator instead of a gatorboy.

The eyes continue to snake through the water looking so much like an alligator that all the hair on my neck stands at attention. I'm not wrong, but if I were wrong, this would be a very dangerous place to be. The closer he comes, however, the more certain I am that it's Phin. I'm just not sure how much of Phin is left.

"It's him," I say again, but edge away from the pond just the same. "But stay where you are anyway."

"Don't have to tell me twice." Candy doesn't sound convinced. "I'm trusting you not to get eaten, Saucier. And if that trust is misplaced, so help me, I'll tell all your worst secrets at your funeral."

Candy's moved so far away I can't tell where she is anymore. I keep my eyes on Phin and his weaving progress.

Water spills up and over his unblinking eyes, watching me as much as I'm watching them. Nearer the bank, more of his face rises, until he's visible to his bare chest. He's not so completely transformed as Abigail, but he's close. His shoulders are ridged and glossy with scales, and when he raises his hands I see that they, too, gleam with black claws, pale green webs running between his fingers. His lips are pulled tight over sharp teeth, scaled and somewhere between green and yellow. It's a gruesome grin and not at all like Phineas. He stops two feet from the bank.

"Phineas? Phineas, do you know who I am?"

I watch for some sign of recognition, but I can't make any sense of his rigid features. I take one step closer.

"I know you do. I'm your sister and you don't want to hurt me. You've never wanted to hurt me. You've only ever protected me, and I'm sorry I let you do it for so long." I take another smaller step forward. "I'm so sorry."

Water slips over his unblinking eyes and down his cheeks like tears. In a motion so slow I'm two years older by the end of it, he reaches out with one clawed hand. He rests the tip of a single claw on the silver bracelet around my wrist. His face is unmoving. He's trapped inside that contorted body and this is the only way he can tell me he knows who I am.

"Yes." My smile comes with tears in tow. I swallow them and clench my shaking hands. "Please, let me bring you home."

A hollow sound starts in his throat, a wet noise that struggles to find purchase in his mouth. "Hooongh."

I nod. "Yes, home. Please, come home with me. Come home so you can take the Chevelle to the racetrack and get yourself to Tulane. Come home so you can live the life you're supposed to live, Phin."

Around us, Shine glows in all the colors of the swamp. Little tendrils tickle my ankles and climb the side of my leg. I hear them whisper, calling me to *stay, stay, stay*. It's warm and comforting, and so much of me wants to curl up in the shade of the everblooming cherry tree and go to sleep. I could stay here with Phin and we'd be as happy as we've ever been. Safe and protected.

"Saucier!" Candy's voice is a cold splash of water. She's gotten impatient and a little freaked. "Whatever it is you're doing, would you hurry up? This place is really starting to wig me the hell out."

I offer the peach to Phin. It reflects the pink of the cherry blossoms and the gold of the swamp lights hanging overhead, but it's a dull thing and I think that's because its magic is on the inside.

"Eat this," I say.

Gingerly, he takes it with the tips of his claws. One pierces the peach and juice spills down his scaled hand. His jaws open wider than should be possible, and he devours the peach in one loud bite.

And then we wait. Long, horrible minutes tempting Fisher to return.

Just when I think it hasn't worked after all, Phin's body gives a shudder. His shoulders jerk this way and that. His jaw snaps. And he sinks into the water with a horrible groan.

I reach for him with a shout, but my feet slide on the muddy bank and I splash into the water, smashing my knee against something hard and immovable. Muck and who knows what else brushes past my shins and calves. The soft bottom of this little pond wants to pull me down inside it.

I should climb to more solid earth, but instead I reach for Phineas. I must find him.

My hands grasp only slick roots and debris. I swing them through the water again and again, becoming increasingly frantic.

But after several minutes, I stop splashing and the water goes still.

THE SWAMP REVEALS NOTHING.

The water is as dull as the clouds above. Wasting Shine hangs motionless in the air. And Phin doesn't surface again. I don't understand how this could have gone so very wrong. The peach was meant to release Phin, not kill him. I search the water desperately for him, but the swamp reveals nothing.

"Sterling." Candy's voice is soft and taut.

I find her standing exactly where she was a minute ago, several feet from the cherry tree with the bag of peaches slung over her shoulder. She's gone so pale she's nothing but a shock of white and blonde against the swamp. And she's staring at me with her mouth open wide enough to catch flies.

"Sterling," she says again, this time with wonder. "I—I

remember. Him. Phineas. I remember."

Laughter swells in my chest and emerges in one loud bark. "It worked! I can't believe it, that peach worked!"

Candy's laughter is baffled and more enthusiastic. Her uncertainty is plain on her face, but she gives me a faint smile.

"Craziest shit I've ever . . ." She trails off, looking over my shoulder. "Well, where is he anyway?"

There's no time to dwell on the fact that I have no answer. The swamp begins to rumble and hiss. All the Shine begins to glow more brightly. Eagerly, it coils and uncoils, rolling through the earth and climbing through trees with such speed that more bits than usual break off into the air. And from the tall, scrubby plants at the edge of the clearing, a gatorgirl slides on her belly.

Only one at first. She noses around the trunk of a fat cypress, crushing its straw-like knees flat beneath her, and stops with claws pressed into mud. More follow. Easily a dozen. Gatorboys and gatorgirls, all of them with jaws parted and bellies to the ground. They look primed for attack, but instead of moving, they release a discordant hiss.

Candy's eyes are wide as saucers. I try to scramble up the bank, but my injured knee gives out and my shins crash against the mud wall. My nails dig into muck and my arms shake as I pull myself to my feet.

By the time I've worked my way into a perilous crouch, the rumbling, snapping, and popping have stopped.

"Sterling, what are we going to do?" Candy asks, her voice fearful.

"Yes, Sterling," another voice says, and my backbone goes stiff straight. "What *are* we going to do?"

When I look up, Candy stands with her bag clutched to her chest. Her body's as rigid as my own and her eyes keep moving over the row of gatorbeasts. Standing right behind her, with a grave smile carved into his face, his eyes alight with malice, and all the Shine of the swamp worshipping at his feet, is Fisher.

Shine curls around Candy, reaching for her, then shying away. Fisher, however, doesn't shy away. He considers her like he might a piece of meat.

"Sterling," she hisses, oblivious to Fisher's presence. "What do we do?"

"Don't move," I say, knowing anything else might get her killed. Just because she can't see Fisher doesn't mean he can't hurt her.

"She's a good friend to you. And I must say she is intriguing," Fisher muses. He begins to run a finger through her hair, but withdraws sharply before touching her. Exactly like Shine. Exactly as I'd hoped. "I don't know that I've ever met another like her. But do you want to know what I find even

299

more intriguing than a sightless girl, Sterling?"

My eyes slide to the pond, which is flat as ever. There's no hint of Phin anywhere.

"Ah, I see that you do." Fisher takes three steps toward the pond. "There I was, trying to make a deal with that obstinate boy for my sister, and here you were trying to slip your brother from beneath my very nose. Do you know what that makes me?" A storm darkens in his eyes. "Upset."

He extends a hand over the water. His palm begins to glow as he bends to reach beneath the surface. When he stands again, Phin's body rises with him. The full length of him hangs in the air, tense and alert and helpless. Just like Nathan. And fully human.

Phin struggles, kicks at the air and his captor. It's all useless and Fisher knows it. *Have I really gotten this far only to lose him?*

"No." I want to move, but fear holds me tight.

"What have you done?" The question's for me, but Fisher studies Phin's human face. "You stupid girl, do you know what you've done?"

Phin's dark blue eyes catch mine. I know that look. I know it from a hundred midnights spent letting him stand in front of me to catch Dad's punishment with his own small body. It's his way of telling me to stay put, he'll take care of it. He'll take care of me.

But that's what got us here in the first place. It's time for *me* to take care of me.

Frustration gets my blood going. I can feel my feet and my legs and my arms, and they desperately want to move. In my mind, there's only one thought: *I will save Phineas, I will save Phineas.*

"Yes," I say, shifting my feet. "I've freed him."

Fisher snarls and Shine races to him, distorting his form. His hands turn dark as rotting wood and long, gray claws curl around Phin's neck. The transformation spreads: in from his hands and up from his feet until his entire body is encased in dark scales except for his face, which is the same pale gray as his claws. He blinks and when he opens his eyes again they are wide, yellow things with dark slit-pupils. He grows until he's several feet taller with legs like tree trunks.

With a start, I realize that I've seen this creature before— on the night I first went into the swamp and found Nathan. This creature—Fisher—is the beast who chased me. I think I should scream, but my insides quiver.

"You haven't freed him." Fisher's voice is beastly. An echo of it rattles in my chest. "You've killed him."

His claws tighten at Phin's neck.

"Please, don't hurt him!" I cry. "Let him go."

Fisher is unmoved.

Phin goes limp in the air. His hands fall away from Fisher's and his feet stop kicking, but that's not what drives terror through my chest like a stake.

The glow of magic, of Shine, is leaving his body. As it leaves, he grows more and more motionless, and I know with all the certainty I've ever felt that if it leaves his body completely, my brother will be dead.

I run two steps and leap at Fisher. My shoulder slams into his and we tumble to the ground. I hear the splash of Phin's body hitting the water. My eyes won't focus. I struggle to get my feet under me again, but there are hands tugging me down.

I kick and kick and kick, fighting to put space between myself and Fisher, but the force of his body doesn't budge. He's too strong, too big, and I'm too, too small.

Sticky fingers of Shine wrap themselves around my neck and my wrists, they snatch at my ankles until I'm bound firmly to the ground. Fisher's pale face peers into mine. A low growl rumbles through his teeth.

"This didn't have to end this way." His voice is a sluggish hiss. "I would have helped you."

"You're the one who needs help," I spit, wishing I could do more than state the obvious.

I feel his claws pressing into my sides. I feel the magic of the swamp wrapping around me, and I wonder if he'll trap me here forever or simply kill me.

He presses one hand to my chest and with his other, rips

the bracelet from my wrist. I hear my first name in Candy's voice and have time to marvel. Must be serious for her to use my given name. Then my body floods with pain, and all I see is a wave of Shine lashing at my eyes.

THE PAIN IS UNENDING. A hundred razors skidding through my veins. A thousand needles pressing into every inch of skin. My bones twist, fracturing slowly. I feel the roots of my teeth shatter. My fingers and toes spread so far apart the skin between them tears. Through the pain, I hear Lenora May's voice describing how Fisher transformed her into a gator and I wish it would happen fast.

And then it stops.

I feel nothing but the cold shiver of a pain just passed.

The world around me returns in static. Opening my eyes leaves me nauseated and disoriented. Everywhere I look, Shine swirls in furious eddies. It's impossible to focus. I squint and blink, looking for anything that makes sense in this vibrant anguish. Something inside me spins and spins and spins, and the world screams.

"Saucier!"

Candy. I yell for her. At least, I think I do. I can't feel my own voice.

"Saucier!"

Again, I try to yell. The light is overwhelming. It's impossible to know if I'm turning around, or if my eyes are open when I can't feel my feet or my hands. All I feel is the chaos of the swamp, the wild swirling of a magic so bright I'm lost in darkness.

Fisher. Where is Fisher? And why did he stop? He could be standing over me, enjoying the sight of my torture, waiting for me to gain my feet before filling me with new pain. But I hear sounds of a fight. A shout that sounds like Heath. A plea that sounds like Lenora May. They've distracted him. Pulled him away to save me, and now he'll kill them both.

I won't let Fisher win.

Closing my eyes, I try to focus. I think of my body, huddled against the wet earth, my shoulder aching from impact with Fisher's monstrous body. I think of the smell of the swamp, the rot and sulfur and rain. I think of the sounds I know so well: the small chirp of frogs, the sad, slow call of a black bear. But I can't isolate any one sensation from the din.

Except a pulsing pain in my knee. My knee! The bruise from falling into the pond!

Focusing on that, on the pain radiating down my shin to my toes, I slowly, slowly find my body. Twigs poke into my side and there's a pain thrumming in my head, but now it's a welcome sort of pain. I open my eyes.

A small, dark spot sits in the midst of all this light. It shifts, swings its arms at me and in that movement becomes Candy. She alone is as she should be, repelling the chaos of Fisher's magic as naturally as she does anyone who gets in her way. She's my point of reference. She's shouting my name, gesturing madly, and all the world falls into order at her insistence.

I see the tree first. The cherry tree with millions of pink blossoms winking at the sky, and a skirt of earth-dark Shine spinning in and out of its trunk like roots. Not far from its base, however, Shine draws together and funnels away from the tree. Every vein leads to the same place: Fisher. He may draw Shine to him with magnetic force, but the tree is the bright, beating heart of the swamp. And it's been diverted into him as Lenora May described.

Beneath its branches, Fisher's gnarled form hunches like a wild secret. A figure is collapsed at his feet. Blood seeps through the fabric of a yellow T-shirt. Honey-gold hair, traced pink by the glow of the blossoms above, soaks black in the muddy earth.

Heath.

The realization knocks the wind from me. He looks dead.

Did he distract Fisher from killing me only to get killed himself?

Farther away, Lenora May's got her back to a tree at the edge of the clearing, while all around her, gatorgirls and gatorboys snap their jaws.

I think we've already lost.

My mind is reluctant, my heart anxious—beating so quickly it's as if I'm already running away. I desperately want to grab my friends and get out of here. The only good thing I see is Candy, leaping into the swamp and holding Phin's body tight to her. In her arms, he's alive. Just as she repels all the magic of the swamp, she's trapped what little Shine remains in Phin's body inside of him. But for how long? And to what purpose?

"Candy," I call. "Don't let him go, okay? You hold on tight and do not let go."

She nods vigorously and moves a little deeper in the dark water, dragging Phin with her.

With a look of distaste, Fisher steps forward to cast a golden web over Heath's body. Heath mumbles or groans, and begins to push himself up. I choke on my relief. Alive. He's alive and still fighting.

It takes little more than a flick of Fisher's wrist to send Heath flying into the air. Thick vines tighten around his wrists and ankles, each pulling in different directions until he's strung up like a marionette.

"Stop it!" I shout, pulling Shine into my hands.

Fisher is unconcerned. "I wouldn't," he says, eliciting a small scream from Heath with a twist of his clawed hand. Then his voice softens. "Lenora May, please come here."

She's surrounded by his small army of gators—the people of Sticks who Fisher has trapped and transformed. Who knows how many he captured over the years? Nathan couldn't have been the first, and I know for sure Abigail wasn't the last. How many more creatures under Fisher's control wait for us in this swamp?

Lenora May doesn't move. She makes a small but definite shake of her head *no*.

Heath screams again. Lenora May inches farther away.

"Let them go, Fisher," she says. "And let me save the boy."

"You're being unreasonable, May. The boy's half dead, but you can still join me. We can be happy again, I promise. Now, please. Come. Here." Even without shouting, his words are sculpted and brutal, each one chilling.

"No." She moves back again, repeating the word with her actions. "There's no happiness here, Fisher. Not anymore."

"Damn it, May!" Fisher's shout is echoed in Heath's scream.

"She said no!" Shine warms in my hand. "Net," I say, assigning the magic intent, "bind." I throw my spell, imagining a wide net as it leaves my hand. It spins in the air, opening like a glittering spiderweb, but before it reaches Fisher, it dissolves at the center, falling around him like confetti.

He narrows his yellow eyes and raises a hand. I don't give him a chance to do whatever it is he's intending. Again, Shine flies to my hand. "Rock," I say, "fast." I throw it as hard as I've thrown anything in my life, but this time I don't pause to see if it finds its target. I throw another and another, stepping closer with each one until I've positioned myself between Fisher and Heath.

I'm aware that Lenora May is shouting as she moves behind me, but I don't stop to see what she's doing. I can't, because Fisher is laughing and that means my attack isn't working.

I gather all the Shine I can possibly hold and hit him with everything I have. He keeps laughing and when the last of the Shine falls away, the space between us is nothing but air.

My body shudders, exhausted. I will never be as strong as Fisher. This is his world and it has no choice but to adore him.

"Please, don't stop on my account." He dusts the front of his coat as if we've done nothing more than share a cup of tea and a few cookies. "Or are you tired?"

There's not a single part of him that's worried he'll lose this fight.

Maybe he shouldn't be.

How can I possibly win? My hands are shaking and I feel the ache of every muscle. I don't have the strength to do this. I don't have any sort of power that can match his. I was foolish to think this was anything but hopeless.

I look up at Heath's figure struggling in Fisher's web, at Lenora May stomping in the faces of gatorbeasts, at Candy holding my brother's half-dead body in the water. I see all the threads of Shine rushing to Fisher's form, giving him all the power he needs to control everything that happens in the swamp, and then I remember the only lesson he ever gave me.

He said, *Every time we speak, we influence the world around us. The magic of the everblooming cherry is more susceptible to your will.* It's like aligning electrons, and if I can redirect the flow of Shine, then maybe, just maybe, I have a shot.

But I can't do it alone.

"I'm not tired." I pull a thread of Shine into my hand. "Heath, you tired?"

"Not me," he grunts.

"Cut," I say with an image of severed vines in my mind. And with a quiet, "Please don't hurt him," I throw my spell at the webbing around Heath.

It works. He falls to the ground, and Fisher jumps forward with a snarl, but Heath is already on his feet. He gathers himself up and throws his fist directly at Fisher's vicious face. The attack catches Fisher completely off guard and he stumbles, struggling to regain his balance. Heath's jaw is set. He'll fight Fisher for as long as he's able, even if that's only another minute. But it's a minute I can use. And I know exactly what to do with it.

I dart beneath the tree, casting around for something sharp. A stick, a rock, anything that can do damage, and I spot something gleaming in the mud: the bracelet. It's been mangled in the fight, its once-smooth band now twisted and broken like a dagger. It's perfect.

The sounds of struggle are loud behind me. I don't even have to call for Lenora May. She's at my side in an instant and we kneel at the base of the tree where its Shine is brightest, where Fisher has diverted its natural flow so that it feeds only him. If all the magic of the swamp were a vast lake, Fisher has dammed it so that he controls its wild heart. He's changed it into something terrifying and selfish.

But dams can be broken and rivers redirected.

I stab the destroyed metal of my bracelet into the roots of the tree. Together, Lenora May and I join hands, circling the trunk with our arms. A trembling growl surrounds me and I look up in time to see Fisher's monstrous body charging. Shine bends around him and lashes at me, slicing my arms and cheeks. My legs burn and my heart begs me to run, to make this pain stop, but I grasp Lenora May's hands.

"Break," I scream, and I hear Lenora May screaming her

heart with mine, "Break!"

With one hand, Fisher knocks my entire body into the trunk. I have no breath left, but I don't let go of Lenora May's hands.

With Fisher's body looming above, I hold one word in my mind.

Break.

I SEE MY DEATH IN Fisher's yellow eyes and it's quick. In his fury, he snaps the fragile bones of my neck and feeds my body to his army of gatorbeasts.

I think of all the things I'll never get to do, the people I'll never see again, the kisses I'll never share with Heath, the volleyball games I'll never win with Candy and Abigail at my side.

And I'm so angry I can't even cry.

Then, Shine sweeps past me. I see all the running tendrils shift course, racing away from Fisher and toward the ever-blooming cherry tree as though someone pulled the plug in the tub and all the water's draining away.

Fisher is no longer the gray-clawed beast he was, but the

boy from before, not much older than me, with untiring coal-dark eyes. With a shout, he dives for the tree, scrambling after the trail of Shine, grasping for more.

"No!" he cries, desperation thick in his voice. "Please, no!" But every last wisp of magic eludes him and, with a small choking sound, his panic ceases.

Slowly, he straightens and stands in a horrified stupor, mud caked to his palms and knees. He gazes to where Lenora May lies slumped on the ground a few feet away, resigned to the fate creeping over him.

It's devastating to witness.

Heath staggers against the trunk of a cypress tree. His nose is bloodied and his breath ragged, but he makes no attempt to wipe away the blood.

"Tell her," Fisher says, recalling my attention. He watches Lenora May as if it brings him great pain and says nothing else.

Shine begins to unravel around him. It peels away from him in long, lazy strips, darts away quickly like minnows in shadow, and returns to the skirt of the cherry tree. Slowly at first, and then with a sense of urgency, undoing all of Fisher's work. He grows pale and soft like a cloudy sunset, but his eyes remain on Lenora May.

He opens his mouth to speak again. I can't hear him, so I step forward until I'm an arm's length away. He continues to fade. Without Shine to tether him, there isn't anything to tie him to this world. His body left so long ago, he's been nothing but spirit and Shine. And anger. But it's all gone now. All I see is sadness.

"What did you say?" I ask.

"Tell her," he repeats in a voice so surprisingly tender I can't help but feel sympathy. He's so thin now I can see the lines of cypress trees through him. "Please, tell her I love her."

He's gone before I can promise. Even as full of anger as he was, his last thoughts on this earth were of the sister he loved too much.

FISHER LEAVES CHAOS BEHIND. WITHOUT Shine to sustain them, the gatorbeasts shift one by one, slowly and painfully, into their human forms. Abigail's is the first face I see, but there's also Sheriff Felder, a few of the good ol' boys who were working on the fence the other day, one of the waitresses from Miss Bonnie's, and more I don't recognize at all. They must be so far out of time I wonder how they'll ever find their lives again.

The clouds spread enough moonlight over the water to show panic on all their faces as they realize where they are. Moonlight. At some point in all this, the sun left us all behind to rest for another tomorrow.

"Saucier!" Candy calls from the water. She's still got Phin

in her arms. His body is nothing but dead weight behind her. I dive into the pond. "He's not dead," she gasps.

Together, we drag him to the bank and begin to pull him up. The mud provides no support, but strong arms reach down to haul Phin from the water. Heath leans him against the trunk of the cherry tree while Candy and I scramble up beside them.

Candy springs into action, moving to calm the confusion that's rising in the background.

"What's wrong with him?" I look to Lenora May for answers. As with everyone else, the Shine in him is fading fast, faster now that Candy's not holding on to him. "Why didn't the peach work?"

"It did." She pauses, frowning at Phin's quiet body. "But he and I switched places, and I gave my life to the swamp long ago. The peach cured him, but there was no life left to return to. Only my death."

"Because you have his life," I say.

Her nod is heavy. "I wish Harlan might have known the truth. He found a way out, but not for me, not for someone who gave themselves willingly to this place."

I think of how many hours Grandpa Harlan spent staring at the swamp, humming Lenora May's song. He may have been a little mad, but it might have been worse if he'd given her the peach that killed her instead of saving her.

Leaning forward then, she cups my cheeks in her hands.

Her eyes shimmer with cherry-blossom pink. She kisses my forehead and says, "Thank you for being my sister."

"Don't go," I say. My words sound strange—so thick and slow.

She shakes her head. Her long, wet curls sway between us. "This isn't my life. It belongs to Phineas. I can't keep it from him any longer. I won't."

"But he's dying." I can't look at Phin's dark form, so empty of anything. "If you switch places with him, you'll die."

All around are the noises of people shifting into their human forms, emerging from their confused prisons. Candy's voice rises above them, pacifying their panic, and directing them to follow the sheriff. Lenora May only watches me, a small smile bending her lips.

"You'll die," I say again, helpless.

The swamp whispers and clucks and chitters. So full of life. So vibrant with death.

"I died a long time ago." She brushes my tears with her thumb. "I won't let Phineas bear the burden of my mistakes."

She wraps her arms around me and holds on for a long moment. I've only known her for a week, but with Shine in my veins, I'll remember her for so much longer.

"I—Fisher asked me to tell you he loved you."

I feel her smile against my neck and I'm relieved that the message brings her comfort. "Good-bye, brave Sterling."

She steps away, her face shining with my tears and hers.

The skirt of her gray sundress sticks to her legs when she leans over the unmoving form of my brother and presses her lips to his. When she pulls away, she whispers to him and hums. Grandpa Harlan's song, her song, and my song. She hums until Shine fills the air between them, and the song resonates through the limbs of the cherry tree.

Then she closes her eyes and becomes very, very still.

Except for Heath, all the others have gone. Freed from the magic that turned them into beasts, they've fled as quickly as they could with Candy at the lead.

Shine bends and twists through the ground in a lazy ballet, stretching and tangling. The swamp is setting itself to rights, the Wasting Shine finding its own course without Fisher around to intercept. I wonder if my town will do the same. I wonder if everyone who was here tonight will go back to pretending.

I know I won't. It's fear that makes this place dangerous. It's time people started seeing this swamp for what it is, it's time the people of Sticks, at least some of them, learn that ignoring the bear in your house won't make it go away.

"When will he wake up?" Heath asks, a few feet away.

I think of the day Phin disappeared. It had only taken a few hours for Lenora May to appear at the fence. I say, "Soon."

Around us, the swamp is loud with sounds I recognize and sounds I don't. I settle on the ground a short distance from the tree. Heath crouches before me with a question in his eyes. I shake my head. Last week, I'd have begged him to stay. The thought of being alone at a moment like this would've been terrifying, but now I'm not afraid.

"Okay," he says, pressing his lips to mine in a too-brief kiss. "Call me when you're home." Then he's gone, and it's me and my siblings curled between the roots of the ever-blooming cherry tree and the swamp.

THE BEETLES AND CRICKETS ARE doing their best to lull me to sleep when I hear a hazy, "Hey, Sass."

Phin steps from beneath the cherry tree on shaky legs, dressed in gray canvas pants and an oil-stained T-shirt. I'm in his arms before he can say another word. He smells warm and familiar, a cocktail of sweat and grit and spice. I don't let him go for several minutes.

"Let's go home," he finally says.

I nod, but first step beneath the tree limbs. As with Fisher, Lenora May's body has faded into the swamp. There's nothing left of her but what I hold in my mind—not her real history, but the one we shared, which is real enough.

The bracelet she gave Grandpa Harlan, and Phin gave me,

gleams from the base of the tree and I decide it's as fitting a memorial as any I could make. She made it to protect her loved ones from Fisher's anger, and that's precisely what it did in the end.

Shine is quick to show us the way, but when the partly destroyed fence appears, I stop.

"Phin, promise me something?"

He pauses. In the distance, I can see the red gleam of his Chevelle in the moonlight, as polished as the day he left. There won't be a fuzzy peach hanging from the mirror or a missing hubcap. There won't even be damage from me sticking a screwdriver in the ignition.

"Don't forget," I say.

"I never did," he admits, and climbs into the yard.

I don't follow. I stay with my hands resting on the post of the fence that's done nothing but keep people trapped for so long. Grandpa Harlan built it because he was afraid. The town kept it up because fear has a way of spreading like crabgrass if you don't tend to it.

Phin pauses when he notices I'm not by his side. "What's wrong?"

"Will you give me a hand with this?" I ask, giving the middle plank a good shake. Fisher was wrong about a lot of things, but maybe he wasn't wrong about this. "Grab a hammer."

He gives me a long, wry look, like I'm stirring up trouble, which I guess I am. "How about I grab two?"

He jogs to the carport and returns with two hammers. Together, we knock at the planks until we've created a wide gap in the fence line. For the first time in decades, the swamp isn't caged.

We've just piled the boards behind the carport and stashed the hammers when Mama appears on the screened porch standing in a puddle of light. Her face is shadowed, but her voice is live as a rattlesnake when she calls, "What in tarnation are you two up to with all that whacking? And where do you think you've been? Get inside, both of you."

It's too dark for her to see what we've done to the fence. I imagine there'll be hell to pay in the morning, but I'll be ready for it.

"You hungry?" Phin asks, treading carefully on this old battleground.

"Starving."

WE HAVE AN UNCANNY ABILITY to keep secrets where anyone can see them in Sticks, Louisiana.

Three days after a dozen people tromped out of the
swamp, having floated around in a pond with tails and claws,
it's as if nothing strange ever happened. Candy and Abigail
are over at my house every day with a box of Old Lady
Clary's sticky buns, making and executing plans for the summer. Sheriff Felder and the good ol' boys mend the swamp
fence and talk about the storm that blew in something fierce
Sunday night. There are new faces in town, too. Those Fisher
stole decades ago or more. They've all been folded into the
fabric of our town, neatly and quietly. And all the others
cluck their tongues and shake their heads, turning their eyes

away from the swamp.

I can't tell who remembers what by the way they're all acting. Last week, that would have sent me screaming into a pillow. But this week, I help Mama recover fallen Mardi Gras beads, and wind a string of Christmas lights around the newly repaired fence, complete with a hard-won gate. She doesn't remember Lenora May and that's the part that seems most cruel, but she also doesn't remember missing Phineas or the fact that for one shining moment her husband was the town sheriff.

Heath is the only one who hasn't changed. Every morning he sends a text as soon as the sun's kissed the sky pink. It's always the same. It says, *Phineas Harlan Saucier.* I respond, *Nathan Payola.* And he returns, *Lenora May Lillard.* He brings me coffee shortly after that, always spiced with cinnamon and blissfully free of milk and sugar, and we spend the morning talking about meaningless things like movies and music, filling in the gaps we didn't have time for the week before.

It's easier to breathe after that, but every time I get near the swamp, I feel it tugging in my belly.

The cherry left me with a connection I'll never break. Every day the swamp calls to me, begging me to cross the fence again, to twist my fingers in Shine, and never look back. I wonder if that was how Fisher felt before things got so bad. I can imagine that wanting the power to protect someone he loved drove him to take as much as he could.

In the end, he was more power than he was person and that made him more jailer than protector. I think that's why he looked so sad, so full of pain, just before he vanished.

For a while, it's hard to tell what Phin remembers. He goes through the days as if he didn't miss finals or the race or graduation. Cody comes over on Tuesday to work on the Chevelle, like always. Phin joins Darold and the rest of the boys in their quest to repair the fence, and he starts filling a laundry basket with all the things he wants to take to Tulane.

It's three days before he says anything about the swamp.

He pauses in his work to toss a wrench into the grass and says, "I wish I could have known her. I wish I could have thanked her, too."

"She knew." I think of Lenora May in the kitchen, spots of white flour in her dark hair, and I miss her. "She was a good sister."

He nods. "So are you."

I shake my head. "I haven't been, but I will be."

"Not everyone would've come after me." He ducks his head to flip hair from his eyes. "I scared myself, Sass. That—that morning when I nearly hit you." He looks sideways at the carport and his jaw clenches. There's a small dent in the wall I didn't see before, lasting evidence of that furious moment. "I ran away because I wanted to hurt you and I knew I was losing control. I felt myself turning into *him*. Dad."

"You wouldn't!"

"But I *could*." His eyes are pinched, his lips tight. "The point is I could have and I nearly did. And that . . . is worse than dying."

Tears gleam in his eyes. I've never seen him so vulnerable. Somewhere along the way we agreed that in order for me to be safe, he needed to be the strong one. That was the dark secret rotting in the middle of Phin's chest.

"I used to be afraid that if you left home, I wouldn't survive." I put a hand on his chest, one of Old Lady Clary's bracelets secure around my wrist. "I'm not afraid, Phineas. I'll miss you, but I know I'll be fine. Even when bad things happen, I'll be fine. I want you to go to Tulane and be brilliant."

"How," he asks, "could I be anything else?"

The swamp is louder now than it was before, crouching beyond my open window. The air is calm, but I can hear it sigh and sing. I can feel its magic reflected inside me as if it's the sun and I'm the moon. It tugs at me, urging me to *come away, come away, come away*. This is why Lenora May said it was dangerous to bind yourself to the swamp. This is what Heath has struggled against for so long. Even with a Clary charm on my wrist, the pull of Shine is stronger than ever before.

But so am I.

ACKNOWLEDGMENTS

Had I known the endurance required to publish a single novel at the start of this process, I might have turned back at the door.

I will never in a million years be able to thank my agent, Sarah Davies, appropriately. She is tireless and discerning, and this book would be a muddy, muddy mess without her skilled hand. I would also be a muddy, muddy mess without her.

My editorial team at HarperCollins: Phoebe Yeh, Karen Chaplin, and Jessica MacLeish, whose encouragement, patience, and dedication have been invaluable—I swear I'm done making changes now. Bethany Reis and Susan Jeffers Casel, who are the kung fu masters of copyediting. Kate Engbring, who created the perfect cover for Sticks. And to everyone else on the Harper team I've never worked with directly but am indebted to nonetheless—thank you!

I would be nothing at all without critical readers: Valerie

Kemp, who has likely read this book more times than anyone including me; Sonia Gensler and Kimberly Welchons, without whom this novel would be all arms and no legs; Maggie Stiefvater, for telling me to write something, and then to write it again better; Myra McEntire, Julie Murphy, Elizabeth Schonhorst, Victoria Schwab, and Alexandra Staeben, who all read at lynchpin moments and helped me through them; Carrie Ryan and Brenna Yovanoff for nascent conversations on New Orleans porch swings; and Christine Koval, Steve Smith, and Tiffany Trent, whose early enthusiasm was inspiring.

To the very fine ladies of GFA and the Fourteenery: your unwavering support has been tantamount to sisterhoods of legend. Let's all drive to Vegas and get tattoos.

My boss, Joane Nagel—your support has made a universe of difference.

CK, for building me a whimsical, chilling website (and loving me anyway), and Emily Kennedy, for sharing this journey with me.

My English teachers at Central Kitsap High in Silverdale, Washington: Mrs. Lillis King, who let me write my first novel as my senior honors project, and Mr. Bill Rosen, whose love of literature was contagious.

To my incredible family, for giving me the power of story and a thirst for adventure.

And to Tess, for doing this whole thing with me.

Thank you.

ROI702116818
Fiction Parker

Peachtree